Praise for Rebecca Taylor

Praise for *The Secret Next Door*

"Taylor weaves a twisted tale of 'perfect' women, broken marriages, and sinful secrets that'll chill you to the bone."

—Kristin Miller, *New York Times* bestselling author of *The Sinful Lives of Trophy Wives*

"*The Secret Next Door* is a twisty tale of surprise and psychological suspense that is populated with relatable characters. Taylor has a zing to her writing style as the words fly across the pages...and every last one will have you wondering how well you really know your neighbors."

—Joanna Schaffhausen, award-winning author of *Gone for Good*

"Rebecca Taylor's *The Secret Next Door* is a taut, chilling glimpse inside the homes of an affluent community built on lies, secrets, and tragedy. Taylor deftly balances the tedium of socially connected/emotionally distanced suburban life with its existential insidiousness: one doesn't want to want to relate to these people, which makes it even more unsettling when one does. And the opposing forces of Alyson and Bonnie are deliciously gray, each sympathetic and flawed, and similar enough to one another to raise the tension through the roof. *The Secret Next Door* is a thoughtful and cunning mystery that will hit close to home for legions of bedroom-community dwellers."

—Carter Wilson, *USA Today* bestselling author

Praise for *Her Perfect Life*

"Debut author Rebecca Taylor spins a superb story of two sisters who, despite growing up together, might as well have been strangers. Secrets, lies, and tragic truths unspoken swirl together through the pages, creating a sophisticated page-turner. It felt like sneaking a read of someone's fascinating private diary—and being completely powerless to put it down."

—A. G. Henley, *USA Today* bestselling author

"A beautifully written and intricate novel that delves into the complexities of sisterhood, relationships, love, and the ties that bind. Through her vivid characters, Taylor doesn't shy away from exploring challenging issues, such as grief, shame, and infidelity with great honesty, insight, and sympathy. A very satisfying and emotional journey from an expert storyteller."

—Anita Kushwaha, IPPY Award–winning author of *Side by Side* and *Secret Lives of Mothers & Daughters*

"A compelling debut novel of two sisters and how their ties to each other irrevocably change the lives of those they love. I couldn't put it down!"

—Shelley Noble, *New York Times* bestselling author of *Lucky's Beach* and *Tell Me No Lies*

"[*Her Perfect Life*] will command readers' attention and hearts with this engrossing tale of two very different sisters."

—*Library Journal*

"In this stunning debut, Rebecca Taylor rivets with a story that unfolds bit by bit, revealing layers that herald a much more experienced author. I was captivated until the very end!"

—Courtney Cole, *New York Times* bestselling author

"Compulsively readable from the first page. Rebecca Taylor weaves an expertly layered story of family secrets and builds the suspense to an almost unbearable pace in this modern story of two sisters."

—Kelly Simmons, author of *One More Day* and *Where She Went*

"Sisters. Secrets. Suspense. Taylor's debut is a compelling dual-timeline story that centers around the secrets we keep from those we love, the secrets that are kept from us, and the secrets we keep from ourselves. A page-turner that keeps the reader wanting more until the very last page."

—Alison Hammer, author of *You and Me and Us*

ALSO BY REBECCA TAYLOR

Her Perfect Life

THE SECRET NEXT DOOR

A NOVEL

REBECCA TAYLOR

Published by Sourcebooks Landmark, an imprint of Sourcebooks
P.O. Box 4410, Naperville, Illinois 60567-4410
(630) 961-3900
sourcebooks.com

Library of Congress Cataloging-in-Publication Data

Names: Taylor, Rebecca, author.
Title: The secret next door : a novel / Rebecca Taylor.
Description: Naperville, Illinois : Sourcebooks Landmark, [2021]
Identifiers: LCCN 2021003831 (print) | LCCN 2021003832 (ebook) | (trade paperback) | (epub)
Classification: LCC PS3620.A9653 S43 2021 (print) | LCC PS3620.A9653 (ebook) | DDC 813/.6--dc23
LC record available at https://lccn.loc.gov/2021003831
LC ebook record available at https://lccn.loc.gov/2021003832

Printed and bound in the United States of America.
SB 10 9 8 7 6 5

For Matthew, Beth, and Rod

CHAPTER ONE

Alyson Tinsdale placed her last orange safety cone in the street in front of her driveway just as her five-year-old son, Andrew, flew past her on his two-wheel bike and directly into the road.

"Andrew!" she shouted, doing her best to run after him in wedge flip-flops while she scanned the street for oncoming cars. "Stop!"

Either not hearing or ignoring her, Andrew pedaled faster. His sandy-colored, shoulder-length hair blew back from his helmet-free head.

"Andrew!" she tried again, watching the front tire of his twelve-inch bike hit the opposite curb head-on. A surge of adrenaline flooded her body; her nervous system knew precisely what would happen next, even if her brain was slow to form the words.

He's going to crash.

Matched against the six-inch concrete curb, the bike's small wheel wrecked left. The forward momentum projected Andrew's little body over the top of his handlebars and onto the sidewalk.

Alyson kept running, waiting for Andrew's siren cry to start, cursing her husband, Justin, for taking the damn training wheels off. She hadn't believed how much faster the small bike could go without those two plastic wheels.

Andrew rolled over onto his back and sat up, a bloody graze

spread across the right side of his forehead and down his temple. Looking confused, he saw his bike in the gutter, his mom running toward him, and both his skinned palms—then he started to cry.

Alyson knelt beside him and brushed his hair away from the scrape on his head. "Are you okay?"

"My bike!" he wailed. "It's broken!" Tears streamed down his flushed cheeks.

Alyson scooped him up into her arms, cradling him to her chest as she stood. "It's fine," she promised, shifting Andrew's weight to her hip so she could hold him with her left arm while she reached for the bike's handlebars with her right. She lugged her crying son and his bike back across the street, past her safety cones, and onto their driveway.

When they reached the garage, Andrew stopped crying and squirmed from her grasp. Unable to hold him and the bike, she let him slide down her leg and released the bike onto the pavement.

Andrew's face crumpled into a worried frown when he saw the ripped vinyl seat and the chain hanging loose off the sprocket. "It's broken," he declared again.

"It's not broken," she tried to reassure him. "Just a little banged up." She touched the bloody wound on his forehead. "So are you. We should go clean this up." She would wait to launch into a lecture about wearing his helmet, riding in the street, slowing down, once she got him inside and slathered on antibacterial ointment.

Still staring at his bike, his most beloved possession, and not looking like he had any intention of moving into the house, Andrew touched the tear on the seat. "I need to call Dad," he said.

"He's at work."

"Ask Dad if he can fix my bike."

Alyson hesitated for a few seconds, weighing her annoyance with Andrew for not believing her against her desire to move into the house quickly and get him cleaned up.

Andrew looked up into her eyes. "Can you send him a picture?"

Alyson sighed and nodded as she pulled her phone from her back pocket. The picture she'd like to send Justin was of their son's face, along with the text: I don't think taking the training wheels off was such a great idea.

But Justin would likely accuse her, again, of being *passive-aggressive*.

Alyson pulled up her camera app and aimed her phone at the bike.

She heard the engine before she could see the car. Still at a distance, around the corner her house sat on, a vehicle was speeding up. The roar of acceleration broke the silence of her usually quiet street.

Her body tensed. As the sound grew louder, rage surged through her system that was directly proportional to the pace of the car. It was him, had to be—every day now for a week.

She saw the open-top, electric-blue Jeep round the corner, music blaring, its wheels squealing as it worked to keep hold of the road around the fast turn.

Alyson didn't hesitate this time.

In three quick strides, she stood at the end of her driveway, raised her phone, and shot a series of photos. She captured the Jeep approaching, zooming right past her safety cones and then accelerating up her street until it took another hard right.

She checked the pictures, scrolling to one in the middle that captured the driver's profile. Light brown hair, muscled build, oblivious expression on his entitled face—she had a clear shot of George Sloan speeding, again, past her house on his way home from school. She swiped through several more, somewhat blurry pictures until she found one of the back of the Jeep. She spread her fingers, zooming in, and smiled.

The license plate was clear as day.

"Mom?" Andrew said as he tugged at the bottom of her shirt.

She pulled her thoughts away from what she might do next about her George Sloan electric-blue Jeep problem and looked into her son's scratched-up face.

"I'm hungry."

She slid her phone back into her pocket and reached for his hand. "Let's get you some dinner."

"Did you send Dad a picture of my bike?"

"Yes," she lied. "He's probably driving home and can't text us back. But I'll put the chain back on after I make you something to eat."

Andrew gave her a skeptical look. Alyson imagined him trying to work out in his five-year-old head how his mother, a girl, could possibly know how to do such a thing. As they passed through the garage door and into the mudroom, Alyson closed her eyes and reminded herself that she was pissed off at George Sloan.

And his parents.

Not Andrew, who might have been in the center of that road right as George's Jeep roared through.

There wasn't any way he would have been able to stop in time.

CHAPTER TWO

Bonnie Sloan sat behind the wheel of her Porsche and let her head fall back against the headrest. Anxiety clawed at her throat. She tried to breathe past it, swallow it down, but it felt tight, an insistence in her body that wanted to take flight into a full-blown panic.

She closed her eyes and tried to force her mind off the nasty particulars of the city council meeting she had just left and onto something more pleasant, calm—anything relaxing.

She tried to imagine herself on the beach in Maui eight years ago. She and her husband, Bennet, had rented that condo with the wide balcony that directly overlooked Kaanapali Beach, where her two sons had spent endless carefree hours playing in the sand and surf. George had been nine, Elijah only five—Gracie's birth was still three years into the then distant future. Their lives had been so different then—simpler, really. Bonnie imagined herself on that plush teal-and-white-striped beach towel, the warm sand radiating up through her body and unwinding her every constricted muscle.

But Carl Wayland's red and angry face swam up into her vision and interrupted her thoughts. "If you think for one second that I'll allow that monstrosity to be erected in my backyard, you'll be hearing from my lawyer!"

A massive wave of anxiety swept away her attempt at

remembering happier times at the beach. Bonnie opened her eyes and stared out across the dark and deserted school parking lot she was hiding in. Tonight's council meeting was the first public opportunity the community had to voice their thoughts about the Extreme Golf center breaking ground just west of The Enclave's Highlands development, but Carl Wayland and his coalition of dissenters and complainers had been making their thoughts loud and clear all over The Enclave neighborhood's Facebook page ever since the Extreme Golf land-use proposal had been filed with the city and made public three months ago.

Carl lived in the Highlands part of The Enclave—same as Bonnie. In fact, their multimillion-dollar homes were only one lot apart. Both their yards backed up to the third fairway of the Enclave golf course and enjoyed stunning and unobstructed views of the Rocky Mountains.

Views that would be forever altered as soon as Extreme Golf began erecting their two-hundred-foot steel beams and the netting system designed to catch golf balls flying from their five-story platform. And that was just during the day. At night, their floodlights would be seen for miles, completely obliterating the Highlands's current serene atmosphere—and it wasn't going to help the property values, either.

Bonnie understood Carl's anger; after all, her house was going to be just as impacted as his. But as the elected city council official for Ward Eight, she couldn't simply use her vote to the benefit of the wealthiest constituents with the largest houses and best views in the city.

Because on the opposite side from Carl were all the residents who really wanted Extreme Golf to move in. For the family-friendly entertainment they would get from launching golf balls from the fifth-floor decks while music blared and drinks were served, yes, but also for the tax revenue that would flow in for the city.

And, of course, Bonnie understood implicitly that many of her less wealthy constituents would derive some pleasure from sticking it to the Sloans and the Waylands of the world. She knew many residents saw Carl as an elitist who felt entitled to his multimillion-dollar unobstructed views, even though he did not personally own the land between his second-floor balcony and the Rocky Mountains. She and Bennet were both counting on Carl Wayland not being able to drum up much sympathy for his fight against Extreme Golf.

But Bonnie also understood that Carl Wayland had influential connections, deep pockets, and, as a retired CEO, nothing but time. Squashing the development of Extreme Golf in *his backyard* was now his full-time job.

And even though Bonnie would be staring, daily, at the same monstrosity while standing at her kitchen sink, sitting on her back patio, or gazing out her second-story master bedroom window, she could not let Carl Wayland stop this deal. No matter how much she personally would like to allow that to happen.

She had more at stake than a fabulous view and tens of thousands in resale value from her house.

Bennet was counting on her to shepherd the Extreme Golf deal through.

Bonnie checked the time on her phone: eight thirty. She needed to get home and see if the kids had eaten the dinner she left for them and if Bennet was home from work—the news about Carl and tonight's meeting was going to send him over the edge.

She took a deep breath, started her car back up, and pulled out of the protective nighttime shadows of The Enclave's K–8 charter school.

Whenever she was feeling overwhelmed and extremely stressed out, like right now, the darkest reaches of the school's parking lot were where she always came to hide and think. She had discovered it entirely by accident, years ago, when her middle child, Elijah, was in second grade. Back then, she'd been president of the PTA. Often the first to arrive and the last to leave the school during every function.

It had been the October parent-teacher conferences, and she and the rest of the PTA were running the bookfair in the school's library. Sometime after eight, she had walked out to the parking lot with the last few teachers in the building. By the time she loaded up her trunk, got behind the wheel of her car, and discovered that her battery was dead, everyone else had already pulled out of sight.

The very first emotion that hit her was fear. She was a woman alone, in the dark, in a car that wouldn't start. Everything about her life up to this moment had trained her to believe she was on the verge of being raped, abducted, or, at the very least, robbed. Never mind that she was in the neighborhood she'd lived in, at the time, for fifteen years. Sitting in her car, doors locked, behind tinted windows so dark no one could see her, especially at night.

Bonnie had sat back in her seat and picked up her phone, ready to call Bennet to come rescue her, when another feeling hit her. An emotion so foreign to her current life, she almost couldn't name it.

Calm.

Maybe it wasn't *exactly* calm, but it was near enough to a sense of well-being, something she hadn't experienced in over a decade, that it grabbed her attention.

She was a woman, alone in the dark.

And no one could see her.

Bonnie had stopped dialing her husband and put her phone down.

She sat back in her seat, feeling the muscles that normally roped across her shoulder blades release a fraction of an inch, and noticed how the glow of light from the streetlamps in front of the school didn't reach to the farthest corners of the parking lot. She felt invisible to the outside world, and it felt good. Regularly, eyes followed her everywhere she went.

At five foot eight, with a slender build, C-cup breasts, and a ballet dancer's ass, Bonnie Sloan knew she was a beautiful woman. She held herself erect, wore the right clothes, drove a luxury car, and occupied the home that, situated off the third fairway on a slight rise, was visible to everyone entering The Enclave from the main entrance. Her home was the crown jewel of the Enclave development.

Eyes, they were on her, always. Even in her own home, between Bennet and her three kids, rarely was there ever a moment or a space to herself.

But not here. In this one dark parking space where no one would ever look for her. Here she could, and had, eaten an entire Big Mac, large fries, and a regular Coke. She slouched, belched, and often even passed gas without giving it any thought at all. No one was watching, ever, as long as she was alone, here in the dark.

So when tonight's city council meeting was essentially commandeered by Carl Wayland and several of her other neighbors, she knew she'd need to make a stop before heading home and sharing the news with Bennet.

The Extreme Golf development was not going to go off without a hitch. And if she was going to pull off her run for the Senate, she and Bennet were going to have to be smart, get out in front of the growing public conflict on the right side, and play all their cards well.

Because if Carl Wayland dug around deep enough to discover the truth that he already suspected, it would ruin her and her family.

CHAPTER THREE

It was the last weekend in September, the last weekend the Enclave neighborhood pool would be open for the season. The pool had been a miracle over the last few months; Alyson dreaded not being able to bring Andrew here to get his energy out. The tan lifeguard with the long legs blew her whistle. "Adult swim," she called out across the pool as she reached over her head to tighten her messy ponytail and eyeball every last kid who looked under sixteen.

"No!" Andrew shouted, five feet away from Alyson in the shallow end.

Oh no, please, not now. She didn't feel like dealing with a temper tantrum. Especially not in front of the audience of other mothers camping out around the pool's edge. Alyson waded over to her son, hoping to defuse the situation quickly and quietly.

"It's the rule," she whispered. "Look, all the other kids are getting out too."

"It's not fair."

Alyson sighed. "It is fair if everyone else has to get out."

"But the grownups get to stay."

"And you're not a grownup." An annoyed edge slipped into her tone.

Andrew narrowed his eyes, like he might be gearing up to do battle with her.

Please God, Alyson thought. *Don't make me haul this kid from the pool, kicking and screaming.* Given that her own mother's discipline style had spanned the spectrum from neglect to belt-swinging tirades, Alyson never felt she knew how to strike the perfect measure of authoritative confidence with her own son. When Andrew put up a fight, she often fell back on her heels into avoidance or distraction.

"Andrew!" Gabby Lawrence, Alyson's neighbor and new friend, called from the side of the pool.

Andrew turned his head to see Gabby, smiling down at him from under her large-brimmed sun hat. "Colten is having a Popsicle. Do you want one?"

"Yes!" he shouted, suddenly not caring at all about getting out of the pool. He paddled as fast as he could toward the steps.

"Thank you," Alyson mouthed to her friend.

Gabby winked at her as she took Andrew's hand and helped him up the last two steps and across the hot concrete to her packed cooler.

Colten was Gabby's fourth kid, fourth boy, and it always seemed to Alyson that she knew exactly the right mom-move to make at the exact right time. Alyson would have stood in the tepid shallow end, getting into a power struggle until she was red-faced and embarrassed. Gabby's solution was to walk up calmly with a sugary distraction.

Alyson had no idea which solution was worse. At least Gabby's way allowed her to exit the pool gracefully in front of the ever-watchful neighborhood audience.

By the time Alyson reached their own poolside encampment,

Andrew and Colten were both happily slurping electric-blue Icees from thin plastic bags. Gabby handed Alyson an ice-cold can of spiked watermelon seltzer and a fabric koozie that said, *Not Today, Satan*, to hide it in.

Not that they were fooling anyone, including every other parent also hiding alcohol. Some preferred koozies, others liked Hydro Flasks, and a few simply kept their cans surreptitiously concealed beneath their lounge chairs.

When Alyson had come to the pool with Gabby for the first time at the beginning of the summer, she was worried when Gabby handed her a drink.

"Won't the lifeguards say something to us?"

Gabby only smiled. "See that woman over there? The one in the orange bikini that looks like she hasn't allowed herself a good meal in two decades? That's the lifeguard's mom, and that concoction she's sipping is likely 40 proof. So no, the lifeguard won't say anything. Not unless you get falling-down drunk, and trust me, I won't let that happen to either of us. But it is kinda interesting to watch when someone else does."

When Alyson and Justin had moved into The Enclave four months ago, Alyson had found herself missing the closeness of the girlfriends she'd had in college back in Nebraska. They'd met their freshman year and stayed friends throughout their two years in the dorms and then after, when they'd rented a house together several blocks from campus. It was so much easier to make and keep those friendships over the late-night study sessions and a shared bathroom as they got ready to go out Friday nights.

She was still technically in touch with those four women, but it was mostly through social media. Text messages on birthdays and Christmas. Things between her and those friends had slowly changed after she'd moved in with Justin. And once she'd married him, and certainly after she'd had Andrew, her whole life had become about her family.

Not that her marriage was the only one—almost all her old girlfriends had eventually walked down the aisle and now had children of their own. One of them was already divorced—only three short years of marriage.

Alyson regretted letting the relationships float away. She wanted that sense of sisterhood, that ride-or-die, *girl, I got your back* in her life again. So when Gabby had shown up at the front door to introduce herself, the only neighbor to do so, Alyson felt relieved. She lived across the street and four doors down. Her yard was usually littered with bikes, skateboards, and Razor scooters and crawling with not only her own four boys, but also many of the other kids living in a three-block radius.

None of Alyson's college friends were like Gabby. She often seemed to say whatever she felt in any given moment. Gabby didn't care what the other mothers thought or said about her. Not that Gabby wasn't friends with them too—many of their kids could be found at and around Gabby's house every Sunday. But Alyson got the impression that Gabby liked her alone time. Whenever Alyson arrived at the pool and Gabby was already here, she was never entrenched with the other mothers on the north side of the pool. She was always alone on the south side, happily drinking her hard seltzer while eyeing her kids, perfectly at ease in her solitude.

Alyson was grateful for Gabby's friendship, but in truth, she wanted to meet the other mothers in the neighborhood as well. But she wasn't as confident as Gabby—she had no idea how a woman just walked up to another woman, stuck out her hand, and said, "Hi, nice to meet you."

Never mind walking up to a *group of women.*

Jessica Hampton, one of the other mothers, was floating in her inflatable lounger near the edge of the south side. She shielded her eyes and called out, "Hey, Gabby!"

Gabby lowered her phone, saw who was calling her, and casually raised her hand.

"Are we going to see you at book club this Thursday?" Jessica asked. "I'm hosting."

"What was the book again?" Gabby called back.

"*A Perfect Life*...Clare Collins."

"Oh, right. I don't know... I'm only halfway done, so maybe," Gabby said with a shrug.

"You should come anyway. It's not like anyone cares if you finish."

"Maybe. Let me see if Dennis has plans," Gabby said.

Jessica shifted in her lounger, an expression of disbelief flattening her mouth into a line. "Okay," she said. "Well, I hope it works out for *Dennis* and we see you there." She leaned back against her lounger so the sun could continue cooking her already caramel-colored skin.

Gabby sat back in her own chair again, a smirk playing at her lips. "They can't stand it when I use Dennis as an excuse. It's so not progressive."

"Would he stop you from going?" Alyson asked.

Gabby let out a laugh. "I love my husband, but that man has about as much say about what does and does not happen in our house as the cat. He goes to work, comes home, eats dinner, has a beer and watches a few episodes of something on Netflix, makes sure all the boys are still breathing if the thought occurs to him, then goes to bed. Repeat until Saturday morning when he goes to play golf."

"Then why—"

"It's like girl code. I'll come if I feel like it, but don't count on it. Honestly, I think I just like to give them something to squawk about when I'm not around. It's an unspoken universal truth among them: if you're not there, you'll probably be talked about."

Alyson sipped her seltzer and covertly watched the women across the pool. They all appeared so comfortable, so at ease with each other. She couldn't help but wonder how long they had all been friends. How had they all met each other? Maybe through their older kids? She had thought about gathering the nerve to ask Gabby, possibly, for an introduction—but even that felt weird. "They must really like you—to be so insistent?"

Gabby shrugged. "God only knows why."

"So, do you think you'll go?" Alyson fished, too afraid to ask her friend outright for what she wanted.

Gabby turned her full attention to Alyson. "Why? Do you want to go?" she asked, raising her eyebrows and making Alyson feel a little foolish for some reason.

Alyson took a breath. "Oh, well…I mean, I wouldn't want to *invite myself*. But, I did read *A Perfect Life*. And it might be nice. You know, to get out of the house…for a girls' night?"

Gabby considered Alyson for several seconds, as if something about her suddenly seemed like a revelation. "Sure," she said, and turned back to her phone. "It will be a good opportunity for you to meet other people. I'll send you an invite to the book club group page and let Jessica know we'll both be there. She'll shit her pants."

"Thank you," Alyson said before she bit her bottom lip. She couldn't tell if Gabby was a little annoyed. At her, or just the prospect of going to something she didn't really want to, Alyson had no idea. But a second later, when the Facebook group invitation notification popped up on her phone, she quickly accepted it and felt a warm rush of inclusion. She definitely wanted more friends, and now there was a crack in that door.

"Did you see this?" Gabby leaned over in her lounge chair and extended her phone so Alyson could see.

Alyson scanned the screen. It was something on Facebook, but she couldn't make it out. "What am I looking at?" she asked, taking hold of the phone to steady it.

"Carl Wayland is losing his shit on the Enclave Facebook page."

"Who's Carl Wayland?" Alyson asked, scanning the angry post that had something to do with golf.

"A perpetually pissed off old man who lives in The Highlands. He's got it out for that giant golf amusement park, Extreme Golf, that's slated to be built directly behind his house. Looks like he's trying to get everyone else wound up and ready to support him."

The post had been up for four hours and had only two likes. "And do they?" Alyson asked.

"Not likely. I imagine anyone not living in The Highlands hardly gives a shit. I know for a fact that Dennis would *love* for this to go in."

Alyson read the rant more carefully. She noticed the withering tone, exclamation points, and threats to publicly share emails he'd received about the matter that proved the city council, and *certain specific members*, were in violation of the law.

"It's pretty hateful," Alyson said, handing the phone back.

Gabby nodded and sat back in her chair. "Knowing Carl, it will probably get worse."

"Mom?" Andrew asked from his towel on the ground. "How much longer?"

Alyson checked her own phone for the time. The fifteen-minute adult swim should be up. She glanced up at the lifeguard stand to see if Long-legs was getting ready to blow the whistle and saw that she was instead talking with a guy. Flirting, actually. Tilted head, coy smile, and her body just inside the guy's personal space.

Alyson watched the lifeguard reach out and touch George Sloan's muscled chest, for just a playful moment, before grasping the whistle between her breasts. She laughed again, still not calling an end to adult swim—and her break.

Alyson leaned over to Gabby. "That's George Sloan," she said.

Gabby looked up over the top of her sunglasses. "Yes, the resident golden child."

"Ha. Not so golden, if you ask me," she whispered so Andrew

and Colten wouldn't hear. "He nearly killed Andrew right in front of my house with his fucking ridiculous Jeep."

Gabby's head snapped back an inch, a huge smile breaking out across her face. "I don't think I have ever heard you use that word."

Alyson blushed. "I'm sorry, I just—"

"No, don't apologize to me. I couldn't give a rat's ass how bad your language is. I only hope I'm not corrupting you."

Alyson pulled out her own phone and scrolled through her recent pictures until she arrived at the ones of George speeding up her street. She handed it to Gabby.

"You took photos?" Gabby laughed.

"Yes! He does it nearly every day. I'm sick of it."

Gabby handed her phone back. "What are you going to do? Call the police? Go to his parents?"

"I thought about it…but I know I won't." Alyson didn't like the idea of any kind of *actual* confrontation. "Bonnie Sloan intimidates the hell out of me," she admitted.

Gabby shook her head. "Why? Because she lives in a giant house, drives a Porsche Cayenne, and swans around like she's The Enclave's founding matriarch?"

"Yes, all of that. And basically everything else about her."

"Well, you shouldn't be. It's like my mother always said: any woman trying that hard to make you believe everything is perfect, is anything but. Trust me, Bonnie Sloan's no different from the rest of us mothers trying to keep the wheels on the bus."

The lifeguard finally blew her whistle, and both Andrew and Colten shot off their towels like fireworks.

"I'll watch them this time," Gabby offered as she pulled herself from her lounger and headed for the water.

"Thanks," Alyson said.

With his lifeguard girlfriend back at work, George Sloan sauntered back toward the pool's exit.

No, Alyson Tinsdale was not the sort of woman who went in for the direct confrontation.

But Carl Wayland's Facebook rant had given her an idea as to how she could get George to stop racing up her street without requiring her to really face anyone.

CHAPTER FOUR

Bonnie finished reading through Carl Wayland's barely veiled threat on the Enclave Facebook page and snapped her laptop shut. She placed both hands on either side of her antique mahogany desk and pushed herself to standing. The force sent her leather office chair rolling back and into the built-in bookcase behind her with a crash.

Her expertly manicured fingers curled into her palms, and her knuckles pressed hard into the desk's shining surface. She closed her eyes, took a deep breath, and resisted the overpowering urge to send all files, pens, and planners in front of her flying across the room.

Which, of course, would solve nothing.

Instead, she opened her eyes and focused on the wood paneling and custom-made upholstered furniture all around her. She had hand-selected every aspect of this room, this whole house, with her interior designer twenty years ago. Pieces that had been so on-trend and expensive at the time now seemed both dated and shabby to her.

Twenty years of her life spent within these walls. An encased eight thousand custom square feet that she had so desperately wanted when she was twenty-eight.

And now at forty-eight? It felt like an eight-thousand-square-foot albatross around her neck.

The anxious thoughts made her spacious office feel claustrophobic. Bonnie walked around her desk and out the nine-foot solid-wood double doors, her bare feet cold against the travertine-tiled hallway. She kept moving, silent and quick, past the family room where her daughter, Gracie, was ensconced on the flotilla of forest-green leather sectional pieces. Her pale blue eyes were glued to the eighty-five-inch television displaying the addictively bright colors of Doc McStuffins on Disney+.

Bonnie snuck behind her, not wanting to disturb her five-year-old daughter and ignite an endless barrage of attention-seeking needs. Thankfully, their heavy sliding patio door was practically silent on its track, so she slipped outside without Gracie ever even catching her scent.

But Bonnie's mom-guilt followed her out the door.

It was Sunday. Most of the Enclave parents would be with their kids at the neighborhood pool, enjoying the last weekend it would be open before closing for the season. Exactly like Bonnie had done for years with both George and Elijah. Back then, Bonnie had been the sort of mother who never would have allowed her kids to sit inside on a gorgeous Sunday—or any day, really. Their eyes glued to screens, and their butts fastened to couches.

She hadn't seen either Elijah or George today, but she knew for a fact they would both be in their respective bedrooms, fingers flying across their gaming keyboards while they yelled obscenities into their mic'd headphones. She was reasonably sure she had spewed thousands of judgments over the years about parents who allowed such things to happen in their homes.

Bonnie walked to the edge of her flagstone patio. She gazed over their black-bottom pool, past the split-level fencing covered in imported Italian grapevines, and beyond the lime-colored fairway of the Enclave golf course. On the other side was the plot of land preparing to be broken so that the colossal Extreme Golf facility could begin construction next month.

Beyond all that, the currently unobstructed view of the Rocky Mountain range rose in the distance, along with her ever-growing anger at her husband, Bennet.

Twenty-two years ago, Bennet had led her by the hand to this exact spot. Back then, it had been nothing but a hardscrabble stretch of dirt, surrounded by even more dirt on every side. There were no homes, no pool, no school, no golf course, no The Enclave at all. Only the Rocky Mountains, and this gorgeous view of those purple majesties.

Bennet had gotten down on one knee, pulled that black velvet box from his pocket, and asked her, a small-town girl from the eastern plains of Colorado, to be his wife. She was twenty-six years old and a low-ranking HR assistant for Sloan Investment Group. She knew exactly what every person in the company would think. But whatever hesitation Bonnie may have felt about marrying Bennet Sloan, the founder's son, quickly evaporated the moment he opened that box up. The five-carat princess-cut diamond couldn't help but capture and refract the full spectrum of the Colorado sun high above their heads on that crystal-clear day.

"I thought about doing this at an expensive restaurant," he said, looking up at her with his dark-brown eyes, a single stray curl of his sandy brown hair falling down over his forehead. "But I thought, wouldn't it be better to make this promise on the earth that would be our future home?"

It was the promise, she now realized, that had tipped the balance. A commitment that was vital to her. Even if Bonnie, and certainly not Bennet, knew it: security was the central need of Bonnie's hidden subconscious.

Bennet would take care of her.

Bennet, and his family money, would always take care of Bonnie.

Bennet, and his family money, would always take care of Bonnie, and their children.

No one would ever be scared, or hungry, or have to go to school with a hole in the side of their only pair of shoes.

That five-carat ring, this earth beneath her feet, this home they had built—all of it—the promise Bennet had made to keep them safe.

It was all unraveling.

And Carl Wayland, even if he didn't ultimately realize it, was pulling at the threads.

It wasn't lost on her, now forty-eight years old, that at twenty-six, she would have been *offended* had anyone dare suggest she might want a man to sweep her up and take care of her. Up until Bennet knelt before her, she had always made her own way in the world.

She had long ago left her small Colorado town behind her to attend the University of Colorado Boulder—on a full-ride academic scholarship. She had gotten herself to CU Boulder on her own merit and hard work. Her whole life, no one had ever taken care of anything for her. She had long assumed, and even expected, that was how it always would be.

So no one had been more surprised than Bonnie when Bennet Sloan quietly asked her out for dinner three months after she started working at Sloan Investment. Her original plan had been to work her way up through the Human Resources department. As it turned out, marrying up had been much faster.

And aside from enduring a few snide remarks when their relationship first became public, for the most part, being a Sloan was everything, and so much more than, Bonnie had hoped for.

Until six years ago, when George Sloan Sr., Bennet's father, had a stroke in the night and passed away in his bed next to Marjorie, his wife of forty-nine years. It was two weeks before their fiftieth wedding anniversary party—a party that was quickly reorganized into George's funeral.

If Bonnie had never realized how much the Sloan Investment Group's success depended on her father-in-law's experience and business acumen, she certainly did now. She was now also painfully aware of how her own husband's lack of ability in these arenas was driving the company to its knees. And destroying the foundations of that promise he had made her all those years ago.

Sloan Investment was going under.

Bonnie, and life as she knew it, was going with it.

"Mom?"

Bonnie startled at the sound and turned to see her oldest son, George, standing behind her at the now open sliding glass door.

"I have paperwork I need to fill out for Yale; where's my social security card?"

Bonnie pasted a placidly pleasant expression on her face and headed back toward the house. "In the safe. I'll get it. Do you need any help?"

George shrugged. "Well, I need help getting my social security card out of the safe. Other than that, I don't know yet."

Bonnie took a silent, deep inhale through her nose, her pleasant expression never faltering, and ignored her son's shitty tone of voice. "Okay then," she said, following him into the house. "I'll get the card and bring it up."

"Thanks," he barely mumbled as he headed toward the kitchen and opened the refrigerator door.

"Mom?" Gracie called from the couch, now alerted to her mother's presence.

Shit, Bonnie thought, still not losing that pleasant expression.

"Yes, Gracie?" she called back as she headed back through the family room on her way to the opposite side of the house and the wall-safe in Bennet's office.

"Mommy!" Gracie yelled. She smiled and stood up on the couch, throwing her arms wide as though her mother had been gone for a week instead of hiding for a couple of Disney-distracted hours.

"Hi, honey."

Gracie began bouncing up and down on the couch, her messy curls springing around her head. "Play a game with me," Gracie said. "Let's play house."

"What have I said about jumping on the couch?" Bonnie asked.

Gracie executed one more big jump, folded her legs underneath her airborne body, and landed with a thud on her bottom. "House!"

Gracie yelled, her missing two front teeth gaping behind her wide smile. "You play the mommy, and I'll be the baby."

A shiver ran up Bonnie's spine. She resisted the urge she had to tell her daughter, in no uncertain terms, that she would maybe rather light herself on fire right now than *play house*. Instead, she smiled at her. "I have to get George some paperwork. Look." She pointed to the screen behind Gracie. "*Sophia the First* is coming on. Why don't you start that episode while I go get what George needs? I'll be right back," she lied.

"Promise?" Gracie asked, narrowing her eyes. She had been fooled by this particular parental avoidance tactic before.

Bonnie raised her right hand. "I swear."

Gracie raised her left hand, mimicking her mother's false oath like this sealed the deal, then flounced back into her nest of throw pillows and blankets.

Bonnie slipped away again, wondering for the hundredth time if she should look into hiring a nanny for Gracie. Someone young. Someone fun. Someone who would sit on the rug in their family room and actually play one of the multitudes of board games they had stored away in the cabinet beneath the bookshelf.

She would never say it out loud to anyone other than Bennet, but Gracie had been a colossal accident. When she was forty-two and discovered she was pregnant, Bonnie had wept her way through the entire nine months. She already had her two kids, the most she'd ever wanted or planned for. The sleepless nights, diapers, nursing, constant supervision, and now, Disney shows, had been a thing of her past.

With both her boys long past their toddler years, Bonnie had been looking forward to going back to work of some sort. Doing something for herself and her sanity. At first, the idea of having a newborn again seemed like it would rip that sense of self away.

But when one of the two city council positions in their district was vacated, she found herself, six months pregnant, throwing her hat into the ring anyway. She had already done motherhood one hundred and fifty percent committed, she reasoned. This time, the baby was going to have to spend some time in daycare.

With her husband's family name, and her extensive community connections throughout The Enclave, Bonnie had won that election by a landslide.

Now, at forty-eight, and with Gracie in school full time, her sights were set even higher—a Colorado Senate seat.

Bonnie Sloan had been playing house for long enough.

She opened Bennet's office door and stopped short when she saw his car keys tossed onto the middle of his desk. He was home? She hadn't heard him—he must have come in when she was in the back-yard. She maneuvered around his desk and reached for his framed diploma from Berkeley hanging on the wall to her right. Lifting it from the wall mounting, she placed the certificate carefully in the armchair, punched in the twelve-digit combination, and twisted the handle open. She grabbed the folder containing all of George's essential documents and headed for the back staircase on this side of the house, careful to avoid the living room and her expectant five-year-old.

She was only halfway up the staircase when she heard them.

Voices, still too distant to hear clearly, but a knowing dread filled her anyway. Bonnie moved faster up the remaining stairs, and when she reached the top, she turned away from the hall that led to George's room and toward the one that led to Elijah's. With every step, the sounds grew louder and more distinct. Every angry word became easier to decipher through Elijah's bedroom door.

Bennet was home all right, and he was arguing with Elijah—again.

With George's social security card and birth certificate still in her hands, Bonnie stood outside Elijah's door. She tried to make out exactly what her husband and son were fighting about.

"You think you get to fucking talk to me like that?" Bennet yelled.

Bonnie closed her eyes—she was already too late. Whatever had started the argument, it had now escalated into one of the rage-filled tirades she worked so hard to prevent.

When she caught them in time.

"When you act like an asshole," Elijah shouted, "and just expect me to nod my head and—"

"What did you fucking call me?"

Bonnie placed her hand on the bedroom doorknob, ready to make her presence known and hopefully put an end to it.

"Mom?" Gracie's voice interrupted.

Bonnie turned and saw Gracie, wide-eyed and brow furrowed. She could also clearly hear her brother and father arguing.

"It's okay," Bonnie tried to reassure her. "Go back downstairs. I'll be there in a minute."

Gracie shook her head, her eyes riveted on the door.

"You're a fucking asshole!" Elijah screamed.

Gracie lunged forward, clearly intent on rushing into her brother's room herself, but Bonnie intercepted her. Sweeping Gracie up and into her arms, she held her squirming child the best she could and headed for the stairs.

"Let me go!" Gracie shouted. Her body writhed like a sack of snakes hell-bent on getting loose.

Bonnie held on to her daughter and the banister, trying her best to keep both Gracie and herself from falling. She had managed to get halfway down the stairs when they heard it.

"I fucking hate you!" Elijah screamed.

Then the sound of storming, heavy steps echoed through the second floor right before the thunderous wallop of large bodies that crashed against a wall, the floor—things breaking.

Bonnie let Gracie slide from her arms and ran back up the stairs.

CHAPTER FIVE

Alyson stood at the top of her basement stairs, staring down at the closed door below her. As her mind ran through several options before her, a white-hot flame of annoyance ignited in her chest.

When she and Andrew left the house for the pool five hours ago, Justin had waved off coming with them.

"Daaaad," Andrew had whined, clearly disappointed that Justin would, yet again, not be coming with them somewhere.

"Sorry, dude," Justin said with a smile and messed Andrew's hair. "But I need to mow the lawn and fix a couple of the sprinkler heads."

"Can't you do it later…or tomorrow?" Alyson had asked, trying hard not to whine herself.

"I just want to get it taken care of today. That way, I can head over to the airport tomorrow and see if there are any open flights for the week."

Alyson sighed but said nothing. It was true, Justin had limited time away from his job; the weekends really were the only time to take care of all the things around the house beyond her ability to fix. But it was also true that he spent much of his free time, and their limited funds, continuing to work toward his private pilot's license—a hobby she kept hoping he would one day grow out of.

Andrew, on the other hand, wasn't put off so quickly. "But you *never* come," he complained.

Which was true. Justin rarely joined her and Andrew for trips to the pool, the park, or even the backyard to kick a soccer ball.

"That's not true," Justin had countered. "We just went to the zoo."

Igniting the memory of the zoo trip had stopped Andrew's argument. Defeated, he dropped his small shoulders and stood before his father disappointed without any further attempts to get him to come along.

"Go grab one of the beach towels from the bathroom closet," Alyson said, watching as Andrew headed for the stairs. When she was sure he was out of earshot, she turned back to Justin, who was already moving toward the basement stairs. "That zoo trip was four weeks ago."

"What?" Justin turned back to her, his voice carrying an edge she hadn't heard when he was making his excuses to Andrew. He faced her, resting his hand on the banister.

"We didn't *just* go to the zoo. It was a month ago."

Alyson watched the space between her husband's eyes furrow as he processed her words. She could tell, having been married to him for almost seven years, that he was attempting to parse the meaning of her tone from the simple fact she just stated. It was this meaning, they both knew but never spoke of, that was the real topic of this conversation.

"Okay," he said, either not caring about what she really meant or deciding not to address it straight on. "And?" he shrugged.

She raised her eyebrows so high, she could actually feel the pressure it created behind her eyes. "I just thought you should know, you know, that when your son tells you that you never do anything with us…there's a reason."

His nostrils flared. The movement was slight, nearly undetectable, but Alyson knew this man and all his tells. She felt an electric wave of tension rise up between them, and it made the muscles in her back flex painfully up her spine.

He inhaled. "So what? You don't want the sprinklers fixed?"

"No, I mean, yes…of course I do. Obviously, we have to." It felt impossible to say what lay just below the surface, to speak outright what she was really thinking. Just lately, she'd had a creeping sense that even if there weren't sprinklers, dishwashers, or a leaking faucet to fix, Justin still wouldn't want to spend time with her and Andrew on the weekends. "We just miss you." She lightened her tone and shrugged, wanting more than anything to avoid an argument that would completely ruin the weekend. "So maybe you could meet us there?" she practically pleaded, and hated it. "If you finish soon?"

Justin turned away from her and headed down to the basement. "Yeah, sure. We'll see." He pushed hard against the wood door, and the loud squeak it always made echoed up the narrow stairwell. That sound, every time she heard it, grated on Alyson's every nerve—yet another home project that needed attention. "Have fun," he said before disappearing into the basement, shoving the door closed behind him.

And now, five hours later, here she stood again, staring down at that fucking closed door with her husband on the other side. Her husband, Andrew's father, who had not joined them at the pool and was also not still fixing sprinklers. She was mad, yes, but the anger was an easy cover, a strong emotion that was preferable to the sickening swirl that was churning in her gut.

Fear.

Alyson stared down the stairwell, with both her hands gripped to the handrails, and considered going down there. She imagined placing her hands on that doorknob, pulling the tight door from its frame, seeing for herself why Justin hadn't come to the pool today, why he chose not to go with them most days.

But even the thought of it, staring head-on into whatever was changing him, changing them—whatever it was that kept him down there so much—caused a flight of panic to take wing in her chest. In her experience, there were often uncomfortable consequences that resulted from facing things.

"Mom!" Andrew called from the family room. "I'm hungry!"

Alyson released the handrails and stood up straight. She tilted her head back and looked at the ceiling above her head. "Be right there!" she called back. She took a deep breath, held it, then let it go as she bent her neck to the left, then to the right. Tension had lately developed into tight bands of constricted muscle and tendons across her back and up her neck. The stretch pulled and caused pain to shoot across her shoulder blades, but not release.

As she walked to the kitchen, she pulled her phone from her back pocket to check the time. Three forty-five—too early for dinner, but Andrew wouldn't be able to wait until then. His mood would deteriorate, and he would become crankier and more whiny if he didn't eat soon. She was about to pull open the fridge and think up a healthy snack that wouldn't spoil dinner when her phone buzzed in her hand.

Alyson glanced at the screen; it was a Facebook notification. She swiped it open.

"Moooommmm!" Andrew called again.

"I'm getting it!" she yelled back. "Just a minute!"

The notification was for The Enclave's neighborhood page—Bennet Sloan had posted something. Alyson leaned over her white marble-top island and used her elbows to prop herself up while she held her phone with both hands. It was a picture of Bennet and his son George. Big white smiles, Bennet had his arm slung over his son's shoulders. George held a piece of paper between his hands. The post read: Guess who committed to playing football for Yale next year?

Alyson placed both her thumbs in the middle of the picture and enlarged it on her phone. The blue Yale letterhead, shield, and open-book logo were clear, but the text was too small to be decipherable.

Not that Alyson thought Bennet and George would lie about such a thing—of course the Sloans' oldest child would be attending an Ivy League school next year. Even if Alyson had a hard time imagining George having the academic and athletic competence to pull off such a feat on his own, she had no doubt the Sloans' money and influence were able to escort him all the way to society's upper limits.

No, Alyson wasn't focused on the validity of the text; she was studying Bennet's and George Sloan's faces. Reading their eyes, the lines around their mouths, the angle of an arched brow. She was hunting for a sign to quiet the storm of injustice rising in her blood. Some symptom of strain, buried unhappiness, a shitty father-son relationship. But other than George's amusing and age-appropriate teenage, aw-shucks embarrassment, Alyson could only find evidence of a father who was beaming with pride for his son. A son he clearly loved very much.

"Moooooooommmmmm!" Andrew wailed from the family room.

Alyson closed her eyes and put her phone facedown on the marble. Annoyed, she let go of any thoughts of preventing the ruination of dinner and made four quick strides to her walk-in pantry. She yanked open the frosted-glass door, grabbed the box of Cheez-Its from the shelf, and strode into the family room where Andrew was transfixed by an episode of *PJ Masks*. Alyson popped open the box lid, unfurled the inner plastic bag, and handed her five-year-old son the whole box.

Without taking his eyes off the screen, Andrew simultaneously took the box from his mother with one hand and reached into it with the other. Alyson waited several seconds for a "Thank you," or some kind of acknowledgment at least, but when Andrew didn't look at her even once, and clearly wasn't going to, she said, "You're welcome."

Andrew turned his head slightly, as if hearing a strange noise, but his glazed eyes never left the screen. He placed three Cheez-Its into his mouth and chewed them with his mouth open.

For a moment, she considered grabbing the remote off the

couch next to him and turning the TV off altogether. She imagined Accepted-to-Yale George Sloan didn't sit around dropping cheesy cracker crumbs all over the Sloans' likely impeccable house while staring dumbfounded at the television half his life.

Not even when he was five.

But Alyson already knew what it would cost her to make such a bold move with Andrew—he could tantrum for hours when really triggered. Abruptly shutting off his show would do just that, and that wasn't something she felt like dealing with right now.

After all, she had already spent the entire afternoon entertaining him and keeping him happy. She needed a break.

Of course, if Justin wasn't preoccupied in the basement, he could help her parent their strong-willed son. At the very least, they could trade off every once in a while.

Leaving Andrew to his show, and keeping the peace, Alyson returned to her phone on the kitchen counter. She pulled up Bennet Sloan's personal feed and clicked on the pictures. There were hundreds.

Alyson scrolled through the gallery, whizzing past holidays, birthdays, vacations, sports events—it was all here. Bennet Sloan spending his life with his arms around his children and his wife, Bonnie. Public, visual documentation that he loved them, enjoyed being around them, and wanted other people to know it! Why else does a man take the time to post these treasured family moments to share with his friends?

Bennet Sloan was a good father with a good family.

Justin Tinsdale was hiding, for reasons unknown, in their family's basement.

Alyson's heart beat hard in her chest as she left Bennet's page and navigated back to The Enclave's neighborhood page. A nervous dread trickled through her veins as she clicked in the new post box, typed her message, added her photos, and hesitated for only a split second before her thumb hit Post.

She placed her phone back on the counter in front of her. She took a step backward, as if trying on some level to separate herself not only from what she had knowingly just done but also any personal investigation into why she had done it.

Without wanting to give it any real thought, she bent down, opened her wine fridge, and slid out the half-empty bottle of chardonnay she had started last night. She poured the perfectly chilled, golden liquid into one of her wedding gift goblets. One clear thought rose above all her small attempts to justify her actions.

She was tired of the Bonnie Sloans of the world. Those perfect women, with their doting husbands, huge houses, imported cars, and Ivy League–bound children. It would do this neighborhood some good to realize that not everything was so perfect about people like the Sloans.

Alyson took a sip from her glass and felt, for the first time all day, some of the tension roping across her shoulder blades release. "It's a public service," she whispered to herself and took a drink.

Yes. The public had a right to know the truth.

CHAPTER SIX

Truth be told, Bonnie Sloan fucking hated social media. Even though her face, and life, was plastered across multiple platforms because of her political campaign, personally she thought they were a blight to humanity, common courtesy, critical thinking, and rational thought. A simple-minded, multi-tentacled monstrosity that maimed, destroyed, and killed careers according to the shrill will of mob mentality.

She received a text message from Jessica Hampton late Saturday afternoon, right when she was in the middle of dealing with Bennet and Elijah's latest battle of wills.

Umm, have you seen what someone posted on the Enclave page? It's about George. You should take a look.

That night, after Bennet left to catch his flight to Atlanta to meet with both developers and potential investors, Bonnie sat at her mahogany desk. She gazed at the picture of her son's distinctive electric-blue Jeep posted to The Enclave's Facebook page. Bonnie had read this woman's rant about her son's deplorable driving habits: speeding, music blaring, complete disregard for the safety of small children. She found that she could not disagree with any of it.

George drove like an asshole—it was a simple fact.

No, being a pragmatic woman at heart, Bonnie couldn't argue with—*what was her name?*

Alyson Tinsdale.

No, she couldn't argue with Alyson's assessment of George's driving. What she did find irritating was the way this Alyson had chosen to handle her complaint.

Publicly.

Also, the whole thing read as incredibly disingenuous. Alyson had begun her public scree with, Does anyone know this driver?

Yes, Alyson, *everyone* knows this fucking driver. They know him, his car, his house, his mother, father, brother, and sister. They know his girlfriend, the school he attends, the sport he plays, his GPA, and—thanks to Bennet's most recent brag post—that he will be attending Yale next year.

What is hard to believe, Alyson Tinsdale, is that you *really* don't know any of this.

Because Bonnie suspected she did. This was nothing more than a passive-aggressive, chickenshit, social media pitchfork attempt to incite the neighborhood mob to like, comment on, and cow George, or maybe the Sloans as a whole, into contrite submission.

And if that was the case, well, there was a critical piece of information that Alyson Tinsdale, being new to the Enclave community, was missing.

Bonnie Sloan, having dedicated herself body and soul to this neighborhood, was the queen of its mob. By the time Jessica had alerted her, the post had been sitting on the page for hours, and it had only one like.

By Carl Wayland. And of course, he liked it—the neighborhood Don Quixote was on his quest to bring Bonnie and Bennet to heel.

Bonnie clicked on Alyson's profile and scrolled through her page. She didn't know her, but the name was ringing some bells. She stopped on a picture of Alyson crouching down and taking a selfie at the Enclave park with her young son, Andrew, who looked to be about five.

And then it came to her. Alyson's son was in Gracie's kindergarten class. Bonnie sat back in her chair and scoffed out loud. There was hardly a day that passed without Gracie coming home and reporting on Andrew's behavior in the class.

Oh, the hypocrisy.

Bonnie closed her eyes and considered the multitude of ways she could make this woman's life a living hell in this neighborhood. It would require almost no effort at all.

She leaned forward again and closed her laptop with a snap. But, unlike Alyson Tinsdale, who was young and rash, Bonnie had acquired a measure of restraint over the years.

Her phone buzzed against the wood desk. It was Jessica again.

Just occurred to me, this is the woman Gabby Lawrence asked me to invite to book club this week! What should I do?!

Bonnie thought about it for half a second before responding.

Invite her. I'd like to get to know her better.

Oh my God, you really are a politician now! 🙄

Ha, ha. She's young, and she's new. I'm giving her the benefit of the doubt.

Well, you're a better person than I am. If I were you, I'd hop right on that post and hand that bitch her ass.

As much pleasure as that might give me, I suspect it would end up making my life more difficult right now, not less.

Okay, grownup. You have a point. Sending her the link to the book club page now.

Plus, age had also taught Bonnie to try like hell to keep her enemies as close as possible. They were easier to influence when they were within arm's reach.

Someone knocked at her office door right before opening it. "Mom?" Elijah asked, sticking his head through the crack. "Are you busy?"

"No," she said, putting her phone down. "Come in."

Her youngest son slipped through the door and closed it behind him, turning the lock on the handle. When he turned back around, she could see the storm collecting in his features half a second before his eyes filled with tears. "Did Dad leave?" he asked, and whatever emotional restraint he'd been hanging on to broke with his words. The tears he'd been so obviously trying to hold back ran down his face.

Bonnie stood up from her chair. "Come here," she said as she rounded her desk and met him in the middle of her office. She opened her arms, and her son lunged into her embrace, nearly knocking her off balance with his recently acquired size and strength, which he had no idea how to manage yet.

In so many ways, Elijah was still a little boy. But he was now operating in a body that had grown four inches over the summer and added twenty pounds. He felt huge in her arms as he sobbed into her shoulder.

"It's okay," she said, rubbing his back and trying to help him calm down. "It's all going to be okay."

"Did he leave?" he asked again.

"Yes," she said. "His flight takes off about six."

She held him the best she could, the weight of him pressing into her. Elijah had always been the most emotionally volatile of all her children. Comforting him had been infinitely easier when he was still small enough to crawl into her lap.

"I'm sorry, Mom," he said.

"I know you are."

"Do you think he's sorry?"

Bonnie sighed. "I'm sure he is," she said. But in truth, she thought it was equally possible that Bennet was still in a rage over this recent dogfight with his son.

Elijah pulled away from her, his eyes downcast. "Can we call him?"

Bonnie ran her fingers through her son's sweaty, disheveled hair. "How about we wait until he lands in Atlanta? He's probably trying to get through security…or boarding." *But most likely he's sitting at the bar in the United Red Carpet Lounge having a scotch and soda.* "Better to call once he's settled in his hotel room."

Elijah looked even more crestfallen, but he nodded in agreement.

Bonnie wiped his face once more. "Are you okay?"

He nodded and took a deep breath. "I'm going to ride my bike to the lake…maybe fish for a while."

"Okay. Be careful."

He let her kiss his cheek, then turned and left.

When she was sure he was gone, she closed her eyes and let all her very real worries and fears settle into the lines of her face. She took a breath, and then another, trying her best to practice what her twice-weekly guided meditation sessions preached to her. She wanted to center herself, balance the chaos, stop resisting the reality of life as it was.

Quite frankly, it felt fucking impossible.

Her eyes flew open, and an anxiety that refused to be kept at bay settled beneath her breastbone. It seemed to her that just lately, the universe was attacking her life on every conceivable front—like an autoimmune disorder dispatching disease-fighting antibodies to attack all the once healthy and thriving aspects of her life.

She was exhausted. Never more than on days like today, when everyone around her was losing their shit and taking the stress of their existence out on each other. Meanwhile, she was required to reroute everyone back to emotionally stable ground in addition to never, ever, ever losing control of her own shit.

She felt like the captain of a jumbo jet plummeting to earth. Always maintaining an outward appearance of detached control while urging the broken machinery of their life to skid to a halt on a grassy field instead of imploding into a fiery inferno on the side of a mountain.

It was never her turn to release the yoke, throw her hands over her head, and start crying and screaming about all the many scary circumstances of life.

Bonnie left her office and padded on perfectly pedicured toes to her kitchen. Once she had interrupted the firestorm of Bennet and Elijah's argument and sent them both to their respective corners, she had called Bennet's mother, Marjorie, to farm out Gracie for a sleepover with Grandma. Escaping the drama, George had jumped in his Jeep and driven away of his own volition—undoubtedly to his girlfriend's house. So now, with Elijah at the lake and Bennet at the airport, she had the house to herself.

They had received their monthly wine shipment today, and the bottles were still waiting in the butler's pantry for her to sort and take down to the cellar. She grabbed one of the cabernets, not bothering to digest the accompanying information card about maker, region, flavor, and scents—she didn't care right now. She placed the bottle beneath her counter-mounted corkscrew without bothering to cut the foil first. With one swift pull, the cork popped from the bottle and ejected onto the floor. She left it there, grabbed one of her bowl-shaped wineglasses from the cupboard, and headed out to her back patio.

The days were getting noticeably shorter now. The sun had set behind the mountains in the distance. A vibrant spectrum of reds, oranges, yellows, blues, and purples swirled and blended with a collection of high-hanging clouds. A natural display so spectacular it looked more like an artist's creation than anything that could be real. Bonnie poured her wine and noticed that her swimsuit from her morning swim was still hanging on the back of one of her patio chairs where she'd left it to dry.

She took a sip from her glass as she plucked the now dry suit from the chair and glanced into her side neighbors' backyards. She didn't see anyone out, but just to be safe, she retreated into the recesses of her covered patio before taking off her clothes and quickly slipping her suit on.

Next to the shed that housed the pool's pump, she grabbed one of the folded towels from the cupboard and flipped on both the underwater light and the pool's waterfall. She laid her towel on the stamped ebony-stained concrete at the water's edge and then sat down with her glass and bottle to watch the skies over the Rocky Mountains shift and dance with color as the sun dipped farther west behind them.

Bonnie slipped both her feet into the water and leaned on her left arm while her right kept hold of the glass. She loved this view. Given different financial circumstances, she would be riding right next to Carl Wayland. Galloping along on his quest to preserve their ability to walk out their back doors and gaze into this wonder of a view every day.

But because her circumstances, and her family, were tethered to Sloan Investment, she wasn't in the position to make decisions based solely on what she desired. Her choices had to be smart, calculated carefully, and, above all, perfectly defendable from any and all public criticism.

She couldn't afford to be an object of scrutiny right now.

She was taking another sip from her glass when movement to the right of her periphery caught her attention. Bonnie turned her head. Two backyards over, a lone figure stood in his own yard, staring up at the Rocky Mountain skyline before him. Bonnie watched as he looked left, noticed her as well, then lifted his own glass in acknowledgment to her before taking a sip and then a seat in one of his outdoor chairs.

Carl Wayland had never hated Bonnie or her family, but he was a man long accustomed to getting what he wanted. There wasn't any way Extreme Golf was erecting their monstrosity between Carl and his mountain view without a fight, and Bonnie knew it.

Bonnie finished the rest of her wine in one large swallow, planted both her hands on the smooth concrete beside her, and hoisted herself up and into the pool's warm blue waters. In one movement, she slipped all the way under.

As she held her breath, her arms and hair weightless and floating up around her, it occurred to Bonnie that—despite the fact that it would completely destroy Sloan Investment—a part of her secretly rooted for Carl Wayland to win his war.

CHAPTER SEVEN

Already dressed and ready for school, Elijah sat on the edge of his bed, staring at the closed door to his room. His stomach twisted into its ever-present knot, and he tried using the deep breathing strategies the school counselor had taught him.

With sharp, angry claws, the anxiety fought back. Pulling at his insides, racing through his bloodstream, disassembling him at his core. His mind, unwilling to be silenced, landed with a thud on an "anxious thought." With that foothold, his thinking took off in a dead sprint through all the other worries that drove his heart rate faster and faster. Feeding that voracious, unhinged entity that existed at his core, hell-bent, it flapped its enormous wings and launched him into a terrified panic.

Elijah rocked. Back and forth, back and forth, trying with everything in him to hang on. *Please, please make it stop.* Tears ran down his face. His breaths were shallow, but he tried to blow one out in a fast stream anyway, the weak air losing force and leaving a spray of spit on his lips.

A hard, two-part knock at his door made him jump. The sound of his door opening, exposing him, untethered him from the last strings of control he had. George ducked his head into his room.

"If you want a ride—" When George witnessed Elijah mid-spiral, his face darkened. "What the fuck is wrong with you now?"

A flood washed over Elijah, blinding him, igniting him, and his rational mind slipped down behind some ancient evolutionary force once designed to protect him at his most vulnerable. Elijah flew off his bed, fists raised for his taller, stronger older brother. Obscenities he could neither hear nor comprehend erupted from his mouth like a person possessed and speaking in tongues.

George shifted his stance and was ready before Elijah was even halfway across his room. Once in contact range, George stepped to the side, grabbed both of Elijah's wrists, and used his uncontrolled flailing momentum against him. Pulling him farther, until he passed George and fell to the floor outside Elijah's bedroom.

Confused, Elijah was on his stomach, and George moved in behind him. Dropping a heavy knee into his back, George grabbed both of Elijah's arms and twisted them painfully behind his back.

Elijah screamed, bucked, twisted, and tried pitifully to kick his brother with the backs of his heels.

"Calm down, psycho!" George yelled.

"What is going on here?" Their mother's voice broke through the riot.

"Get the fuck off me! You fucking motherfucker! Get off me!" Elijah screamed, his own voice reverberating off the walls all around them.

"George," their mother said. "For God's sake, get off him!"

Elijah saw his mother's feet rush toward them.

"I'm not getting off until he calms down!" George said.

Elijah writhed, kicked, bucked, all while a steady high-pitched scream rang from his mouth. The weight on his back increased for a second, then was gone. His hands were free—he was loose. He flipped onto his back, feet scrambling, arms swinging. He stood up—his fist connected with something.

He heard his mother's voice cry out.

Elijah ran through the loft to the far corner, pressed himself into it, and shrank into a ball. With his hands over his head, he peered out at the image of his mom sprawled backward on the floor, her hand cupping her face as blood poured between her fingers.

"Mom?" His mouth moved, but no sound passed his lips.

Elijah watched his brother look down at their mother; she was hurt, bleeding—and it was Elijah's fault. Whatever composure George had been hanging on to vanished, and he turned toward Elijah in rage. Shoulders hunched, fists clenched, he came at Elijah. "You fucking little shit! I'm going to kill you!"

Elijah buried his face in his arms and waited to feel the impact of George's fists.

"George!" their mom commanded. "Stop!" Her voice, deep with authority, was like a bucket of ice.

Elijah peeked out from between his forearms and saw his enormous brother frozen in place, halted by the weight of their mother's injunction.

She stood to her full height, blood still pouring from her face, and moved into the space between Elijah and George. "That is enough. I've had enough. I will handle this, George."

"Have you seen yourself? He fucking hit you."

Elijah stared at the carpet where his mother stood. Three drops of blood fell and soaked into the soft, cream fibers. She lifted the bottom of her nightshirt and wiped a smear of blood from her face. "Yes, I'm aware. But you beating the crap out of him isn't going to solve anything. It's only going to make it worse."

"Well, someone should beat the crap out of him. What kind of psycho hits his mom?"

"Please," she begged. "Just walk away and let me handle this."

George stood, wide stance and ready, for several more seconds, then shook his head and stormed from the loft and down the stairs.

Once George was downstairs, Bonnie turned toward Elijah and crouched before him. Her hands reached out, laying her palms flat against his hands, which gripped his hair by the fistful. She took a ragged breath. "What happened?" she whispered.

He looked up into her eyes, then at the blood smeared all across her face. A feeling so profound tore through him on a tidal wave of regret. "I don't know," he sobbed and shook his head. "I'm so sorry, Mom."

She sat on the floor next to him, pulled him into her arms, and rocked him gently while he cried. "I know," she whispered. "I know."

His mom had almost let him stay home from school. "You've already missed so much," she explained. "It's not even October, and you've had five absences. I don't think I can even keep you out anymore without a doctor's note." Her voice was calm—she was simply stating the facts. She didn't scream and yell at him, not like his father. She hardly ever even raised her voice at him. Which just made the reality of what had happened this morning all the worse. He wished she would get mad, shout at him, call him the piece of shit he knew he was.

At least it would make sense to him.

Her kindness and a seemingly bottomless well of patience for his freak-outs made him feel so guilty, so utterly undeserving of her love.

His dad and brother were assholes to him, all the time, but Elijah understood the language of rage they used. They hated him. It was a concept he could relate to.

Lack of conditions—that seemed to be the best way to wrap his mind around his mother's love. For thirteen years, no matter what he did, said, threw, or broke, he never once looked into her eyes and saw anything but love. It terrified him, utterly, to think that one day he would go too far even for her. One day he might look into those eyes and see that even she had finally given up on him.

He wanted to do better, really. He wanted whatever was wrong with him to get fixed. But he didn't know how.

His mother pulled her Porsche up to the school's front entrance and shifted into park. She reached into her purse and pulled out a folded note. "I probably shouldn't go in," she said, handing him the paper.

"Because of your nose," he said.

His mom flipped down her sun visor and opened the mirror. "Yes." As she gazed at her reflection, her fingers prodded carefully at the bruised and swollen flesh.

He watched her, still horrified at what he had done to her—even if it was an accident.

She closed the mirror and turned to him. "It looks worse than it is. I'm sure this will be healed up in no time at all."

"Is it broken?" His voice cracked on the last word. The thought threatened to send him into yet another emotional tailspin.

She held his gaze with a firm and reassuring expression. "It is for sure not broken, so don't worry about it. You know it was an accident. I know it was an accident."

"George doesn't think it was an accident."

His mother took a deep breath and sighed it out. "I'll worry about George. Right now, I need you to focus on being calm. Deep breaths, no catastrophic thoughts."

Just then, an enormously catastrophic thought occurred to him for the first time that morning. "Dad is going to find out."

His mother licked her lips. "No. No, he's not. Okay? Listen to me—it's over now. Done. We are moving on. I will talk to George, make him see reason. And Dad is for sure not finding out about any of this."

Elijah looked down at the folded paper clutched between his hands.

"I wrote that you had a doctor's appointment this morning." She tapped the paper with her long, pink, painted nail. "So that's why you're late. Now tell me, why are you late this morning?"

Elijah swallowed; he hated to lie. "I…I had a doctor's, doctor's… doctor's appointment."

His mom smiled at him, leaned across the center console, and kissed his cheek. "Okay. It's all going to be fine. Right as rain, and by this afternoon, this morning will be a distant memory."

Elijah nodded, not believing a single word of what she said—she only wanted him to feel better.

And not freak out again.

He lugged his heavy backpack up off the floor between his feet and ran his arm through one strap as he opened the door. Holding his note, he stopped before getting out and held it up to her.

"Maybe we *should* make a doctor's appointment. For real," he said.

His mother looked at him, her eyes squinting slightly, as if she were only now noticing something about him that she never had before. She nodded. "Yes…I think maybe that is a good idea."

Elijah stepped out of the car and onto the curb. About to close the door, he stopped. "Can you call them today?" he asked, looking into her eyes.

Her index finger tapped twice on the steering wheel. She hesitated, but only for a moment. "Yes. I'll go home right now and call."

Elijah closed his eyes, nodded once, and shut the door. His mother's promise brought him some small sense of reassurance. They would go to a doctor. Get some help. An expert would examine him, tell him what was wrong with him and, most importantly, how to fix it.

Because he didn't want to live like this anymore.

CHAPTER EIGHT

Alyson stood on the sidewalk and double-checked the house number against the Facebook invite on her phone. Once she felt sure it was correct, she walked up the recently repaved driveway to the flagstone path. Evenly spaced landscape lights lit the way through the twilight evening to Jessica Hampton's front door.

Gabby had insisted the Enclave book club was a casual affair. "I'm wearing yoga pants and flip-flops, so don't stress, okay." But stress was precisely what Alyson did. Gabby was clearly already socially well established in this neighborhood, an insider with these women—whether she wanted to be or not. Given the way the women at the pool regarded Gabby, she could pull off wearing her pajamas if she chose to.

Alyson couldn't help but feel she had something to prove, but she didn't want to *appear* like she was trying to prove anything. She had combed her closet for over an hour that afternoon looking for some magic combination of fabrics that said *I'm relaxed, but not a slob. I'm smart, but not frigid. I like to have fun, but not too much fun, not crazy moms-gone-wild.*

Basically, she wanted to look like the woman they would all be dying to be friends with—just exactly the right amount of everything.

In the end, she decided she needed to be an only slightly better dressed Gabby—who actually *did* want to hang out with them. So she chose her cutest pair of jeans, a solid cream silk shirt, and paired it with a long silver chain that landed right at the top of her well-supported cleavage. On her feet: easy, but stylish, black flats.

She had pulled a mid-priced merlot from her wine rack, sliced the selection of cheeses she'd picked up at the grocery store, and paired them with some rolled charcuterie onto her chilled slate cheese board. Careful to remember her copy of *A Perfect Life* by Clare Collins for the discussion, Alyson arrived at Jessica's ten minutes after seven—ensuring she would neither be the first person there nor so late that it would seem rude and make her entrance awkward.

She arrived at a front door flanked on either side by large planters filled with billowing fall mums and pressed the button on Jessica's video doorbell system.

While she waited, Alyson noticed that along with the early mums, Jessica had already hung an autumn-themed wreath on her door. Despite the fact that it still felt like summer and the temperature had blazed upward of ninety-five degrees that afternoon. She had the feeling that tomorrow, the moment the calendar turned to October 1, Jessica's house and front porch would be dressed and ready for Halloween.

She had been standing for several seconds beyond what felt normal, especially since Jessica should have been expecting people. Her earlier fear crept back; maybe this was the wrong house. Alyson eyed the video doorbell again, its sizeable round fisheye camera staring back at her.

Or maybe they were all watching her from Jessica's phone.

Alyson stood perfectly still, suddenly afraid like a girl in middle school. Were all the popular girls pointing and laughing at her without her even knowing it? She resisted the overpowering urge to turn on her heel with her meticulously crafted charcuterie board in hand and return to the safety of her own car.

"Hello?" someone said suddenly and interrupted her paranoia. "Hello, Alyson?" The voice erupted from the small speaker on the doorbell.

She was being watched, right this minute. Alyson smiled at the camera. "Yes, it's me."

"Sorry, come on in. The door's open."

Alyson nodded, maybe to herself, maybe to Jessica watching her on her phone, perhaps to no one at all. It was impossible to know what the appropriate social etiquette was with a doorbell. Still, she opened the front door like she was told.

Alyson consciously wiped her feet on the natural fiber porch mat. Its message, Home Is Where the Heart Is, welcomed her right before she ducked her head into the house first, as if testing the atmosphere for oxygen. Expecting someone to be there to greet her, and seeing that there wasn't, she stood upright and entered Jessica's house.

A second later, Jessica rounded the corner at the far end of the hall and greeted Alyson with an apologetic smile. With both her palms raised at either side of her body, as if to say *I don't know what happened*, Jessica shook her head in exasperation. Her small frame slipped quick as a fish toward Alyson.

"I'm *so* sorry," she exclaimed. Lunging forward, she removed the platter from Alyson's hands. She gave her a brief one-sided hug like they actually knew each other. When she pulled away, her expression did seem genuine as she crinkled her nose. "We haven't had a new person in ages, and everyone just walks right in. I wasn't thinking and had turned the bell to mute on my phone." She guided Alyson down the spacious hall, across rectangular, gray slate tiles set into a herringbone pattern, beneath the gargantuan wrought iron chandelier hanging from the twenty-foot ceiling, past several individually lit pieces of *real art* hanging on the walls. When they arrived at the corner Jessica had appeared from, Alyson could hear the collective sound of women's voices.

"We're all in the kitchen," Jessica explained. "Which is where book club always seems to happen despite our best efforts to move to more comfortable chairs."

They rounded the corner, and Alyson had her first glimpse of Jessica's colossal kitchen. It was filled with members of the Enclave book club—about fifteen women ranging in age from late twenties to early sixties. They bustled to unwrap dishes, uncork wine, pull necessities from the industrial-sized refrigerator, whisk a sauce on the six-burner gas stove, or simply stand in pairs with wine in hand, talking.

Alyson didn't see Gabby among them.

"Honestly," Jessica said quickly before jumping back into the fray. "If you decide to come again, just walk right in. Doesn't matter whose house, really." She placed Alyson's platter on the counter closest to them, then raised both her hands to the group. "Ladies! Hello, everyone!"

It took a few seconds, but eventually all the women slowed their current activity, or stopped talking and turned toward Jessica. "Our guest is here. For those of you who don't know her, this is Alyson Tinsdale. She and her family moved to The Enclave at the beginning of the summer and her son..." Jessica stopped and turned to Alyson. "You have a boy, right?"

"Yes," Alyson nodded.

"He just started school at The Enclave Academy." Jessica turned again to Alyson. "Kindergarten?" Jessica clarified.

"Yes," Alyson nodded again, wondering how it was that Jessica, who didn't know her at all, seemed to know so much. "His name is Andrew. And my husband is Justin," Alyson included.

"Well, there you have it. Book club, meet Alyson. Alyson, meet book club. Please just dive in and make yourself comfortable." Jessica finished with a smile before reentering the center of her kitchen and taking control of a half-constructed vegetable platter.

Alyson was still holding both the wine she had brought and her copy of the book. She noticed all the other bottles everyone brought clustered on the rectangular kitchen table, along with both chardonnay and cabernet crystal stemware that sparkled under the overhead lights. She made her way around the exterior, high-top counter where Jessica had placed her platter and went into the kitchen. She put her bottle next to all the others and wondered if she should pour herself a glass.

"Do you prefer red or white?" someone asked her, her hands reaching onto the table for a bottle of the open chardonnay and a merlot.

"Probably the white to start," Alyson said. Grateful someone was starting a conversation with her, she smiled and turned toward the woman, who plucked one of the chardonnay stems and poured Alyson a glass of the chilled white wine.

As the woman handed Alyson her glass, a sickening swell of anxiety made Alyson feel weak.

"I'm Bonnie Sloan," the woman said, and her fingers brushed against Alyson's as they exchanged the glass. "Welcome to book club." She smiled and took a sip of her own blood-red wine.

Alyson felt her heartbeat, hard and fast, in her chest. "Hello," she managed. "Thank you," she said, raising her glass slightly before taking a tiny sip. She was utterly uncertain of what might happen next.

Was Bonnie about to confront her? Make a scene? Alyson didn't think she could handle that. Correction: she *knew* she couldn't. Had she known, or even suspected, that Bonnie Sloan was a member of the Enclave book club, she never would have come tonight.

Why? Why had she posted that picture of George Sloan speeding down her street?

In the moment, she had been filled with a sense of suburban vigilante justice. And now, standing here awkwardly in front of his mother? Who was maybe about to do the one thing Alyson hated the most—confront her. If that was the case, Alyson now deeply regretted her impulsive, angry act.

Bonnie's barely there smile coupled with her relaxed hold on her glass signaled a pleasant detachment. It was her eyes, focused and intense, that let Alyson know Bonnie knew exactly who Alyson was and what she had posted about George. "Your son goes to the Academy; he's in kindergarten?" she asked.

"Yes." Alyson smiled big. Like she was having a casual get-to-know-you conversation with another woman. "He's in Mrs. Sinclair's class."

Bonnie raised her eyebrows and her smile widened. "Of course he is," she said. Her tone dipped its toe into sarcasm and hinted at the anger Alyson could only imagine lurked just beneath her calm, perfectly groomed exterior. Bonnie took a breath, like a self-correction, and said, "What I meant to say was that my daughter, Gracie, is also in that class. They probably know each other."

That's great, Alyson thought, wishing she had figured out this important detail before she had set out to publicly humiliate Bonnie's oldest son. "How fun," she said quickly. "Maybe we should plan a playdate for them sometime."

Bonnie masked the disappearance of her chilly smile with a drink from her glass. Still, her eyes communicated her feelings perfectly all by themselves. *You must be out of your fucking mind.*

"Hey there," someone interrupted. Alyson felt a hand on her back and turned her head to see Gabby's smiling face appear beside her. "You made it. Sorry I was late."

"Don't worry, I got her started," Bonnie said, pointing to Alyson's glass. "I'm going to go check on my squash soup, make sure it's not burning." She excused herself and left Alyson and her anxiety alone with Gabby.

Once she'd left, Gabby turned toward the table and poured herself a huge glass of the Bordeaux. "Did she say anything to you about what you posted?" Gabby whispered so only Alyson could hear.

"No," she whispered back. "God, do you think she will? I'm so stupid. I wish like hell I hadn't done it."

Gabby stood back up and faced her, a smile planted on her lips, but her eyes looked worried. "We should talk," she said, then took a big swallow from her glass.

Gabby turned to face the busy kitchen. "Jessica," she called.

Jessica was standing at her island talking with four other women, eating some of the appetizers and sipping her wine. When she heard Gabby call for her, she turned and lifted her chin.

Alyson watched Gabby place her index and middle finger up to her mouth and raise her eyebrows in a silent question.

Jessica smiled and pointed to the small cupboard high above her fridge. "Behind the cookbooks," she said.

"Thanks," Gabby mouthed. "Take your wine out to the backyard, I'll be there in a second."

"You smoke?" Alyson asked, forgetting to hide her tone of astonished judgment.

"What?" Gabby pressed her fingers to the turquoise crucifix at her chest and pulled her head back in mock indignation. "Me? Of course not. Now go wait outside for me while I go bum a smoke from my non-smoking friend's secret stash."

Alyson watched Gabby knowingly grab a folded stepstool from one of Jessica's cupboards and take it over to the fridge so she would be able to reach the high cabinet. Alyson topped up her glass and did as she was told, making her way back out of the kitchen and through the family room to the sliding glass door that led to Jessica's backyard.

Since Alyson had adjusted to the air-conditioned house, the still-hot end-of-summer evening air felt suffocating by comparison.

She looked out over Jessica's sparkling sapphire pool and beyond the split rail fencing that separated the elaborately landscaped yard from the lush fairway of the Enclave golf course. In the distance, dark-gray clouds were rolling in over the Rockies, and Alyson could see that sheets of rain were blanketing the foothills. It would probably reach their neighborhood within the hour. Alyson took a deep breath to steady her nerves. Seeing Bonnie here was a surprise she hadn't anticipated. Coupled with the fact that Gabby seemed rattled when she found her standing and talking to Bonnie—and Gabby never seemed rattled—Alyson was now slightly terrified.

When she heard the door open behind her, she took a big drink of her wine and turned to face her friend.

"Hold this a second." Gabby handed her glass over while she pulled a single cigarette and a small BIC lighter from her shorts' pocket. With the cigarette hanging between her lips, Gabby cupped one hand to block the slight breeze while the other flicked the lighter. In two puffs, the cigarette was lit. She returned the lighter to her pocket, blew a stream of smoke sideways from her mouth, and took back her glass of wine. "Christ," she said as she closed her eyes, took another drag, blew it out, and then took a drink from her glass. She opened her eyes and focused all her attention on Alyson. "I needed that. Now let's talk about the situation here."

Still slightly flabbergasted to learn that Gabby smoked, Alyson pulled her disbelieving eyes from the red-hot end of Gabby's cigarette and focused instead on her words. "Do you think she saw what I posted on the Facebook page?" Alyson whispered, hoping that maybe she had misread Bonnie's tone and body language.

Gabby nodded her head. "Oh yes, along with everyone else in the neighborhood."

"Now see, I don't think so. It's been up for almost three days now, and not a single person has commented on it. And last I checked, only one other person had liked it."

Gabby looked directly into Alyson's eyes. "Trust me when I tell you that just because no one commented, and only *Carl Wayland* liked it, does not mean that everyone hasn't read it. Everyone in The Enclave knows that was George Sloan's Jeep, and I imagine very few believe you didn't know it too. I'm your friend, but honestly, the whole thing reads like a cheap public jab at the Sloans that is trying to be passed off as *I'm just a neighbor trying to do her part.*" Gabby took a swallow from her glass and waited for Alyson's defense.

But she didn't have one. Because what she did was precisely what Gabby described. A cheap public jab because she was too scared to confront the Sloans, or anyone really, face-to-face. Alyson stood, staring over Gabby's shoulder at Jessica's patio furniture with pale blue cushions. "I wish you had told me to take it down as soon as you saw it," Alyson whispered.

"I'm barely on Facebook—I only just saw before I came here tonight. And the only reason that happened was because I was checking the book club page for updates on what food everyone was bringing. But everyone else, they've read it and they're not commenting or liking it because they don't want to appear like they're standing in your corner."

Alyson felt sick. Real, honest-to-god nausea. "I should leave," she blurted, wanting nothing more than to run away from this house, this moment, and all the women inside it who were clearly already friends with Bonnie Sloan.

"You can't run," Gabby said. "You said you want to make friends with these women. So the only option left to you at this point is to make it right."

Alyson's eyes zeroed in on her friend's face. "But he does speed down our street every day! He nearly ran over Andrew."

Not unsympathetic, Gabby nodded. "All that is true. But was the way to handle it a public shaming? Or a private conversation with Bonnie?"

Alyson's shoulders sagged, and she closed her eyes. "I'm such a shitty person."

Gabby slung her arm over Alyson's shoulders. "You're not a shitty person," she said. "But you are kind of a coward." She squeezed Alyson close. "Luckily, it's not terminal, and it can be remedied by doing the one thing you fear the most right now."

"Talk to Bonnie Sloan?"

"Talk to Bonnie Sloan…and take the post down."

CHAPTER NINE

SHE FELT COLD, AND SO SHE REACHED FOR THE BLANKETS THAT MUST have slipped off of her in the night. Instead of finding her duvet, her hand connected with a cold, hard surface.

What was going on?

Alyson tried opening her eyes and was punished for it with a searing bright light. Why were the lights on? And why did she feel like she'd been hit in the head? Awareness dawned in small increments and with it a mounting sense of dread.

Her face was pressed against cold tiles.

She was facing the base of a toilet.

Alyson pushed herself to sitting, igniting a rage of protest in her head as blood rushed over her skull in thumping waves. She was in her downstairs bathroom, passed out on the floor next to the toilet that she had obviously gotten sick in.

"Mom? Are you okay?"

Alyson turned her head, her every muscle aching from too much wine and a night spent on the floor. There was her son, standing in the doorway in his blue sleeper pajamas that zipped from his foot to his neck, his expression both confused and worried to find her here. He moved toward her, the rubber traction on the bottom of his feet making a sticking sound against the tile. When he reached her, he placed one hand on her forehead.

"Are you sick?" he asked, staring into her eyes, waiting for a reasonable answer.

Heavier footsteps landed on the wood floor outside the bathroom, and Justin appeared. Already dressed for work in one of his blue oxford shirts and dark-blue neckties, he swept his eyes over her in one movement. "Yes, Mommy's sick," he said to Andrew, reaching his hand out to his son. "I'll get you some cereal before I leave."

Andrew hesitated for a second, like he was maybe not sure he should leave her.

"Go ahead," she whispered, her voice not capable of anything more robust. "I'll be right there."

Andrew took Justin's hand, and they left her to collect whatever dignity she might be able to scrape together. When Alyson stood up and caught her reflection in the mirror over the sink, she was horrified at the sight of herself. She was still wearing the jeans and blouse she'd so carefully chosen to make just the right statement with the Enclave book club last night. She examined her untucked and rumpled attire. There was a large, brownish stain cascading over her right breast; it didn't look like it would be washing out anytime soon. Her makeup had slid off her eyes and onto the baggy flesh beneath them. Her hair stood out in a wild and tangled mess.

Alyson turned on the faucet, closed her eyes, and cupped the freezing water onto her face. How had this happened? And what exactly had happened? She racked her tender brain, trying to force it to re-create the memories from last night.

She needed to know exactly how ashamed she should be while standing with Andrew at morning drop-off.

"I'm leaving," Justin said behind her. "I have a meeting at eight, and I can't be late."

Alyson grabbed the hand towel from the ring next to the sink and scrubbed at her eyes as she turned to face him.

"Okay," she said, like this was just any other morning on any other day.

"Are you going to be okay?" His tone was matter-of-fact and not sympathetic in the least. He raised his eyebrows as he took a sip of coffee from his travel mug.

"Yeah." She waved her hand and shrugged. "I'll be fine."

Justin stood there a moment more, like maybe he was considering something else he might add, then turned toward the garage without another word. She was relieved when he walked out the door, grateful for the chance to collect herself in private while getting Andrew ready for school. But less than a second later she heard the door open again.

"Are you aware that your car is not in the garage?" he called back into the house.

No, she was not aware of this. "Yes," she called back. Given how drunk she was, she must have walked home from Jessica's last night. "Don't worry, it's only a couple blocks away at Jessica's."

With no further response from Justin, she heard the garage door close again.

In the kitchen, Andrew was seated at the island counter, eating a bowl of Honey Nut Cheerios. Cartoons played on the TV in the family room. Alyson glanced at the clock on the stove. They had half an hour before they needed to walk out the door for school.

Actually, since she'd left her car outside Jessica's house, they would be walking to school this morning—she had fifteen minutes to get Andrew dressed and get herself ready to show her face.

There was little time for anything besides a ball cap, a quick powder to the face, and sunglasses to hide her bloodshot eyes. She threw on a pair of Lululemons, her most flattering sweatshirt, and tried her best to pretend her brain wasn't collapsing in on itself inside her skull.

"Why did you leave your car at your friend's house?" Andrew asked when they were only steps beyond their front drive.

Because I was blackout wasted and trying to be responsible, I guess. "One of my tires was flat," she lied. "So I'll need to get it fixed today while you're at school."

She felt the pressure of his gaze as Andrew looked up at her for several seconds, probably weighing her words against any and all evidence he had witnessed this morning. Whether he believed her or not, he didn't say another word about it. She watched as he ran ahead of her, always most content to be just out of her arm's reach, and kicked several of the small landscape rocks that had escaped their border and were scattered across the sidewalk.

Alyson considered which of the women from last night she was most likely to run into at drop-off. Bonnie Sloan was the first and most likely, since her daughter and Andrew were in the same class. Just the thought of seeing her after their brief encounter last night made Alyson's guts squirm.

It was true—much of what happened last night was a mystery, and a terrifying one, to her. But she did distinctly recall that when she and Gabby had come back inside after their heart-to-heart on the patio, Bonnie Sloan had already left. Alyson had been relieved to escape facing Bonnie again and having to apologize.

Partly because of the sheer humiliation of it—mostly because she didn't one hundred percent feel like she should. Gabby thought that Alyson's posting the picture of George Sloan in his Jeep was wrong. Alyson wasn't completely sold.

Someone needed to teach that spoiled brat a lesson. Then again, maybe Alyson wasn't the person who should be holding that class for him—or schooling him in public.

If she was completely honest with herself, she seemed to feel a deep-rooted but unexplainable bitterness toward the whole Sloan family, even before she knew it was George tearing down her street. There wasn't any single particular thing but a collection of thoughts that drove her to both loathe and fear them.

She supposed it was possibly their money. And their huge house, expensive cars, expensive clothes, successful careers, high-achieving children, physical beauty, and authority in general that made Alyson uncomfortable. No, more than merely uncomfortable, she realized.

Alyson was jealous. Of everything about them.

She stood next to Andrew, who had stopped at the corner to wait for her to cross the street. Without prompting, he reached up his small hand and placed it in hers.

The truth was, in comparison to Bonnie Sloan, Alyson Tinsdale felt very small, unaccomplished, and inconsequential.

"Mom, look. A fire truck!" Andrew said and raised his hand to point.

Alyson raised her gaze in the direction of his finger. Across the street, past the park next to the pool, and on the far side of The Enclave's private lake, a fire truck was slowing to a stop next to two police cruisers with their lights flashing.

Andrew yanked hard on her hand. "Is there a fire? Can we go over there?" he begged, a radiant excitement erupting from his expression. "Please! Please, Mom. Please can we go see them?" He pulled harder, grabbing her wrist with both hands, trying to change their course away from the road that led to school and toward the entrance to the park.

"Andrew." She laughed a little but knew immediately that this wasn't likely to end well. "No, we can't go over there." She smiled at him and kept her voice light, but there was a high probability this would lead to a meltdown right in the middle of the road.

"Mom! We *have* to."

Her brain fought against her hangover to come up with a good diversion. "We can't. Look." She crouched down next to him, placing one arm around his waist as she lifted him up. "It's not just the fire truck—there are police there too. Can you see them?"

He nodded his head.

"The police are working, doing their jobs to keep people safe. They won't let us just go over there and interrupt their important work to look at a fire truck."

He wilted in her arms from the disappointment but didn't argue with her logic. Police *were* important—there was no fighting this truth.

As they looked on, an ambulance rounded the distant corner on the far side of the lake and pulled up next to the police.

"I don't see a fire," Andrew said. "What are they doing? Was there an accident?"

Now just as curious as her son, Alyson squinted into the distance and tried to see what the emergency responders were doing over by the lake. "I'm not sure," she said. They were too far away for her to make out what was going on, but several people in uniforms were near the water's edge.

"Am I going to be late?" he suddenly asked.

His question broke through Alyson's curiosity.

"Because Mrs. Sinclair will make me turn my stick to yellow if I'm late."

They started walking again, faster now, while Alyson pulled her phone from her pocket. Crap, the late bell was going to ring in three minutes—there was no way they were making it on time.

"Are we late?" he asked again.

She could hear the worry in his voice. "It's okay," she reassured him while they picked the pace up to a jog. The increased blood pumping to her brain shredded through her frontal lobe and sent sharp spikes of pain into her temples. "People are late sometimes. I'm sure Mrs. Sinclair won't make you change your stick for that."

"She will. She said she will. I'm always on red…she doesn't like me."

This statement, and her pulsing brain, made Alyson stop jogging. "Andrew, wait. Stop for a second. What do you mean? Of course she likes you. She's your teacher."

Several feet away from her, he stopped too and shook his head. "I don't think so," he whispered. "Every day I get on red. Nobody else does, just me. She says I'm too hipper active. I don't know how to control myself."

Alyson stared at her son and watched as his eyes filled with tears while they stood on the sidewalk a block away from school. "She said you're *hyperactive*?"

He nodded, and several tears broke loose and rolled down his baby pink cheeks. "And now nobody wants to sit with me. I have to sit by myself."

She didn't breathe. Her mind raced, and her chest constricted as she imagined Andrew, for weeks now, sitting in class every day. Alone. Being called things, by his *teacher*. Sitting *alone*. Other kids not including him. The teacher *publicly* excluding him. Rage billowed inside her. She took two steps forward, picked up her son, and turned around.

"Where are we going?" he asked.

"Home," she said.

"But won't I get in trouble for missing school?"

"Nope." She kissed his cheek. "Mom's going to take care of everything."

CHAPTER TEN

Alyson had begun her angry email to Andrew's teacher five times. She would write a sentence, then delete it. Three sentences, delete. The fifth and final time, she managed two whole paragraphs before realizing she had blown far off course from her intended message. Delete.

She wanted to ask Mrs. Sinclair how the woman dare presume her son had ADHD. And *furthermore*, what sort of teacher said this to a child? And the rest of the class! And did she realize her actions were leading other children to be hateful, to exclude, to make her son feel like everyone at school hated him?

Including you, Mrs. Sinclair.

But every time she read back over her words, she never got it quite right. She wanted this woman to understand how both she and Andrew were feeling. And she wanted Mrs. Sinclair to feel equally bad for what she was doing in return.

Alyson worried she wasn't coming at this task in a way or with a tone that would lead Mrs. Sinclair to truly experience remorse. She felt it far more likely that Mrs. Sinclair would simply now slap Alyson with some derogatory label of her own.

Helicopter Parent.

Enabler.

Or Justin's personal favorite, Passive-Aggressive.

Annoyed, and still hugely hungover, Alyson closed her laptop in frustration and placed it on the coffee table in front of her.

Next to her, Andrew was curled on the couch with his favorite blanket, secretly sucking his thumb, and watching *Toy Story 3* for the hundredth time in his life. She leaned over and kissed his head while gently pulling his thumb from his mouth. "I'm going to get more coffee. Do you want anything to eat?"

He nodded his head, eyes never leaving the screen. Alyson waited several seconds for an elaboration she knew she wouldn't get. Finally, she sighed. "Do you want pancakes?"

He nodded again, then lifted his blanket to his face so he could hold it as cover in his fist while returning his thumb to his mouth. Alyson ignored it, and her feelings of guilt. With her mug in hand, she pushed herself off the couch and toward the kitchen.

Her phone, charging on the counter, pinged with a new text notification. She flipped it over to see the screen while pouring another large cup of her favorite hazelnut-flavored coffee three-quarters full.

The text was from Gabby. A pang of shame shot through her, and she placed her phone back facedown.

She grabbed her vanilla-flavored creamer from the fridge, then filled the rest of her cup with the syrupy-sweet liquid. It transformed her coffee into a rich, caramel-colored, hot intoxication of caffeine and sugar. An aromatic combination that was her definition of bliss most mornings.

But it was going to take far more than a great cup of coffee to shake all the emotions clouding her head right now. Alyson took a sip, allowing herself a small comfort from the mug's heat cradled against her palm, then braced herself as she opened Gabby's text.

Fully expecting some admonishing words for whatever embarrassing thing she may have done or said last night, she was relieved to see Gabby's actual words.

How are you feeling this morning?

Alyson put her mug down and typed her reply with both thumbs.

Actually, not too bad. I remembered to drink lots of water when I got home.

Which was, of course, complete and utter bullshit. But just in case she'd managed to pull off being blackout drunk, and no one but her was any the wiser, Alyson wasn't going to be the one to unnecessarily out herself—not even to Gabby.

That's good, because you really had a lot to drink last night. I thought you probably passed out...do you remember anything?

Alyson stared at Gabby's words and wished she could dig a hole and bury herself inside. She hadn't fooled anyone and now dreaded hearing about exactly how embarrassed she should feel. She debated continuing with her lie and pretending everything had been fine—of course she remembered—or simply confessing to Gabby that last night was a complete blur and begging her to help Alyson mitigate any damage she may have done.

Hello? Gabby prompted.

Alyson sighed. No, I don't really remember anything. I obviously drank way too much and ended up walking home. I feel terrible. Did I make a complete ass of myself?

Alyson waited to hear Gabby's response, detailing some horrific scene that would accelerate her spiral of shame. It was taking Gabby forever to answer, which made Alyson worry that there was a litany of terrible social crimes she had committed. Had she slurred her words? Stumbled? Fallen down drunk on Jessica's floor in front of everyone? Had she overshared or emotionally exposed herself in some way? Alyson steeled herself to hear it all, so when Gabby did finally respond, her simple question surprised her.

You walked home?

I must have. My car wasn't in my garage this morning.

Alyson watched for Gabby's response, which again seemed to be taking forever.

Did you get it from Jessica's? she finally texted back.

Yes. Andrew and I walked over there this morning.

Andrew? Did he stay home? Sick??

No...long story. I'll call you later about it.

Since he stayed home, you probably didn't see the cops and emergency vehicles at the lake this morning?

I did, actually. But no idea what was going on.

Looks like there was some sort of accident. It's all over the Enclave FB page.

Piqued and also relieved that whatever happened last night at book club was maybe not the most interesting topic of conversation that morning, Alyson closed her message app and opened Facebook. She clicked on her groups, and then the neighborhood page. The first post was about whatever was going on at the lake—a question by Annie Bleecher. Alyson spent half a second trying to remember if this was one of the women she'd met last night before continuing into the thread.

Does anyone know what is going on at the lake this morning? Saw lots of police and fire vehicles parked on the west side, just past the park, when driving Jordan and Emily to school this morning. Is everything okay?

Her question was followed by several others expressing that, yes, they too had seen them, but no, they also had no idea. This went on for fifteen or twenty posts, everyone reiterating the same thing before Alyson found the one with more information.

Todd Singleton posted:

I have it on good authority that a body was found near the lake this morning.

"What?" Alyson blurted out loud into her empty kitchen.

"Mom?" Andrew asked as he craned his neck over the back of the couch, his expression a question.

"Nothing," she said, giving him a warm smile. "It was just something I read."

Satisfied, he turned back to his movie and his thumb.

Alyson returned her attention to her phone. The "good authority" comment had hijacked the rest of the comments. Everything else sprang from there. Some expressed shock, others disbelief, while some even seemed angry that Todd Singleton would say such a thing. They demanded to know what "good authority" his information was sourced from. It was irresponsible to start and spread unfounded rumors on this site. The poster even suggested the administrators should actually take the whole thing down until more reputable and official information was made public by the police or news.

Todd Singleton, probably not aware of the firestorm his tiny post would create, had stayed silent on the comments right up until the angry one criticizing him.

Todd Singleton: My good authority, and source, if you will, is the simple fact that it was my two sons who found the body on their way to school this morning. I was simply trying to let the community know that something very serious is going on. Rest assured that I won't be saying anything else until the official reports are made public.

The comments trickled to a stop after that. One vulgar soul dared to ask Todd: Did you ask your sons if they recognized the person? Can you give us a bit more information? Gender, age, ethnicity, etc.?

This, along with probably everyone else, made Alyson cringe. She put her phone down to continue charging on the counter and turned away. She needed fresh air, so she carried her coffee to her back door and went outside.

Alyson stood on her gray, concrete slab patio and stared at the weathered and splintered wood fence separating her overgrown yard from the neighbor behind her. Her patio set was still soaking wet from last night's torrential rain. She watched as several large drops of water fell from the rust-colored cushions into the large puddles below the chairs. She tried not to compare her spare and functional yard to Jessica Hampton's suburban oasis. Last night, entering Jessica's home, seeing her furniture, art, appliances, in-ground pool, and professional landscaping—it was the first time she realized just how vastly different the homes in The Enclave were.

In April, when Justin was offered the job in Denver, they had started making weekend trips from Omaha to find a house. She knew the moment the real estate agent brought them into the Enclave neighborhood that this was where she wanted to live. This beautifully planned, already established golf course neighborhood had a private lake, pool, tennis courts, miles of walking paths, five parks, and the only public charter school around with a perfect ten rating. This was where she wanted Andrew to grow up. A safe and beautiful community with access to the best, free education for miles.

"We can't afford it," Justin had flatly stated before the real estate agent could even get him in the door.

"Well, now," Alyson countered while trying to hide her embarrassment. Did he have to say things like "can't afford"? "It doesn't hurt to at least take a look."

Justin, shaking his head, had looked at Alyson like she was insane. "I don't see the point." He shrugged, looking again at the sales sheet in his hand, his eyes focused on nothing other than the list price. "It's fifty thousand more—"

"Well, I'm going inside, okay?" she interrupted and slipped quickly out the car door. She was both unable and unwilling to listen to him talk about the money they didn't have in front of the agent who was driving them around town in her Mercedes.

Alyson stood on the front drive, staring up at the three-bedroom, three-bathroom, pale blue home with hardwood floors, marble countertops, and a decent-sized backyard where Andrew could play. This was her house—she knew it before even walking through the door.

"It backs to the golf course?" she asked the agent.

"No. None of the Enclave homes at this price point are golf course lots. There is one for sale four streets over, but it's about a hundred thousand more—"

"If we win the lottery in the next two days, we'll let you know," Justin said.

Alyson smiled, her insides squirming.

"Well let's head inside this one. It's adorable. A great starter home in this neighborhood. And hard to find! These usually go quick. The schools are wonderful, so lots of young families want to get their foot in the door here."

Every word the agent said both described their exact situation as well as made Alyson feel like she was in a life-and-death competition for this house. She imagined a hoard of other families charging through The Enclave's gates, hoping to steal her family's opportunities and brighter future from her.

Before they had even seen the finished basement, Justin was eyeballing the listing sheet for the next home on their list. It was clear to her that if she was going to get her husband on board, and fast enough not to lose out on this house, she was going to have to think of some sales tactics outside their agent's capacity.

When they opened the door to the expansive basement, Alyson was overjoyed to see that the previous owners had already finished the space and had done a beautiful job. There was a whole other living room space, wet bar, additional bedroom, and three-quarter bathroom not accounted for in the listing.

"Wow," Alyson had said. "What a great man cave this would be." And when she glanced sideways at her husband of seven years, she saw the first fissures form in his resolve against this house. "None of the other houses we've seen had the basements finished already. What do you suppose they spent on this, Justin?" she asked, allowing full naiveté to enter her tone. "Like, ten thousand?"

He scoffed at her ignorance. "Hardly." He placed a hand on the wet bar's mahogany top and inspected the woodwork of the cabinets. "For the whole space, and this quality, I'd say sixty...probably seventy at the least."

Alyson's eyes widened in exaggerated awe, and he nodded, letting her know it was true. So when she turned away from him, with a victorious smile on her face, she felt confident that with only minimal nudging, Justin would, in the end, sell himself on this house.

Even if for reasons utterly different from her own.

The next day, their full-ask offer was accepted, and the Tinsdales had taken possession of the house at the end of May.

She'd been so busy over the summer—unpacking, buying new pieces of furniture, exploring the community pool and parks with Andrew, getting him registered for school—there hadn't been time to wonder if they'd made an impulsive and costly mistake. She felt reasonably sure, based on several of his comments over the last four months, that Justin had some serious buyer's remorse.

She stared at the two pre-planted bowls of petunias she'd bought earlier in the summer, that she too often forgot to water, that were now shriveled and sad. They were so far gone, and so near to the colder fall weather, she realized she would probably just let them die. The whole summer, these poor plants had cycled in and out of near-death because of her inconsistent care. Next year, she'd do better. But it was a relief to now, finally, let these ones slip away. She considered picking them up and walking them, right now, around her yard to the rolling garbage can on the side of her house. Except there were still three or four flowers and a handful of greenish leaves in both pots—maybe it was too soon to just give up and throw them away.

A dread settled over her, upsetting her stomach and making her feel both jittery and vaguely afraid. She tried to pinpoint its origin. Deciding first it was the hangover, then the news about the body by the lake, or probably the fact that Andrew was struggling at school, then her mind landed on the image of her husband's mildly disgusted expression before he left for work that morning. There was also still the fear of not remembering what she had done, how she may have behaved in front of all those women last night.

Her mind now cartwheeled through a smorgasbord of stress. She pulled out one of her patio chairs and sat down, only remembering the cushion was still soaking when she felt the water seep through the butt of her yoga pants. She jumped up, sighed in exasperation, and closed her eyes. Her current state was obviously due to all of it. She was glad she had decided to keep Andrew home with her today. They would stay in their own bubble, shut the door, close the blinds, hunker down in their home—their safe space—until the storms outside dissipated and passed them by.

Suddenly, everything felt so dangerous to her.

"Hello?"

Alyson jumped up from her chair, hand clasped to her chest, and spun toward the voice coming from her own back door.

"Oh, God!" Gabby said and raised her hand in apology. "I'm so sorry."

Alyson let out a breath and laughed out loud. "Oh, Gabby. You scared the crap out of me."

Gabby walked out the screen door, pulling the glass door closed behind her. "I'm sorry, really. I tried calling, but you weren't answering your phone, and I guess it kinda freaked me out." Her expression was serious.

Alyson wrinkled up her forehead at her friend. She didn't care about Gabby just walking into her house—they both did this pretty regularly when they knew their husbands weren't home. But it wasn't like Gabby to worry about something as minor as a missed call. "Because I didn't pick up my phone? Sorry, it's charging inside. I didn't hear it."

Gabby hesitated for several seconds, her eyes narrowed, and Alyson had the impression that Gabby was evaluating her, like maybe she thought Alyson might be lying. But then the moment passed and Gabby shook her head. "You didn't see it?"

"See what?" Alyson asked and started pulling the cushions from the chairs so they could dry faster.

"The police released some information about the body found by the lake."

"Oh, God," Alyson said. "Is it someone you know? A friend?"

Gabby was pale as a sheet, Alyson now realized. She had the blank expression of a person in shock. Alyson reached for her friend's hand. "They didn't release the name," Gabby whispered. "They want to make sure the family is notified first."

Alyson gave her friend a confused look. If she didn't yet know who it was, why did Gabby look so upset? "Well, what did the police say?"

Gabby gripped Alyson's hand and looked her in the eye. "They didn't say who it was, but they did confirm…it was a kid. A boy between twelve and fourteen."

CHAPTER ELEVEN

After Gabby left Alyson's house—Dennis was taking her to get some work done on her car—Alyson sat on the couch with Andrew. She pulled him into her side with her arm protectively around his little body. She checked her phone every ten to fifteen minutes for any updates on the boy who was found.

The neighbor page had gone silent like Alyson had never seen. It seemed everyone realized that posting anything at all would be completely inappropriate while everyone waited to see if it was someone's kid they knew.

By dinnertime, there was still no official word on who the child was, but the information had leaked out through private text messages. Someone who knew the family told one other person in complete confidence, who felt less compelled to honor the family's privacy than she felt compelled to inform her best friend—and so it went until around five thirty, when Gabby called Alyson.

"Alyson, Jessica just told me…it was Elijah Sloan," she whispered.

"Oh, God," Alyson said, her hand instinctively moving to her stomach. "Bonnie must…I can't even imagine."

"No. Me, either."

"What happened?" Alyson asked.

"I don't know. The police still haven't said if it was an accident or…or what happened. I'm going to go feed the kids. Figure out a way to tell them…Grant. Jesus, they've been friends and in classes together since kindergarten. But if I hear anything else, I'll let you know."

"Okay," Alyson said and hung up. She checked her text messages to see if she'd missed anything from Justin. She'd texted him hours ago, letting him know what had happened at the lake, but she hadn't heard anything back from him. She looked at the clock above her stove, and it was now almost seven. He was usually home between six and six thirty, depending on traffic.

A child was found dead in their neighborhood. Why on earth hadn't he gotten back to her?

Are you almost home? Dinner's ready...should I wait? she texted him again.

The timer keeping track of her chicken in the oven sounded, so she put on her oven mitts and pulled the golden-brown bird out. "Andrew," she called. He was playing with his trains in the living room. "Dinner's ready."

She took two plates from the cupboard and dished up green beans and mashed potatoes with gravy onto each. Andrew, always picky about meat, would eat a few pieces of white meat as long as she slathered it in gravy. She placed the two dishes onto the table as he walked into the kitchen and took his seat.

"Where's Dad?" he asked, eyeing his plate for his first complaint.

Alyson checked her phone for a message, sighed, and poured Andrew a glass of milk. "He's not home from work yet. So it's just us, I guess."

She gave him his milk, poured herself a glass of wine, and sat down to eat dinner without Justin.

An hour and a half later, she was standing at the sink and loading the dishwasher when she heard Justin come in through the garage door. Andrew was already bathed, in his pajamas, and asleep. There hadn't been a single text from Justin telling her he would be late, or why.

"Hi," he said as he walked into the kitchen.

Alyson, almost always terrible at hiding her emotions, couldn't help the set of her jaw and furrowed brow. She made a point of turning around and looking at the clock on the stove, then returned her attention to her business in the sink. "It's eight thirty," she said.

Justin stood, his stance wide, glaring at her profile. "You're right, it is eight thirty."

She turned toward him and cocked her head. "Did I miss a text from you?"

"Not as far as I know," he shrugged.

"So?" she asked, resisting stating the obvious because it felt like that was what he was trying to goad her into doing.

"So what?"

"So why are you only now getting home, and why didn't you bother to let us know you'd be late?"

"Oh, I don't know. But maybe I can also ask you why you didn't bother to tell me you were going to get shit-faced drunk at some *book club* and pass out in the downstairs bathroom last night." He turned and left the kitchen. "Don't think for a second you're going to hold me accountable to standards you yourself are unable to live up to," he yelled from around the corner.

Stunned by his venom, Alyson stood paralyzed, her arms limp at her sides as she heard the heavy footfalls as he retreated down to the basement. The sound of the door being shoved into its frame signaled the end of the argument.

Alyson gripped the counter's edge with one hand as her shoulders drooped. She felt like she'd been slapped. For half a second, she considered drying her hands, storming down those stairs herself, looking Justin in the eye, and really having it out. She would stand there, taking up his space until he finally told her what was wrong.

Because something *was* wrong—with her, with him, with them. Something had moved into their home, their marriage, something she had never experienced before—but she didn't know what.

And based on Justin's behavior over the last few months, she wasn't sure he even cared enough to try to figure it out.

Alyson took her already washed wineglass from the drainer, turned it right side up, and pulled the cork from the half-full bottle of wine on the counter. She poured herself another full glass, took it to the family room, and curled up on the couch, intent on distracting herself from worry with a movie.

But as she scrolled through the guide, trying to find something to make her forget, the words became blurry and impossible to read through her tears.

It was past ten, and she was halfway through *Becoming Jane* when a text message came through on her phone. It was Gabby.

Sorry this is so late, but thought you'd want to know. The police have begun investigating Elijah's death as a homicide. I'm just sick about this. I can't tell you how many times that boy has been at my house over the years. I can't imagine how or why this has happened.

Alyson read the text twice and placed her phone back on the table without responding. Tomorrow she'd tell Gabby she didn't see it till morning. Right now, she simply couldn't deal with anything else.

A child had been murdered in The Enclave.

Alyson poured herself the last of her wine, laid her head against the back of the couch, and started her movie back up.

She had a feeling Justin was going to sleep in the basement bedroom tonight.

CHAPTER TWELVE

Alyson looked up the loud, crowded hallway filled with other parents and their kids. She had scheduled their parent-teacher conference for seven o'clock so Justin could make it after work. She checked her phone: it was 6:58. Justin still wasn't here, and there wasn't any message either.

It had been two weeks since their argument, after which, Justin had spent three nights in the basement bedroom. They had spent four days slipping around each other in a wordless avoidance, neither willing to be the first to break the silence and concede. On the fifth day, Alyson had caved and asked Justin, "I have to schedule Andrew's parent-teacher conference… Should I do it in the evening so you can come?"

"Yeah, I'd like to be there," he said.

And from those two sentences, they had spent the last week building a thin bridge of conversations. Short, necessary exchanges that eventually led them back to communication that sort of resembled their routine existence. But their lives in the house felt tenuous and strained, like one strong wind would blow it all to bits again. Alyson felt every loose thread in her marriage and was terrified of examining the fabric too closely. It was easier to pretend everything was fine. Somehow, smiling, agreeing, and never bringing up any frustrations or disappointments felt less dangerous.

Outside the classrooms, the hallway walls of The Enclave Academy K–8 were filled with row after row of student academic work and artwork. There were three rails of corkboard, spaced two feet apart, that ran the length of every hallway wall outside the classrooms. Pinned to these were the essays, self-portraits, and All About Me projects of the students. Publicly displayed so parents could take pictures and feel proud of the work their child had accomplished over the first quarter.

And, of course, compare how their child ranked against other kids' abilities.

Alyson stood outside Mrs. Sinclair's classroom, scanning the wall for Andrew's Me and My Family project. This was a project she hadn't seen, so it must have been completed solely at school. A surprise for parents on Parent-Teacher Conference Night.

But her eyes were drawn to the project of one of the other kids. It was pinned to the center of the row at eye level. Detailed and carefully drawn, this project stood out from all the rest. The five family members were not merely scrawled onto the center of the page. This project was a beach scene, complete with sand and rolling waves in the background. The sun high over their heads was a swirl of yellows, oranges, and reds that shined down on the parents, lying in towel-draped beach chairs. Two children looked to be playing baseball while a third sat, legs sprawled in the sand, building a sandcastle. The project was titled "My Family at the Beach." Each figure had his or her name inked with a steady hand beneath: Mom, Dad, George, Elijah, Me.

A chill ran through Alyson as she stared at this family picture.

The kids hadn't put their names on the front of the projects, so she couldn't be sure. She glanced up and down the hallway, then reached out and gently flipped up the bottom edge of the page.

Gracie Sloan had written her name and date, 9/28, on the back.

Alyson snatched her hand away, catching herself in what felt like a vile act of morbid curiosity. Gracie had completed this project three days before her brother's body was found next to the lake. It had been exactly two weeks, and the police had not made any arrests.

"Here's mine," Andrew said and pulled on her hand.

Alyson turned her attention to where Andrew pointed. On the very last row, in the farthest right corner, hung Andrew's work. She smiled at him and crouched down so she could get a better look. What she saw made her heart sink. There were three crudely drawn figures. Disjointed circles floated on the page, and from these floating heads sprang arms where other children had drawn ears. For the legs, two uneven lines extended from the bottom of the circles and stretched down the page, entirely out of proportion.

Above each of these disfigurations were their labels, scratched onto the page with great effort. Each letter twisted and disjointed from the rest of its word: Mom, Dad, Me. Alyson had noticed vibrant backgrounds above, below, and behind many of the other children's work. Andrew had a small, wobbly circle near the far-right corner, and a tiny, singular tuft of grass, more blue than green, next to his dad's feet. The most remarkable aspect of Andrew's family art was the absence of color. An expanse of mostly blank white page—unexplored, underdeveloped, and out of step with the others hanging on the wall.

"It's beautiful," she said, hugging him and kissing his cheek. She watched her son, staring at his work with a frown on his lips, like even he was seeing it for the first time and found it not what he expected. He turned and looked into Alyson's eyes, scanning her for evidence of the lie between them.

"It's not good," he declared. And before she could stop him, Andrew's hand whipped out from his side and ripped his picture off the wall, crumbling it into a ball between his small hands.

"Andrew," she admonished, but in a whisper. Alarmed by the behavior, afraid he'd again make a scene in public, she pulled the crinkled and ripped page from his hands and stuffed the evidence into her purse. She hoped all the other parents were too distracted with their own perfectly behaving children to notice hers gearing up for what felt like an imminent meltdown.

"Mrs. Tinsdale?"

Alyson turned to see Mrs. Sinclair standing in a doorway, looking down at her and Andrew across the hall from her room. She glanced once at her smartwatch. "Ready to get started?"

Alyson stood, already feeling at a disadvantage. "Yes, of course. I was just waiting for my husband."

Mrs. Sinclair grimaced. "Well, hopefully he'll get here before we finish and be able to join in. Unfortunately, my schedule is packed all the way till eight, not a minute of wiggle room. Please come in, and we'll get right to it."

Alyson scanned the busy hallway one more time, hopeful she'd see Justin rushing toward her and Andrew—hell-bent on being here with and for them. A united family front.

But there wasn't any sign of him.

"Mrs. Tinsdale?"

"Yes, I'm coming."

Alyson hadn't been inside Andrew's classroom since the back-to-school night before the start of school. She was amazed at how much had changed in eight weeks. That night, the room had stood mostly empty. The whiteboard took center stage and was surrounded by bare walls with a fresh coat of soft cream paint.

Tonight, she could see that the class and Mrs. Sinclair had spent the last several weeks at the epicenter of an explosion of primary colors. The walls were lined in large swaths of bright solid paper, partitioned and bordered into rectangles that framed out a variety of subjects and learning directives. The small desks were grouped into arrangements of four or six, and large, multicolored shapes hung over each collection.

Mrs. Sinclair led them to the back of her room, where a kidney-shaped table was pushed near the wall. She maneuvered behind it, where she took a seat in the large office chair like she was the commander in chief over this Lilliputian domain.

"Please, take a seat." She gestured to two of the six tiny seats pushed into the external curve of the table. She pulled a purple folder from the stack of three left on her desk—the remaining scheduled conferences, Alyson realized. The tab of the very bottom folder was visible, labeled: Gracie Sloan. Alyson wondered if the Sloans would be coming to parent-teacher conferences. Had Gracie even been back to school since her brother's death? Maybe they had booked the very last time slot, hoping to avoid the questions and condolences they would surely have to endure.

Mrs. Sinclair, noticing Alyson's focused gaze, placed her hand over Gracie's file tab and slipped it farther beneath the one above. She then opened Andrew's file and turned it around so it faced the seat directly across from her.

Taking the cue, and slightly embarrassed to have been caught so openly curious about the Sloans, Alyson pulled out the seat and sat. Andrew, acting clingy, elected to stand behind her shoulder and lean into her arm.

While Alyson gazed down at the folder of work, grades, and testing before her, Mrs. Sinclair reached to her right and picked up an apple-shaped kitchen timer. Glancing up at the wall-clock to their left, she then twisted the apple's top and set the ticking mechanism back on the table. The continuous and rapid clicking marked the seconds Alyson had left.

"So, let's get started," Mrs. Sinclair said as she took the lead and pulled out all the papers in the folder. "I like to start by reviewing some positives. When Andrew started in August, he knew one letter sound out of forty-four. This, of course, caught my attention and so became a focus of concern for these first weeks."

Alyson, suddenly hot, felt a bead of sweat run down her lower back.

"However, it's my understanding that Andrew didn't attend preschool?"

Alyson looked up from the chart of consonants, vowels, and letter pairs before her and shook her head. "No," she said like a confession. "I kept him home with me."

Mrs. Sinclair gave her a strained smile. "Well, I'm happy to report that since starting kindergarten, Andrew has made wonderful growth." She pulled one of the pages from the folder and placed it before Alyson. "At our last assessment, Andrew was able to correctly identify eighteen letter sounds." Mrs. Sinclair leaned sideways in her chair to look at Andrew. "I'm very proud of all the progress we've made, even with some of the challenges."

Alyson felt her son sink further into her side.

She looked up from the paper in front of her. "Challenges?" she asked, annoyed with the scared tenor of her own voice. Where was Justin?

"Well." Mrs. Sinclair stacked her pudgy hands on top of each other on the table before her. "We are struggling with behavior in the class... and out at recess...and in the cafeteria at lunchtime. We are trying several behavioral interventions." Mrs. Sinclair lifted her hand and gestured to a single desk about three feet to Alyson's left. "He has his own space, right near me, so we can work on focusing on our own work and not disturbing the learning of others." Mrs. Sinclair leaned again in her chair, peering around Alyson's body to direct her words at Andrew. "And many days, it seems to be helping. Isn't that right, Andrew?"

Andrew, still hiding, said nothing. Alyson felt his face turn into her back.

"But I'm very concerned." Mrs. Sinclair lowered her voice and addressed Alyson directly. "His behaviors are getting in the way of his learning and keeping him from making the progress he could be."

Alyson's brow wrinkled, and the tips of her fingers touched the letter sound page. "But you said he had made good progress."

Mrs. Sinclair nodded her head, but her eyes opened a fraction wider. "Yes, and the growth is encouraging, but he is still very behind the other children."

"What do you mean? Where should he be?" Andrew's drawing on the wall outside the class now seemed particularly telling.

Mrs. Sinclair took a deep breath, both her hands flattened onto the table, her fingers spread wide. "Of course, all the children are at differing levels and abilities. And most of the others had the benefit of preschool…for several years even before starting kindergarten, so many of them were reading higher-level text before they even started."

Alyson felt the blood drain from her face. "They're reading? Books?"

Mrs. Sinclair nodded, her mouth a flat line of sympathy. "Yes, but I don't want you to think they're all reading three-hundred-page chapter books. It's really only a handful at that level. Many of the students are still in the early readers, working on the kinder sight word lists and decoding. My worry is that, with Andrew, we're still spending much of our time on just the individual letter sounds. Never mind the blending and sight word foundation he'll need to start tackling even the early readers. I feel that his behavior is slowing the academic progress down even further, causing him to fall further and further behind his peers. Which, I think, is increasing the negative behavior. He knows he's not performing at the same pace as the other kids. It upsets him, thus more behavior issues, and less academic progress." Mrs. Sinclair shook her head. "We're in the middle of a vicious cycle."

Alyson felt a knot forming in her throat, a hot ball of fear and helplessness. She didn't know what to say. As she shook her head, her eyes welled up and blurred the pages before her. Was this her fault? Should she have sent him to preschool, worked with him on his letters? A tear broke loose, rolled down her cheek, off her chin, and landed with a wet splat on the blue inked page.

"I know it's difficult to hear," Mrs. Sinclair said as she reached for the box of tissues on her left and placed them before Alyson without missing a beat. "I've been teaching for thirty years, and these discussions are never easy. You might consider speaking with your pediatrician. Generally, when there's this level of concern about focus and impulsive behaviors, they will give you an evaluation to fill out and another one for us here at the school."

Alyson remembered her son's words from two weeks ago. The anger she felt about what he had said, how the other kids were treating him, how *this woman* was treating him, returned. She swallowed back her tears and straightened her back. "Because you think he has ADHD." Her tone was now clipped and defensive.

Mrs. Sinclair, sensing the shift, sat back an inch in her chair and squared her shoulders. Her empathetic expression was replaced with a calm but chilly one. "Of course, I'm not a doctor—"

"No, you're not. You're a kindergarten teacher who has led my child to believe that there is something wrong with him." Alyson pointed to the single desk beside them as evidence. "You've excluded him, allowed the other children to exclude him, and *publicly labeled him* with ADHD, and now the other kids say that to him."

Mrs. Sinclair, her face now a blank and unreadable mask of professionalism, gathered the pages on the table and replaced them into the purple folder. "If the other students are excluding him, then I will address it with the class as a whole. But you should know, the other students may be avoiding Andrew because, when he becomes emotionally escalated or doesn't get his way, he will often scream in their faces. He has also, on several occasions, hit other students. I assure you, I have never publicly labeled Andrew in any way. Still, it can be difficult to control what other parents say based on what their own children tell them about what happens in class."

Andrew hit other kids? Alyson felt like she'd been slapped. "What? Why wasn't I made aware—"

"I have made many attempts to call home. Unfortunately, it's always immediately picked up by a generic voicemail. You may want to verify that the number the front office has on file is correct. Additionally, I've sent six emails, as well as sent copies home of the Think Sheets Andrew has had to fill out for you to sign. But I've never received any of those back, so I'm uncertain if they've made it to you."

Alyson shook her head.

Mrs. Sinclair picked up a pen and a pad of sticky notes beside her and handed them to Alyson. "If you could please write down a viable phone number and email address where you can be reached, I will forward all my previous email attempts to you. I will also be sure to use that contact information from now on."

Alyson took the pen and quickly scribbled her information. When she finished, the red apple kitchen timer rang out between them, signaling the end of the conference.

Mrs. Sinclair placed both her hands on the table and pushed herself up from her chair. "Thank you for coming in this evening, Mrs. Tinsdale." She extended her hand across the table, and when Alyson took it, Mrs. Sinclair gave her a single limp shake before she quickly dropped her hand. "I'm sorry your husband was unable to join us. The data in the folder is for you to keep. I will be in touch."

Dismissed, and not knowing what else to say, Alyson gathered the folder, took Andrew's hand, and turned to leave without even saying goodbye. As they left the class, another family waited patiently at the door to enter.

"Hi, Andrew," the little girl said as they passed.

"Hi, Deepali," he said back.

Alyson felt the eyes of the parents on her, watching for some sign of a typical social exchange between adults whose kids were in the same class. She gave them a brief smile and averted her eyes, never even slowing her rapid exit. Alyson wanted to get her son out of this room, out of this school, as fast as possible.

"Can we go to the bookfair?" Andrew asked.

She pretended not to hear him.

"Mom?" Andrew pulled on her hand and tried to stop moving his feet, using his body as an anchor to slow her down. "You said!" he shouted as she tried to pull him past the entrance to the library where the bookfair was on display.

Unable to keep him moving, she stopped, took both his hands in hers, and crouched down to face him. "Not now," she hissed. "We'll come back tomorrow," she lied.

Andrew's face crumpled in anger. "You promised!" he screamed, his voice echoing down the hall. He yanked both his hands from her grasp as he dropped to the floor, then scrambled to his feet and bolted into the library.

Several other parents nearby gave her sideways glances. A few had sympathetic knowing looks. But none said a word as they surreptitiously waited to see what she would do next.

For several seconds, she stared into the bookfair. Feeling completely mortified and also silently telling herself that temper tantrums were normal, every one of these parents had been in her shoes. Probably.

She considered her options:

Chase after him, pick him up, drag him out kicking and screaming.

Act as if nothing had happened. Follow him inside and buy him something he didn't deserve.

Or walk away. Stand up, turn toward the front entrance, and head for her parked car. Open the door, sit in the driver's seat, and wait for her five-year-old son to realize she wasn't coming this time.

"Hey, there you are."

Alyson turned away from the library entrance and looked into her husband's face.

"Sorry I'm late," he said, sounding fairly sincere. "Traffic was terrible… Can we still talk to his teacher?"

Alyson stared at Justin, simultaneously relieved and annoyed. "I already went to the conference." She handed him the purple folder and Andrew's mangled family project from her purse. "He's behind academically, has behavior problems, and just threw a fit and ran away from me into the bookfair." Alyson took her keys from her purse. "I'm going home now."

"Wait, what?" Justin asked, his expression clouding as he looked between the papers in his hands and her face.

"I'm going home," she repeated. "I'll meet you and Andrew there when you're done at the bookfair."

And without another word of explanation, she walked up the still busy hallway and out the school's front door.

CHAPTER THIRTEEN

Bonnie stood outside Elijah's bedroom door. Her hand flat against the paneled wood, she imagined him lying on his side, curled beneath his comforter, eyes closed in sleep. His cheeks, round and soft, the palest blush of color hinting at the warmth she would feel when she placed her hand against his face.

Losing the strength to keep it up, her head dropped forward. Her hand slid down the wood as her legs gave way and left her slumped on the floor, her face pressed to the door. The grief, it never left her. Like a tide, it rose, swelled, abated—but it never stopped. It had no bottom, no end, and when it washed over her, its icy swells were black as ink. It filled her, overwhelmed and consumed her. Bonnie was drowning in a riptide of grief and had no will to swim.

Her son was dead.

It didn't matter how many hours she spent here, remembering him, imagining him on the other side of this door—he wasn't there. He would never be there again.

The reality was too much to bear. She couldn't wrap her mind around it. She had no wish to believe it. How could it be true that her Elijah was dead?

It wasn't fair.

It wasn't right.

Please, God, please, she thought over and over and over. Morning, noon, night—*Please, God, please.*

But it didn't matter. Nothing changed. He wasn't here. Elijah was gone forever. However much she begged, she would never see him smile, hear his voice, or hold him in her arms again.

Exhausted, confused, Bonnie lay down outside his door, closed her eyes, and, for the hundredth time today, wished herself dead as well.

CHAPTER FOURTEEN

It had been a month since Elijah Sloan's body was found, and the police still had no leads. Several parents had posted on the Enclave Facebook page that they weren't going to allow their kids to go trick-or-treating tonight. Others planned on driving to neighborhoods farther away. A few parents reasoned that, since they would be with their children, they weren't going to allow the perpetrator "to win by making us hide in our house and live in fear." Which prompted an avalanche of argument from both sides: The Timid vs. The Brash.

Alyson read every comment on the Halloween post, her own feelings pulled first one way, then the other. She was afraid, terrified actually, of the fact that whoever had killed Elijah Sloan was still out there. But she had moved to this neighborhood, and was currently yoked to a mortgage beyond their financial means, for the specific reason that she wanted her son to grow up in a *safe* neighborhood. A neighborhood where she felt confident Andrew could ring doorbells and be greeted by fellow parents—dressed as witches and Obi-Wan Kenobis—smiling and doling out handfuls of mini Kit Kats and Snickers.

Not snatched off the sidewalk and dragged off to some basement prison.

Alyson fastened the Velcro tabs on the back of Andrew's Spider-Man costume. She silently worried about the gap of exposed skin running along his spine, where the cheap red polyester fabric didn't fully come together. She had tried to get him to at least wear a T-shirt, *maybe his thin thermal leggings?* But he *refused* to wear anything but his Spider-Man underwear under the flimsy costume.

As soon as the last Velcro tab was secured, Andrew snatched up his plastic jack-o-lantern bucket and sprinted away from her. Before she could get up and out his bedroom door, his small, red-socked feet were alternating down the carpeted stairs.

"Hold the handrail!" she called, and rushed toward the stairs herself. Bracing herself, she watched him leap the last three steps and land in a crouch on the wood floor below.

Justin walked toward the front door with a bowl of candy in his hands. He smiled at Andrew and laughed. "You ready?"

Andrew held out his arms in front of him, his middle and ring fingers folded into his palms as he posed and shot a pretend web at his dad like Spider-Man.

Justin's hand covered his chest like he'd been shot. "Ah, you got me, Spider-Man!"

"Daaaad," Andrew complained. "It's not a gun."

"Oh, right." Justin smiled and tousled Andrew's hair. "I forgot."

Alyson walked down the last few stairs. "You need your shoes," she reminded him and handed over the tiny Spider-Man tennis shoes.

Andrew dropped to the floor, shoved both his feet into the shoes without undoing the straps, and sprang back up with his trick-or-treat bucket in hand. "Gracie said the houses on her street pass out the big bars. I want to go there first."

Alyson closed her eyes in a moment of exasperation as she quickly unpacked her son's sentence. Gracie Sloan must be back at school, and Andrew must have spoken with her. Alyson wondered what exactly Elijah Sloan's five-year-old little sister knew about his death. And what information, exactly, she might have shared with the other kids in her class, including Andrew.

"I need my coat first," Alyson said and turned to the closet. "And so do you," she whispered under her breath.

Andrew threw his head back and collapsed in a fit of frustration onto the floor. "Mooommm, all the good candy is almost gone! Gracie said you have to be first to get the big candy bars!"

"It's not even dark yet," Justin said as he gazed out the long, thin windows that flanked each side of their front door. "And we haven't had a single kid yet. You'll for sure be first," he said and reached a hand down to Andrew, who seemed to really be considering the logic of his dad's assessment.

Alyson slipped into the arms of her coat and decided she'd just carry Andrew's for now. No sense bothering to have the fight until it was absolutely necessary. She'd wait and see if the cold helped change her son's stubborn mind. "You'll pass out the candy?" she asked while keeping her eyes focused on her coat's zipper.

"Yes," Justin said, his tone clipped. "I said I would, didn't I."

Alyson nodded. "Okay then," she said, and walked to the door. "See you later," she added, everything about her unsure of how to be with this man whom she'd been married to for seven years. Suddenly it felt like living with a stranger—or a bad roommate. She felt fairly sure that the reason Justin had offered to pass out the candy while she took Andrew trick-or-treating was that he had every intention of retreating down to his subterranean compound.

Andrew rushed past her and out the front door. Alyson took a breath and looked into her husband's eyes. All the questions she had rolled up inside her. *What is wrong? With you, with me…with us? How big is this wrong? And what do you do down there? How bad is it? Is it life-changing? Marriage-ending?*

All the questions she was too afraid to ask—too afraid to have answered.

"Bye" was all she said.

Justin raised his hand and turned away.

She crossed their small porch and the two carved jack-o-lanterns she and Andrew had butchered in the backyard. It was only twilight, and the warm glow of the small tea lights was just beginning to show through the wide, toothy grin on hers and the small gash of a mouth on Andrew's. He waited impatiently at the bottom of the porch stairs, bouncing on the balls of his feet to get started.

"Mom, hurry."

"I'm coming, I'm coming."

Andrew's intended destination: The Highlands development. Gracie Sloan's neighborhood, where the custom homes were enormous, and they passed out whole chocolate bars, was two blocks away. It was clear by the way he skipped fifteen feet in front of her and never once even paused to consider stopping at any of the Enclave starter homes on their own street, that her son was on a mission. It only took her a few seconds to realize that no other kids were trick-or-treating on their street either.

It was early, not even dark yet. But as they reached the end of their street and turned right onto the main road that circled through the neighborhood, she still hadn't seen one other child. The awareness ignited a small flame under her ever-present anxiety—it was their first year in The Enclave. Were there some unspoken Halloween social norms they were breaking here?

She took Andrew's hand as they crossed the street and slipped her phone out of her coat pocket. She should have texted Gabby earlier.

Hey there, are your kids trick-or-treating tonight?

She waited for the response, but there was no slowing Andrew down. As they rounded the corner into the Highlands development, Gabby still hadn't replied—but Alyson did see other kids.

All younger, like Andrew, out with their parents early, but the sight of them was enough to ease her anxiety. They weren't the only ones. Obviously, Gracie Sloan hadn't steered Andrew wrong; her street was the best street when it came to the candy—and it seemed like a lot of kids knew to hit up the largest homes first.

As Andrew ran up the brick path to the first house on the corner, Alyson's phone buzzed in her hand. It was Gabby's text response.

God yes. Michael Myers could be standing on our porch with a knife, and my kids would run right toward him.

Ha! Are you already out?

No. Kids are still getting ready, and Dennis is on trick-or-treat duty this year. I'm passing out candy and having a glass of wine as soon as they're all out the door–hopefully soon! Want to come over?

I wish. Out with Andrew, and Justin is at home.

Well, come over when he's done if you're up for it. My die-hards stay out till people stop answering the door.

Okay, I'll text you when we're done.

Andrew was heading back toward her, brow furrowed. She watched as he navigated between the lit paper lanterns that lined the brick walkway, and she planted a broad smile on her own face.

When he reached her, he didn't say anything and only held up his plastic bucket as evidence.

Alyson peered inside and saw one Tootsie Roll and a bite-sized PayDay. "Well, I'm sure not *every house* passes out full-sized candy bars," she tried to reason.

Andrew rechecked his bucket and, apparently deciding to continue on despite this colossal disappointment, turned to head up the street to the next house.

The next two large houses were similar to the first: Smarties, tiny bags of candy corn, and fun-size chocolates. She could see that Andrew was beginning to think Gracie Sloan had been lying to him about full-sized candy bars. But as the early evening gave way to twilight and more costumed children began to fill the sidewalks and rush the houses, Andrew's disappointment was replaced with an excited smile. Thrilled to be Spider-Man, prowling the streets for candy after dark.

Along with the darkening sky, the temperature dropped. Alyson pulled the zipper on her own coat higher and called after Andrew as he ran down the front path of one house and then up the sidewalk to the next. "Andrew!" she shouted and held out his coat. "It's getting cold."

Barely acknowledging her existence on his crusade for sugar, Andrew yelled from twenty feet away. "I'm not cold!" His half-full plastic bucket bounced against his leg as he ran up the lighted path of the next home.

Alyson sighed and waited patiently for him at the end of the long driveway. A line of kids had formed outside this particular house, so Andrew had to slow down and wait for his turn. Alyson noticed a few other parents waiting around, some surreptitiously sipping from insulated tumblers likely filled with beer or wine. God, why hadn't she thought of that?

One of the other moms looked up as she took a sip from her cup and met Alyson's gaze—a flash of recognition passed between them. In that split second, Alyson considered looking away, pretending that she didn't realize this was Jessica Hampton—which would, of course, be stupid.

She had been to Jessica's home, gotten drunk, and left her car on the street—pretending not to know who Jessica was right now would be a weird and socially costly mistake. Alyson smiled quickly. "Jessica?" she asked, her tone full of fake surprise.

Jessica smiled back. "Alyson?"

As they moved toward each other, smiles fixed, Alyson could tell Jessica had been weighing the same response: acknowledge each other or pretend to have not recognized each other.

"So great to see you," Jessica gushed and reached out a hand that brushed Alyson's forearm. She suddenly turned and then called back over her shoulder, "Courtney! Look who it is!"

Alyson watched the woman turn her head to see what Jessica was yelling about. She had been bent over speaking with a small, red-wigged mermaid; when she realized what was going on, Courtney stood up. "Oh!… Hi!" She raised her hand—the one not holding her own tumbler—and walked over to join them.

"You remember Alyson Tinsdale…from book club last month."

"Yes, absolutely." She leaned over and gave Alyson a one-armed hug. "You were the life of the party; how could I forget you?"

Alyson swallowed but kept her smile. "Yes, it was such a good time. Thank you again for inviting me." She hated everything implied by Courtney's statement. *You were the life of the party* seemed like code for *You were the new girl who got blackout drunk and had us all talking for days.* Not even in the ballpark of the first impression Alyson had been hoping to make.

Never mind that she had zero memory of this woman—at all.

"It's so weird," Courtney continued. "Jessica and I were *literally* just talking about you, like five minutes ago." She shook her head in disbelief. "It's like we manifested you into the moment."

Talking about her?

As if reading her anxious, insecure thoughts, Jessica interjected, "Well…not *talking about you,* not really." She glanced at Courtney, obviously hoping she'd get a clue.

"Oh no, I mean—" Courtney placed her free hand over her heart. "Not gossip…not that there's anything to gossip about…"

Jessica took over the explanation. "Courtney hosts a Christmas Garage every year. We were just saying that we should make sure to invite you and your husband. What was his name again?"

"Justin," Alyson answered, feeling some sense of relief that the conversation was taking a different direction—and they seemed to be inviting her to something. "What's a Christmas Garage?"

Courtney laughed. "Exactly what it sounds like. I decorate our garage in the gaudiest, leftover Christmas crap that I buy on sale after the holidays. Put up a tree. Fill the fridge with beer and wine. And invite the neighborhood to come hang out, drink, watch football, play games… It's a lot of fun, really."

"It sounds like it." She smiled warmly, suddenly very motivated to be included in this Christmas Garage despite having only heard of it moments ago. "Beer, football, and Christmas? Sounds right up my husband's alley," she lied. She couldn't remember the last time they had even gone out with anyone else, let along *hung out* with a group of neighbors. What friends they did have, mostly from high school and college, got left in Omaha when they moved. As far as she knew, Justin hadn't made a single new one here in Denver. Although he had gone out for happy hour with someone from work that night he came home late. Wasn't it the same day Elijah's body was found?

"It's settled, then," Jessica piped up. "Courtney will send you the information for Christmas Garage, and you'll bring Justin along so we can all meet him as well."

Andrew rushed toward her just then, a smile filling his whole face. He reached into his jack-o-lantern bucket and pulled out a full-sized Hershey's bar. "Look!" he yelled at Alyson.

"You got one," she said, realizing that must be why there was a line outside this particular house.

"That's Carl Wayland's house," Courtney explained, nodding to the house Andrew just came from.

"He's a vampire," Andrew said. "He had pointy teeth and blood all over his chin."

"That sounds exactly like Carl," Jessica said with a smirk on her lips, then took a drink from her tumbler.

"And Gracie said they're passing them out at her house too!" he yelled and pointed to the enormous home two doors down. "She's going to take me!" he blurted, then turned and ran up the street before Alyson could say another word. She watched him join a little girl dressed in what looked to be a Doc McStuffins costume.

"Wait," Alyson whispered, her voice dying on her lips as the realization hit her. She turned to Jessica and Courtney. "Was that Gracie Sloan?" The two children raced toward what Alyson assumed was the Sloan house.

Both women nodded.

A second of solemn, silent knowing fell among them all; both Jessica and Courtney took sips from their cups. Alyson was just about to follow Andrew to the Sloan house when Courtney's and Jessica's kids—trick-or-treating together—returned from Carl Wayland's house. "We're heading that way too," Jessica said and nodded in the direction of the Sloans'. "Want to finish this street together?"

"Sure," Alyson said. A warm flood of inclusion filled her. Maybe she hadn't made a complete ass of herself at book club after all. "Thanks."

They all followed after Andrew and Gracie together, the kids running en masse ahead of the adults.

As they approached Bonnie and Bennet Sloan's house, Alyson noticed another woman, younger, maybe early twenties. She was carefully tracking Gracie and seemed to be the adult in charge of her trick-or-treating. "Who's that?" Alyson whispered to Jessica and Courtney as they waited for their group of kids to make it through the enormous line leading up to the Sloan house.

"She's one of Bonnie's campaign staffers," Jessica said. "So is he." She nodded to the Sloans' front door. A twentysomething man dressed in jeans and a tall, purple wizard hat passed out full-sized candy bars to the hordes of kids pressing into and receding from the enormous porch.

Alyson gave Jessica a quizzical look.

"Bonnie, Bennet, and George left for the evening. This just stays between us..." Jessica gave both Courtney and Alyson serious looks.

"Of course!" Courtney exclaimed.

"Yes...I would never," Alyson promised.

Jessica nodded. "Bonnie wasn't ready. To face the kids, the parents...everyone. She was just going to turn off the house lights and skip Halloween altogether this year. But..."

"But Gracie is five," Alyson offered.

"That, and her campaign thought it was a bad move. Something about appearing too broken."

"Oh my God," Courtney whispered. "Her son was murdered. They have no idea who did it, and it's barely been a month since it happened. What? Is she just supposed to get over it?" she finished in a hiss.

Jessica shrugged and shook her head. "She came over to my house yesterday; she's—now this *really* doesn't leave here—she's a complete wreck. Obviously. And I would be too."

"So would we all," Alyson offered.

"I can't even imagine having to go through this in private, never mind while in the middle of a campaign," Courtney said.

"Well, this is where they are. Running from their home while staffers pass out candy and make sure Gracie gets a somewhat normal Halloween," Jessica said.

"It must feel like a nightmare," Alyson whispered.

"It must be like living a nightmare," Courtney corrected.

"And I don't think there will be any waking up, for any of them, anytime soon," Jessica finished just as all their kids came running back down the Sloan driveway toward them.

Including Gracie Sloan.

Alyson and Andrew spent the rest of Halloween with Jessica, Courtney, their kids, and Gracie on the streets in the Highlands development, and the next block over. The staffer charged with keeping an eye on Gracie was obviously very hands-off. Never once saying hello, she only looked up from her phone to make sure the five-year-old made it from house to house. Alyson imagined her, young and idealistic, excited to work on Bonnie's election campaign, slowly becoming disillusioned and resentful about babysitting duty.

Alyson, enjoying being a part of the in-group, allowed Andrew to stay out later than she had planned. By the time people were running out of candy and switching off their porch lights, Alyson realized she was pretty beat. When she checked the time on her phone, she saw that she had missed two text messages from Gabby.

Whenever you're ready, I've got a bottle of wine open and ready.

Then, forty-five minutes later, a second, follow-up text.

Well, sorry to have missed you! I'm heading to bed...but let's hang another time!

In her excitement to be invited to stay with Jessica and Courtney, Alyson had completely forgotten about her plan to go over to Gabby's.

Sorry! she texted back as she and Andrew passed by Gabby's house on their way back to their own. *Ran into Jessica and Courtney and completely lost track of time. Let's get together tomorrow after drop-off.*

Walking up their driveway, Alyson saw that Justin had turned off the porch light. "I guess Dad passed out all the candy," she said.

"Wait until he sees how much I have!"

Alyson pushed open the door; Justin had turned off the hallway entrance lights as well. She reached for the switch on her left so she and Andrew could navigate their way without falling all over themselves.

The candy bowl sat, exactly where she'd left it on the entrance table—still full of candy. The whole rest of the first and second floors were also dark, which only meant one thing. Justin was in the basement. And by the looks of the still full Halloween bowl, he'd been down there all night.

"Look, Mom!" Andrew exclaimed, digging his hands deep into the center of mini Snickers, Kit Kats, and Reese's Peanut Butter Cups. "Can I keep it?"

Alyson forced back the tsunami of angry disbelief rushing over her and compelled herself to smile at Andrew and use a light tone. "Of course not, silly. You have too much candy already."

"Well, why do we have so much left? What are you going to do with it?"

"So many questions! But it's late, and you still have school tomorrow."

Andrew's shoulders sagged, and just like that, all his Halloween joy faded away. "I hate school," he declared.

Great. Now she would have to battle Andrew into bed while also being pissed off at Justin for bailing on Halloween. And not only Halloween. Justin was bailing on everything: her, Andrew, their whole fucking life, as far as she could tell.

Alyson nodded at Andrew; she knew he hated school. She just didn't have the first clue what to do about it other than worry, constantly. "Let's get you ready for bed," she whispered. "And if you brush your teeth and put your pajamas on without arguing, I'll read you a story."

Andrew started up the stairs, his precious bucket of candy clutched in his hand. "Where's Dad?" he asked.

"I don't know."

CHAPTER FIFTEEN

Bonnie opened her eyes. Her bedroom was washed in the bright, hard light of the afternoon sun. A spike of panic shot through her. She bolted upright, her eyes scanning her bedside table for the clock. Her eyesight was blurry, and she couldn't focus on the digital numbers.

"Shit," she said, pressing the pads of her fingers onto her closed lids like the pressure might help. She rubbed the thin, papery skin around her eyes, then grabbed for where she hoped her glasses would be on the table. In her rush, her hand knocked and nearly spilled the tumbler of vodka and orange juice she had poured herself after dropping Gracie off at school.

Her hand connected with one of the lenses, and she snatched the glasses up and shoved them onto her face. Even with them on, she still had to squint to make out the time: 12:43. Bonnie let out her breath and fell back against her pillows. She hadn't overslept; she still had over two hours before she'd need to pick Gracie up.

The relief she felt was brief. It only took a few seconds for the harsh reality of her new life to settle back over her; the ever-present grief washed back in on a tidal wave of awareness. Bonnie rolled onto her side and pulled her knees tight into her chest. She didn't want to move, breathe—she certainly didn't want to think. Not about anything.

Not even Elijah.

It had been four weeks since his body was found. Her every waking thought and emotion had been about him. Reliving every moment of his life. From the moment she found out she was pregnant with Elijah, his birth, breastfeeding, rocking him to sleep, his first tooth, tantrum, and day of school. Helping him learn to read, write, ride a bike. Watching him swim for the first time. Bonnie had spent the last several weeks living in the past, poring over every photo she could find and every memory in her mind.

It hurt. Every second of it. It was a pain she had never known. Deep, buried in her veins, carried within her cells. The feelings of irreparable loss grew inside her every day. It wound tight around her spine, pulled at her tendons, flooded her lungs. She both craved relief and was terrified of the day when that relief might come.

What would it mean to get over this? She didn't want to even imagine feeling better.

How could a mother ever feel better after this?

Her cell chimed and vibrated on her bedside table: a text.

Bonnie stared at her phone. She hated it. Its insistent rings, chimes, chirps, each one an attempt to pull her back into the world. A constant reminder that the rest of the world had not stopped, had not even slowed down. To everyone else, Elijah's death was a news article, a segment, an abstract train wreck happening in another country to another family—another mother. It meant almost nothing to them.

Her phone buzzed again, kindly letting her know that she had missed the first alert.

Bonnie pushed herself up to sitting and picked up her glass of vodka and orange juice, swirling it a few times because the alcohol and juice had separated while she slept. She took three large gulps, then reached for her phone.

It was Chelsea, her campaign manager. Bonnie closed her eyes; she had come to hate Chelsea over the last month. Of all the responsibilities, obligations, and demands trying to drag her back into her life, the campaign and its shepherd, Chelsea Braine, was the one Bonnie avoided the most.

It had barely been a week after Elijah's body was found that Chelsea and her team had approached Bonnie with an elaborate plan to keep the campaign on track for the state Senate seat they had all been working so hard to capture. Bonnie had sat with Chelsea and four other members of the team in her living room, half-listening to their brief condolences, and then the clumsy segue into a containment and management plan. There had been a media strategy presented that involved advice and direction on everything from Bonnie's wardrobe to the facial expressions she should make while speaking about Elijah's murder. She was instructed to state her confidence in law enforcement. Her belief that they would find the guilty party quickly. And finish on a note about her ability to carry on in the face of the "unspeakable tragedy" and her "strengthened resolve" to "serve her community" and further the "good work" she had planned for their great state.

She had sat in the corner of her mammoth sectional, her feet curled beneath her ever-shrinking frame. She hadn't showered in days, her hair hung in greasy, limp strands around her bare face, and she couldn't remember how long she'd been wearing her blue sweatpants and black T-shirt, but she knew she'd slept in them now for several nights without bothering to change in the mornings. She had tried to align her present self, this ghost of a woman she had turned into overnight, with the beacon of confidence and fortitude Chelsea was working to coax her back into.

But she couldn't.

Not even on some distant horizon of her grief could Bonnie visualize the shadow of this woman Chelsea and her team were describing. Bonnie didn't want to see her—never mind become her again. So she sat in the corner of her couch, sinking deeper into its protective cushions, losing track of their pointless plans, the thread of their words; even the sound of their voices eventually faded into a nonsensical background of incomprehensible noise.

An hour later, they stood up from their seats in her living room as if they were one unit, all smiles of reassurance. "We'll get through this, Bonnie. I promise," Chelsea had said, reaching out her hand, and when Bonnie made no move to take it, Chelsea let it drop awkwardly to her side. "We'll call you tomorrow—start getting everything set up," she finished. Then Chelsea and whoever the other four people were turned and walked out of the Sloan living room, down the hall, and out the front door.

Bonnie didn't have the faintest idea what Chelsea was talking about—and she didn't care. Not then, and not now, three weeks later.

Bonnie stared at Chelsea's long text, not able to muster even a hint of the motivation necessary to decipher the paragraph of details it contained. She picked up her tumbler, finished off the last two inches of vodka and orange juice, and decided to tell Chelsea what she obviously should have said weeks ago.

Bennet would be furious—she assumed, anyway. He had been splitting his time between his mother's house and Atlanta, desperately trying to convince the potential investors there that everything was fine, still running, ready, and moving forward—secure. When in truth, his grand plans for keeping Sloan Investment from completely going under were anything but assured. Every day their finances got worse. Since his father's death, Bennet had made one wrong business decision after another. His latest Hail Mary wouldn't be any different from the hundred terrible choices he'd made leading up to it. It had taken years for her to fully understand, but now, when it was all too late, she finally did.

Bennet had run them aground, and whatever faith she'd once had in her husband vanished in the days after learning their son was dead. As far as Bonnie was concerned, an atomic bomb had detonated in the middle of their house; no one should have survived. She certainly hadn't.

And yet, one day after the funeral, she overheard Bennet on his phone. In his office, behind closed doors, he was having a conversation with someone. She stood outside the door, waiting to hear the sound of grief in his voice, a father's sorrow about the unbearable loss of his son.

"Yes, that sounds great. I have a few personal things I need to take care of here, but I should be out there no later than the eleventh… Yes, of course! That sounds great… Okay, until then," he finished and hung up the phone.

Bonnie had stepped away from the door, her shock over listening to Bennet describe Elijah's death, the funeral—the fucking grief that was killing her—as "a few personal things" sucked the marrow from her bones. Didn't he *feel* it? She pressed her hand to the center of her chest, willing herself to take a breath that wouldn't come.

Like this? Did he know this pain?

Seconds later, he opened the door and jumped when he saw her. "Bonnie! Jesus," he said, exhaling on the word. "You scared the shit out of me. Are you…? What's wrong?" he asked, reaching his hand toward her.

She recoiled, her body finally able to take a desperate breath. "What's wrong?" she repeated his question. "What's. Wrong?" she said again, trying to process his words, her feelings, their whole fucking life together. "I don't know," she said, her head shaking once before she turned for the stairs and their bedroom. She had locked the door behind her.

She hadn't slept a single night next to Bennet since.

She placed her glass back down and held her phone between her two shaking hands. She didn't even bother to read Chelsea's latest text—there wasn't any point.

I'm dropping out, she texted back, then placed her phone face-down on the table, stood up, and went downstairs to pour herself another drink.

CHAPTER SIXTEEN

GABBY'S HUSBAND, DENNIS, LEANED IN AND WHISPERED IN GABBY'S ear. It made her smile. Then she nudged him with her elbow and shot him a knowing look—*behave*.

Alyson watched them from across the garage and felt an acute stab of jealousy. She wanted that, right now, a husband who looked at her just the way Dennis looked at Gabby. They were a team, partners, best friends—his love for her so evident to anyone who cared to look. The way they leaned into each other, shared covert, knowing glances. Their bodies always seemed in communication with each other, like a secret language only they could hear.

Alyson witnessed the electric connection between them. Gabby and Dennis really loved—and were still very much in love with—each other. It was palpable enough to make Alyson take a deep breath, swallow a large gulp of her wine, and turn away from watching them.

"You came!"

Alyson turned toward the voice and saw Courtney standing before her, decking her own garage halls as Mrs. Claus—a sexy, tipsy Mrs. Claus with her white faux-fur-trimmed, red velvet dress that ended mid-thigh.

"Yes," Alyson said, with a huge smile that in no way matched what she was feeling. "This is amazing."

Courtney looked around her bedazzled garage with pride. "It really kind of is. I *love* Christmas, obviously."

"I can't imagine how long it must take to put all this up."

"Oh, well, some of it stays up all year—all the white lights, for sure. Those are nice anytime, if you ask me. But I start the moment Halloween is over, and honestly, I'm pulling boxes from storage every day. I keep adding things right up until New Year's Day. Then, on January second, I just reverse it. Taking a little down every day until Valentine's Day."

Alyson thought about her own scarcity of decorations. A second-hand artificial tree from her parents and a hodgepodge of ornaments that somehow ended up making their Christmas tree look even barer than it did without them. Courtney's garage looked like a Christmas village; Alyson wondered what the inside of her house looked like. "It sounds like a lot of work," Alyson said with a smile.

"Oh, it's loads of work!" Courtney leaned in and briefly placed a knowing hand on Alyson's shoulder. When she pulled away again, she shook her head. "But I love it. Every second of it. I would do this for a living, if only someone paid me."

"And your husband? He doesn't—"

"Mike? Oh my God!" Courtney turned and pointed to a group of men drinking beer from bottles and standing around one of the high-top tables. "See that guy in the red blazer?"

He was impossible to miss. His jacket was the exact shade and texture of Courtney's dress. Only in addition to the white fur cuffs, it was embedded with tiny multicolored lights set to blinking. He glanced away from his conversation and noticed them looking at him. He flashed a dazzling white smile and raised his bottle in a distant cheers to them.

Courtney raised her wineglass in return and kissed the air before turning back to Alyson with a shake of her head. "Honestly, I think he maybe loves it even more. Plus, when the door is open, all the neighbors are always welcome to stop by…that goes for you and Dustin as well, you know."

"Justin," Alyson corrected her with a smile.

"Oh, right! Sorry. Jesus, my head and names. Speaking of Justin, where is he? I've never met him." Courtney extended her neck and peered around the room, looking for someone she wouldn't recognize even if she saw him.

Alyson scanned the room of Christmas sweaters and bright red and green oxford shirts until her eyes landed on Justin in his faded black T-shirt. She watched him standing near the open garage door, only halfway inside, watching all the kids—including Andrew—out on the street kicking balls and playing tag. He didn't have a drink, but at least he was holding a plate of finger food from the buffet table.

She watched him for several seconds, reluctant to point him out for Courtney's assessment. He didn't belong here; anyone could see that. Furthermore, everything about him, from his clothes to his posture to his facial expression, clearly communicated that he didn't want to be here.

"Oh, that must be him!" Courtney exclaimed, following Alyson's eyeline. "He's handsome," she said with a wicked smile. "Where'd you find him?"

Alyson turned away from Justin and found another smile she couldn't feel. "We went to college together. University of Nebraska."

"Oh, big Cornhuskers fans then." She took a sip from her glass. "There are loads of people in the neighborhood with Cornhuskers magnets on their cars. And someone's always posting on Facebook about one Nebraska game or another. There are probably tons of people you guys can connect with around here. Ooooh, we could even host a Cornhuskers game day here in the garage!"

"Yes, that would be fun," Alyson said. Desperate to be included, she didn't tell Courtney that, actually, she and Justin didn't watch football. Or baseball, or basketball, or anything whatsoever that involved uniformed teams and balls. They never had. And yes, they were here today at her Christmas Garage, drinking and eating and waiting for the Broncos game to start. But that was only because Alyson wanted to make more friends. And yes, Justin had agreed to come along, begrudgingly and only with much complaining about the "ridiculousness of a Christmas party the first weekend in November."

"It's just supposed to be a fun neighborhood thing," Alyson explained. "Courtney starts it in November, and it goes on through the Super Bowl."

"That makes it more stupid," Justin said as he buckled Andrew into his booster seat in the back of the car. "Not less."

Alyson had sighed but said nothing as she slid onto the passenger seat, closed the car door, and stared at her reflection in the side mirror. She had decided she wanted to try to get Justin more involved with their life. Because based on even a casual observation of the last five months, this wasn't something he was intrinsically interested in doing.

Courtney reached out and placed her hand briefly on top of Alyson's. "Perfect!" she gushed. "It's all set then."

"What's all set?"

Both Alyson and Courtney turned and found Jessica Hampton and Gabby standing behind them.

"A Nebraska Cornhuskers, Christmas Garage, game day extravaganza," Courtney proclaimed, with what seemed to be real enthusiasm.

"Oh! You know who would love that?" Jessica added loudly. She looked around, as if checking to see who might be listening in, then added in a whisper, "Bennet Sloan." She let that sink in before continuing. "Actually, so would George. They both love watching college football. I mean, obviously, right. Since George is so good."

"I heard he only sat out for one game—right after they found..." Now it was Courtney's turn to check their surroundings to make sure she wasn't overheard. "Found Elijah's body," she mouthed, too afraid to even whisper the dead boy's name. "Then," Courtney continued in her regular voice. "George got right back in the game."

Alyson couldn't tell if Courtney found George's dedication to his sport in the face of such a devastating family tragedy admirable or abominable. Her tone and raised eyebrows could really be interpreted as either.

"I'm sure there is a lot no one knows about what they are all going through right now," Gabby said, her own tone suggesting that Courtney should probably just shut the fuck up.

"Well, I do know that Bennet's been sleeping at his mother's house over in Cherry Creek. And George has been staying at his girlfriend's parents' house most nights," Jessica continued. Either not hearing Gabby's subtle warning to change the subject, or not caring,

Jessica went ahead and steered the conversation right past appropriate concern for her neighbor—and friend?—and straight into gossip. "Bonnie's holed up alone in that huge, dated mansion. Falling to pieces, really. Did you know she dropped out of her Senate race? Just quit. No explanations, from what I hear. She sent a text message to her campaign manager. Can you believe that?"

"Yes," Gabby said, her tone flat and bored. "Actually, it makes perfect sense to me." She finished her drink in one long swallow and slammed her glass onto the tabletop, hard enough to make the other women jump. "I'm going out back to have a smoke," she said and walked away without another word.

"What's her issue?" Courtney asked.

Jessica shrugged and waved Gabby's reaction away. "Whatever. She's obviously already drunk—*big* surprise there. I hope Dennis is planning on driving home. Lord knows she can't afford *another* DUI."

"What?" Alyson asked.

Courtney cleared her throat loudly and gave Jessica a sharp look.

Jessica rolled her eyes and continued. "Whatever. Gabby's always been sensitive," Jessica explained. "Especially about Bonnie. Let her go suck her cigarette and cool off. She'll be back."

Alyson digested what Jessica said and found it hard to believe. Knowing Gabby, Alyson felt pretty sure she hated to stand here listening to women—who acted like they were Bonnie's friends when she was around—gossip about her, and her horrible tragedy, when she wasn't. But there simply wasn't any way Alyson could even imagine herself saying something so bold to Jessica and Courtney. Maybe later, once she was more established in the neighborhood and with these women. But right now, she really wanted to just get along. "What about Gracie?"

"Oh, right!" Courtney placed her hand on Alyson's forearm. "Yes, poor little Gracie is also stuck in that house with her mother. God knows if or how she's being looked after. Since Bonnie quit the campaign, I doubt any of the staffers are dying to continue providing free daycare while waiting for Bonnie to pull it together."

"My son's in the same class as her—Gracie, I mean."

Both women pivoted their heads toward Alyson; she had their full attention. "I see her most mornings. At drop-off."

"Bonnie?" Jessica asked.

Alyson shook her head. "No, Gracie. Well, sometimes Bonnie too. Briefly, if she's helping Gracie get out of the car. Mostly it's just her car; the tint is really dark. And she hasn't walked Gracie into the building since…well, since that day."

They both stared at Alyson a second longer, like they were considering what to say or ask next. It was Jessica who broke the silence. "We went to the funeral, sent over a beautiful arrangement of white roses, a condolence card. And I've sent her, gosh, I don't know how many texts since. I haven't heard a single word from Bonnie since that night at book club."

Courtney gave a sharp inhale of breath. "That's right. I completely forgot that we were all at book club the night before…oh, God. Do you think it could have happened while she was at your house?"

Jessica shook her head and shrugged. "Who knows? I mean, really. Who knows anything, because the cops don't seem to have a clue as to who did it, and whatever information Bonnie and Bennet have, they're not sharing." Her expression had a pinched, angry look. She picked up her glass of wine, took a quick drink, then held it in one hand while her other arm crossed protectively over her breasts. "We have kids too," she hissed. "Kids that are probably also in danger from whatever monster it was who did this." She raised her eyebrows and shrugged. "Do I feel sorry for Bonnie and Bennet? Yes, of course. I mean, who the fuck wouldn't. But I'm also pissed off, obviously, because I know they know something. And that something could maybe help keep our own kids safe. So I get that her whole fucking world is falling apart right now, but Jesus Christ. Doesn't she want to try to prevent it from happening again?"

Courtney was staring, mouth ever so slightly agape, at Jessica. Like she couldn't quite believe the other woman had so completely broken rank and spoken out—and not covertly—about Bonnie Sloan. Seconds ticked. Jessica's angry monologue hung in the air between them, taking up space and waiting to be processed.

Jessica squirmed and stretched her neck. She took another drink from her glass, then caved. "I mean…obviously, I'm just concerned. It keeps me up at night," she said, her voice pleading with them to take up the mantle she was holding out.

Courtney's expression was sympathetic, but she continued to stay silent. She was unwilling to commit and officially go on the record as judging Bonnie Sloan over how well she wasn't handling the death of her son.

"It keeps me up too," Alyson practically whispered, stunning herself with her sudden foray into this territory—she had everything to lose in this community if she chose the wrong side. "I wish they'd find the guy, or whoever it was."

"Obviously it was a guy," Jessica added, encouraging Alyson to keep talking. "It's always some guy."

"Maybe someone could talk to her?" Alyson offered. "Explain how this is impacting the whole neighborhood? Someone she's really close with? I'm sure that's not her biggest concern, obviously. Still, I bet if someone she trusted explained how we're all feeling, she'd be willing to open up about the details. At least share anything that might help us be on the lookout for our own kids."

Jessica shot them both an expression of exaggerated doubt. "Under normal circumstances...I would say yes. But you're new, Alyson, so I'll let you in on a little secret." Jessica took the last drink from her glass. "The Sloans do not operate under normal circumstances."

Courtney, who still hadn't said a word, gazed wide-eyed at Jessica from behind her own glass before placing it back on the table. "Hey, it looks like we could all use a fill-up," she chirped. She collected all three of the glasses between her two hands. "Everyone still want the cab? I have some chardonnay too. Or Mike made some of his Christmas punch?"

"I'll have the cab, please," Alyson said.

Jessica nodded that she'd have the same. As soon as Courtney left them, Jessica leaned in closer to Alyson. "Let's just say that everything in the Sloan home, and for that matter, the Sloan family business, is not as perfect as Bonnie would like everyone to believe. And knowing what I know..." She hesitated, leaning back for a second as if considering if she should press on, or let this whole thing go.

"Knowing what I know," she whispered and tilted her head once to the right, directing Alyson's eyes to the group of people playing cornhole out on the driveway, "and what other people know for that matter… I'm not sure that what happened to Elijah isn't related in some way to Sloan Investment's financial problems. The man tossing the bean bag right now."

Alyson nodded. He was older, with gray hair and wearing a solid-green sweater over a red collared shirt—festive, but not in the least silly like most everyone else here.

"That's Carl Wayland," Jessica explained.

Alyson met Jessica's eyes. "The guy on Facebook always complaining about Extreme Golf going in?"

Jessica nodded.

"He seems like a grouchy, old nut job."

Jessica shook her head. "Grouchy, yes, sometimes. Nut job? Believe me when I say he's anything but. He's retired now, but for over twenty years, he was the CEO of Ascendant Media."

Alyson wasn't exactly familiar with Ascendant Media, but she had seen the building, and its extensive landscaping. "You think he—"

"No," Jessica corrected her and gave her a look of disappointment. Or like she thought Alyson might be stupid. "But I've talked to him. He may be retired, but he still has a lot of influence in the Colorado business world. He sits on five or six boards of directors. He knows powerful people in this state…he still *is* a powerful person in this state."

Alyson looked again at Carl Wayland. His perfectly groomed gray hair, erect spine, tidy business-casual clothes, measured smile—attending a neighborhood football party in a garage. She realized she never would have guessed everything Jessica had just told her. She glanced around the rest of the party, suddenly feeling like she was very much out of her league. Because if these were the sorts of people a man like Carl Wayland would watch football with on a Sunday—what else didn't she yet realize about any of them?

She looked again to Jessica—who was now accepting her fresh glass of wine from Courtney—and wished she could ask her without feeling foolish.

Just how successful were the people who lived in The Enclave?

"And here you go," Courtney said to Alyson with a smile as she handed her a glass of cabernet.

"Thank you," Alyson said softly.

"What are we talking about?" Courtney asked. "Or should I say, *who* are we talking about?"

"Carl," Jessica said with a slight nod in his direction.

Like an expert in covert gossip, Courtney didn't even flicker her eyes in his direction. "Oh, so we're on to the big, big game, I see."

"Yes," Jessica said. "He stopped by my house last week; Eric and I were hosting the pinochle game. Anyway, I was just about to tell Alyson what he told Eric and me."

"No doubt he was looking for support for his Stop Extreme Golf campaign," Courtney said.

"Of course, but that's not the interesting part. The interesting part was when he told us who had the most to gain—financially, I mean—from Extreme Golf being constructed in his backyard."

Courtney gave Jessica a quizzical look.

"Sloan...Investment...Group," Jessica said, clearly relishing every juicy word before taking a sip of her wine to congratulate herself on getting the gossip scoop first.

CHAPTER SEVENTEEN

Alyson sat at her kitchen counter, sun streaming through the windows. On her computer, she scrolled through the latest Indeed job listings that popped up from her keyword search: Part-Time; Work from Home; Flexible; Remote.

She moved quickly through the job listings for Technical Recruiter, Remote In-Home Solutions Technician, Part-Time Real Estate Assistant, Outside Sales Representative, Music Instructor, and In-Home Teacher. There simply wasn't anything. Either she had no interest or, more importantly, no qualifications.

Yes, that was true. But Alyson could see the larger truth right in front of her. Anyone with two brain cells could tell from the keywords in her search. The biggest obstacle keeping Alyson from finding a job—a job she promised Justin she would get when he agreed to buy this house—was a single, simple fact.

She didn't want one.

This realization, which had only recently dawned on her, brought with it both confusion and shame. What did it mean? She had four years of student loan debt, debt she had enthusiastically saddled herself with because of the belief it would lead her to better job prospects, better pay—a better life than the one she'd grown up with. She had worked hard to get herself to college, and through it, but aside from the few years she'd spent working for a small public relations firm in Omaha before they'd had Andrew, she hadn't put her expensive diploma to any practical, wage-earning use.

It wasn't planned. It's not like she knew beforehand she'd end up feeling this way. But becoming a mom had impacted her in ways she hadn't expected. Alyson hadn't known about the primal, instinctive clutch to protect that would overrun both her thinking and her senses. The sheer impossibility of handing Andrew over to strangers at a daycare, of trusting anyone else to care for him—she hadn't realized the terror she would experience.

Because what if they neglected him? Let him cry and didn't hold him? What if they didn't like him, were mean to him—cruel, even? How would she ever know? He was an infant, unable to speak or walk, or get help if he needed it.

What if, because Alyson wasn't there to protect him, Andrew felt as scared and insecure as she had as a child?

Having a job outside their home made her feel like it would be impossible for her to keep Andrew safe.

She was about to give up and snap her laptop shut, when an email notification slid onto her screen.

It was Justin's mom; Alyson clicked the notification open.

Hey kids!

I just checked flights, and the prices are super reasonable. Soooo, I'm flying down for Thanksgiving! Can't wait to see you, Justin, and my handsome grandson. My flight arrives at DIA on the twenty-second at 8:30 AM. I figured Alyson could pick me up since she's available all day. See you next week!

Love, Mom

Sometimes, like right now, anxiety took hold of Alyson by the throat. She had always thought it had started sometime during seventh grade, when Mr. Riley would relentlessly call her up to the board, in front of everyone, to factor algebraic equations she didn't understand. But maybe it had always been with her. Lurking in her life, watching over her every action, guiding the decisions she did, and did not, make from the back alleys of her mind.

She read over Renee's email again. She noted the fact she had sent it to both her and Justin in conjunction with her explicitly stated excitement over seeing *Justin and Andrew*—not Alyson. When she and Justin had first gotten together, Alyson used to imagine that these underhanded slights were accidental. After all, for almost all of Justin's life, it had only been him and Renee—his father had walked out on them only months after Justin was born. Alyson could understand that, especially under those circumstances, a mother might be protective of her only child, somewhat resistant to another woman stepping in.

But it had been seven years now. Alyson and Justin were married and had a child of their own. And still, for whatever reason, Renee Tinsdale continued to be, at best, chilly toward Alyson. If the last seven years had taught Alyson anything about her mother-in-law, it was, without question, that Renee's backhanded compliments and snubs were anything but accidental. They were far too targeted and frequent to be anything but calculated.

She closed her laptop. If Renee was coming next week, Alyson would need to make sure the guest bedroom in the basement was made up for her. The thought sent a wave of dread through her. Alyson sat at her counter for several more seconds, gearing herself up for—or avoiding—what came next. She finished the last swallows of her coffee, stood up, and was about to head for the stairs when another email notification slid into the top right corner of her screen. The subject line read: Andrew's Behavior Today.

She sat back in her chair, held the top of her head in her hands, and blew out a fast breath. *Why today?* Wasn't it enough to find out that her husband's horrible mother was invading their home for Thanksgiving? Did she really have to deal with Andrew and the *school issue* today? For several seconds she considered not opening the email at all. Or at least not right now. Waiting an hour to see what new horror Mrs. Sinclair was accusing her son of committing.

The woman so obviously hated Andrew; just the thought of it made her ache for him having to spend every day in that room with that woman and those kids. Ever since the parent-teacher conference, Alyson had been teetering between hoping the situation would somehow get better and pulling Andrew from the school.

She had half a mind to not open the email at all and simply drive down to The Enclave K–8 Academy and withdraw Andrew right that minute. Just thinking about it—rescuing him from ever having to go there again—gave her a sense of satisfaction. Control over a situation that otherwise felt beyond her ability to fix.

But then what would they do?

That school was at least fifty percent of the reason she had been so dead set on moving into The Enclave in the first place. If Andrew didn't go there, the only other nearest option was the district elementary school in the neighborhood down the road, Heights Elementary. But that school had only a five out of ten Great Schools rating. In Alyson's mind, she might as well send Andrew into a war-torn country—not that she would ever admit that out loud, not even to herself. But obviously there were reasons The Academy had a perfect ten rating.

She didn't completely understand those reasons. Or how the ratings were calculated. But obviously those numbers, and the disparity between them, meant *something*. Didn't they? The Academy was simply a superior school. Better teachers—except for Mrs. Sinclair—better curriculum, better students.

What would it mean if she had to pull Andrew from that environment?

That he didn't *belong* at The Academy?

The thought, igniting old fears, made her heart race. Because Gabby's kids seemed to be thriving. And Jessica's kids, and Courtney's kids...and Bonnie Sloan had very explicitly stated that Mrs. Sinclair was an excellent teacher. An "excellent teacher" for kids like Gracie. Mothers like Bonnie—wealthy, highly educated...powerful—thought Mrs. Sinclair was an "excellent teacher."

Was Alyson qualified to judge? Did she belong? Here, in this neighborhood, with these women—she felt like an interloper. Trying to make friends. Trying to *get in*. A climber. *A striver.* Her mother used these words with disdain. *Know your place* was the parental advice Alyson had received in high school when she told her parents she wanted to go to college.

Know your place.

Maybe her mother had been right. Maybe she and Justin, and… Andrew, weren't *good enough* for this place.

Old fears flayed open by a single email.

Alyson closed her eyes, took a breath, then another. When she finally opened them again, she focused on her email icon for half a second, then shifted her attention to her web browser. She opened the internet, navigated to Facebook, found the *Courtney's Christmas Garage* group, and clicked it open.

Because she was *in* this group.

She had been *invited.*

These women, the Courtneys and Jessicas of The Enclave, had *included her*, she reminded herself. Her mother's personal hang-ups didn't have to be her own.

She wasn't pulling Andrew from his school. No. She would handle this the way she suspected Jessica, Courtney…Bonnie would handle it.

She opened her email browser, read over the latest Andrew issue, and replied.

Dear Mrs. Sinclair,

I am disappointed to hear that Andrew had a hard day at school today. Of course, his father and I will speak with him this evening, both to get his side of the story and determine what, if any, repercussions he should have at home.

Since you were so rushed during the parent-teacher conference appointment, I feel that it would be beneficial for us to set up an additional meeting with us, yourself, and the principal, to try to come to a solution about how best to handle this moving forward.

Even though Andrew is only five and has only three short months of experience with school, he repeatedly and incessantly tells me that he hates school. That his teacher hates him. That the other children hate him. You may imagine how difficult this is for me to hear.

His father and I only want the best for Andrew. By enrolling him at The Academy, we thought we were doing exactly that…giving him the best elementary education we could. It has become evident to us that there are specific struggles for a student like Andrew in your classroom. He is a very bright, curious, and high-energy boy. He requires stimulation and educational experiences that allow him to be hands-on with his learning. Something more project-based. Worksheets, receptive drills, and rote learning are not his strong suit.

After doing some research, I have begun to suspect that he may be gifted and does NOT have ADHD as you suggested. I would like to request for him to be tested as soon as possible and hopefully identify his tremendous strengths instead of forever focusing on how he struggles to fit into a typical classroom environment that has a hard time meeting his needs.

Thank you, and we look forward to hearing from you and the principal concerning a meeting date and time.

Sincerely,
Alyson and Justin Tinsdale

She read it over, checking for spelling and grammar. Satisfied that it was striking the exact right tone, Alyson included Justin's email address in the cc, so they appeared to be a unified front, and hit send.

She then quickly sent Justin a text message letting him know that the email was supposed to send a message of a "unified front" and that they should discuss Andrew's struggles at school as soon as he got home.

Because, other than the quick rundown she had given him when he finally showed up at parent-teacher conferences, Justin had no idea how much Andrew was struggling at school—both academically and behaviorally. For a moment, she worried about Justin's reaction to being thrown into the deep end of this situation with no preparation.

Within seconds, Alyson's phone buzzed on the counter next to her. She flipped it over and saw that it was a text message from Justin.

What the hell is going on with Andrew at school?

Apparently, Justin had seen the emails.

CHAPTER EIGHTEEN

As Alyson made her way down the stairs, she could feel the temperature drop, and a chill ran across her exposed arms and legs.

At the bottom, she stood outside the door to their basement, her hand clasping the doorknob. Alyson's whole body trembled under the sickening dose of adrenaline and cortisol flooding her bloodstream.

"It's my basement," she said to herself, but her logic ultimately did nothing to help her open the door. It had been weeks—no, months—since she had been down here. How was that even possible? It was never an outright discussion; no physical lines had been drawn. But standing here now, terrified of what fears she might have confirmed if she crossed this threshold, she suddenly realized that the square footage of their home had become compartmentalized.

While Andrew and Alyson had dominion over the first and second floors, the basement had, by either accident or design, clearly become Justin's territory. Every day felt more and more like they were living separate lives. Justin even slept in the basement five nights out of seven during the workweek. He claimed he didn't sleep well in their shared bed. Every morning he woke up and still felt exhausted and then had to work all day.

This hadn't been a dramatic overnight decision, she realized. It was a slow shift, mere inches at a time. Hardly noticeable until the day you woke up and realized your husband was now living in a different room on a separate floor.

That day was today.

Alyson had woken up, again, to the empty mattress next to her. When she went downstairs to get a cup of coffee, Justin had already left for work, without so much as a "Goodbye. See you later." Things between them were obviously getting worse. No amount of her wishing, hoping, or not facing it was going to make it better.

She was going to have to *confront* Justin.

But first, she wanted to have some sense of what she might be dealing with. And it seemed to her that her basement may be harboring some clues.

As ready as she would ever be, Alyson took a breath, closed her eyes, and turned the knob.

It didn't move.

She tried again, then wiggled it, wondering if somehow the tight frame was inexplicably part of the problem. It took several seconds for her to figure it out; the door was locked. She leaned over and inspected the doorknob. It was the same in every way from all the other knobs in their home—except this one had a hole for a key on this side.

Alyson ran her index finger over the rough slot where the key went. She was seventy-five percent sure that this door had not had a handle with a locking mechanism when they bought the house.

Did it?

She stood up and stared at the locked door. Had Justin installed a fucking lock on the door? And even if she was wrong, and the lock was always here—*why* was he locking it? She felt sick. There was no pretending now. Obviously, Justin was hiding something from her.

She tried the handle one more time, just in case—it really was locked.

She turned away, then headed back up the stairs, not at all certain what her next move should be. Her mind spun through a variety of options: search for the key, break the door down, text Justin and ask him what the hell was going on—cry.

In the kitchen, she grabbed her empty coffee cup from the counter, a bright-blue Nespresso pod, and made herself some more hot caffeine. As the machine spun and the whipped coffee began flowing into her cup, she considered the most painful possibility.

Maybe Justin was having an affair. And if that was the case, was it someone from work? It would almost have to be; when else would he have the opportunity—

He could have met someone online.

The machine finished, and Alyson grabbed her cup and the sugary vanilla-flavored creamer from the fridge. As she allowed herself a hefty, calorie-filled pour, she tried to imagine Justin having an affair, but the image wouldn't quite come into focus.

Her laptop sat open on the kitchen counter. She would have to wait to see what was going on in the basement, but she sure as hell could check their bank and credit card accounts.

Alyson situated herself in one of their upholstered counter chairs. She positioned her laptop and coffee directly in front of her, ready to do some research and see what she might find.

She typed in their bank's URL, pulled up their account information, and began scouring statements for anything that seemed suspicious.

CHAPTER NINETEEN

"What exactly are you accusing me of?" Justin asked. With his jaw set and eyes slightly narrowed, Alyson could tell they were on the brink of another fight.

"I'm not accusing you of *anything*," she insisted, hating the way her voice slipped up an octave. A flutter of anxiety took flight in her chest. "I'm just trying to understand *why*. Or even to remember, really—"

"Why *what*?" Justin snapped back, cutting her off from her reasoning.

"Why it's *locked*." Her voice was even higher now, creeping its way far beyond what might still be considered a *reasonable conversational tone* and into *emotional*.

"And why does that have anything at all to do with what you do and don't remember?" Justin shot back, his face an angry mask of annoyance without even a trace of understanding. He was already in fight mode—there didn't seem to be any way of salvaging the conversation, dialing back, rerouting this back to a smoother road.

"I'm not trying to fight with you. I'm simply trying to understand!"

"Don't give me that bullshit. You had your mind made up—like always—about what you believed long before I walked in the door.

You're waiting here—it's an ambush! And you can stand there and act innocent and pretend that—*oh, I just don't know, or remember, or why would you lock that door? I just don't understand*—but it's complete bullshit because you're basically accusing me of something you obviously think I've done and pretending it's a fucking question instead!"

It was true. She thought he was hiding something down there—she'd thought it for weeks now. The locked door seemed like irrefutable proof. "That's not true! But look at it from my perspective! I get an email from your mother—she's coming next week. And I think—oh! I need to make sure the spare bedroom and bath are in good shape. I'm not thinking anything else. But I go downstairs, and the door is locked! Locked! You're the only one who spends any time down there. In fact, you spend almost *all your time* down there. So what the hell am I supposed to think? As far as I can remember, there wasn't a lock on that door when we moved in—and there is now."

"You don't believe me? Fine." He pushed past her and headed for the stairs. "Let's go, right now. See for yourself what I'm hiding!" Justin stomped out of the kitchen and down the basement stairs.

Alyson hesitated; she hadn't expected this. For him to just fling the door wide open without any prior warning. She followed him down the stairs and stood behind him while he fished his keys from his pocket and inserted one into the handle's lock.

"You still didn't answer my question," she said.

"Which one?" he hissed back at her as the handle unlocked in his hand, and he pushed the door hard, freeing it from the too-tight frame. He walked into the basement and threw his arms wide.

Alyson followed after him. She couldn't help her angry glare as she pointed to the door behind her. "About whether you put a lock on the door."

He stared back at her for half a moment, then said, "No. I did not. The fucking door already had a lock."

He was lying. Or at least Alyson thought he could possibly be lying. She immediately realized her mistake had been in asking the question in the first place. She should have led with confidence that there had never been a lock on this door—he put it on. Admitting she didn't remember, that was her error. It gave him a way out—deniability.

"Take a look around. Make yourself at home. Let me know when you find what you're looking for," he finished, then headed back out the door and up the stairs.

"Where are you going?" Alyson called after him.

"Out!"

Alyson listened to Justin's heavy footsteps as he crossed the wood floor above her. He moved down the hallway and through the family room. By the time he made it to the mudroom, it was harder for her to hear, but the sound of the door to the garage slamming behind him was crystal clear.

Her shoulders dropped, and she closed her eyes. *What the hell had just happened?* She honest-to-god did not want to fight with Justin—she hated fights. She could barely stand simple disagreements. So for this to blow up like it did…

Alyson straightened her head and opened her eyes—but what exactly did she think was going to happen? If she was going to prod around the subject of their locked basement door—and yes, Justin was right, she did think he was doing *something* down here—how exactly was the conversation ever going to be anything but what had just happened?

She looked around, took a breath in through her nose, and cocked her head. She was inside their basement—Justin's *space*.

And yes, it was probably unlikely that he would simply open the door, dramatic as it was, if he really was hiding something from her. Then again: what choice had she given him? In the middle of the fight, fueled by self-righteous adrenaline, he was probably betting that simply opening the door and declaring, loud and indignant, that he couldn't believe she would accuse him of being shady would be enough to prove a point.

And it kind of was.

Coming down the stairs behind him, Alyson had felt foolish for thinking he was up to something.

But that was exactly what he wanted her to feel—foolish. Not suspicious.

She walked through the living room space, past the wet bar, and to the door that led to the bedroom where Justin had been sleeping during the week. She placed her hand on the doorknob and turned it.

It was locked.

CHAPTER TWENTY

"What happened to the handle?" Renee Tinsdale asked the second she saw the perfect circular hole in the guest-bedroom door.

Alyson, standing behind her mother-in-law with her suitcase in hand, didn't hesitate to respond with her practiced line. "It was jammed. Something to do with a spring. I had to use a screwdriver and take the whole thing off a few days ago. Sorry I haven't had a chance to replace it."

"Well," Renee said as she continued through the bedroom doorway, "does Justin *know* the door is broken? Because if he knew, this is a simple fix for him. He'd have it right as rain in less than five minutes."

Following behind her, Alyson put Renee's case down and reached for the light switch on the wall. "He knows," Alyson replied, working to keep her tone light. After Justin had stormed out of the house, leaving her to find this door also locked without a single explanation why, she had marched right upstairs, into the garage, and grabbed a hammer. She was halfway down the basement stairs again, ready to pound the shit out of the whole goddamn door if she needed to, when a saner plan arrived. She dropped the hammer on the floor and went back to get a screwdriver instead.

Standing here now, with her judgmental mother-in-law who never missed a hair out of place, Alyson was thankful that a missing handle was the only evidence remaining from that day. She showed Renee where to find the guest bathroom, the thermostat for the basement, and how to operate the remote control for the ceiling fan and overhead lights. "Are you tired from the flight? Would you like to lie down for a while before Justin gets home?" *Please, God, please. Let her need a nap, so I don't have to entertain her on my own for the next three hours.*

Renee turned toward Alyson; her expression could only be described as suspicious. It was like she could read Alyson's thoughts. "No, I don't think so," she said, walking past Alyson and out the bedroom door. "Where's that grandson of mine? Is he in school? I thought for sure he'd be on a break for the holiday. I was disappointed you didn't bring him to the airport."

Behind Renee's back, Alyson closed her eyes. She took a deep but silent breath to gather the strength necessary to play hostess to this woman for the rest of the day. "He's across the street with a neighbor. I'll go get him," she said, following Renee back up to the main floor. "He'll be excited to see you."

It wasn't a lie; Andrew was really looking forward to seeing his Grandma Renee. Why wouldn't he? The woman doted on him, found delight in his every move, his every word. It had taken Alyson awhile to realize it, but she imagined that Renee's current behavior toward Andrew was likely evidence of exactly how she had raised Justin. From the moment her husband left, and maybe even before that, Justin had been Renee's sun, the center of her entire solar system.

Until Alyson had come along.

There were consequences for their particular history playing out in real-time now. Threads of Renee's suffocating style of parenting wrapping around her marriage, choking it of air. Alyson had always felt Renee's presence, her imprint on Justin's thoughts, behaviors—his expectations and experience of what a mother looked like.

Alyson had no idea how she measured up in his head; they never talked about anything of consequence anymore. Maybe they never had.

But since Justin had stormed out of the house and Alyson had ripped the lock off the bedroom door, they hadn't spoken a single word to each other. Not one syllable for seven days.

Alyson got Renee situated at the kitchen table with a glass of water. "I'll go get Andrew now. You're sure I can't get you something else?" She gestured to the glass on the tablecloth.

Renee waved her offer away. "I'll wait for dinner," she explained before turning her gaze out the kitchen window. It was a dismissal—from the set of her spine, the tone of her voice, the superior expression—the wave of her fucking hand. Renee had dismissed Alyson's hospitality like she was a lady in waiting, not Justin's goddamn wife, not the owner of this fucking house.

Alyson turned and retreated, her skin crawling. She exited her front door, careful to close it quietly behind her, and wished like hell she could just leave. Walk across the street to Gabby's house and stay there with Andrew for the rest of the week. Let Renee have her precious Justin. Let them bask in their mutual love and adoration for each other. Because right now, Alyson didn't have the faintest idea how to do any of this.

How the hell was she supposed to pretend everything was fine in front of this woman for an entire week? Her marriage was on fire. Burning to the ground all around them and Alyson was supposed to nod, smile, and cook a fucking turkey. A turkey that would, without a doubt, be dry and not in the least like how Renee would have made it.

The more she thought about the week ahead of her, the more impossible it seemed. As she crossed the street separating her house from Gabby's, she noticed the pounding pressure growing inside her head. It was true—Alyson never enjoyed spending time with Justin's mother. But this was absolutely, hands down, the worst week of their entire marriage, thus far, for Renee to be visiting.

She and Justin weren't speaking to each other, they weren't sleeping with each other, and they barely acknowledged the existence of each other right now. Renee would be taking up residence in their only guest room, a.k.a. Justin's space. What was going to happen when he came home tonight? How would they act? Where would he sleep?

Alyson pressed Gabby's video doorbell and considered confiding in her. She needed to talk to someone. Say all the thoughts spinning through her head out loud; test the weight of them against someone else's capacity to judge their meaning.

Once upon a time, Justin had been that person she talked to. Sitting across from each other at their favorite off-campus coffee shop, shoulder to shoulder at the bar down on the corner from their apartment in Lincoln—they had been best friends.

Thinking of those days, her and Justin in college at the University of Nebraska, holding hands, kissing goodbye before class—it was like remembering two different people. A couple she used to know. The difference between who they were and what they had become left her vacant and off-balance.

Was her marriage actually ending? Was this how it happened?

One unresolved argument after another until two people who had once loved each other now couldn't bear to sleep beside each other. And couldn't bring themselves to utter a single syllable about it.

Gabby wasn't answering her door.

Alyson stepped forward and rang the bell again. She waited several more seconds and was about to open the door herself—what if something was wrong?—when it finally swung open.

She stared down at Andrew and Gabby's youngest, Colten. Their smiling faces were smeared with what looked like blue frosting. "Hi, Mom!" Andrew said before both boys ran away again.

"Wait!" she said, leaning through the door. "Andrew!"

"My mom said to come in!" Colten shouted.

"We're busy, Mom!" Andrew added as both boys rushed down the hallway and disappeared around the corner.

Alyson sighed and wiped her feet on the outside mat before stepping inside. She closed the door behind her right as Gabby peeked her head around the same corner the boys had disappeared behind. Gabby held her cell phone to her ear with one hand and motioned for Alyson to come in with the other.

Gabby's eyebrows were arched high as she listened to whoever was talking to her on the phone. She stared into Alyson's eyes, silently communicating something was going on, then shook her head and mouthed, *oh my God.*

"What?" Alyson whispered. Now standing at the entrance to Gabby's kitchen, she could see both Colten and Andrew were kneeling on bar chairs at the marble island, an entire box of blue frosted sugar cookies open before them.

Gabby raised her index finger at Alyson, *just a second*, as she listened to whatever was still being said. "When did this happen?" Gabby asked. "How do you know for sure—"

Alyson listened to the one-sided conversation and debated whether or not she should put a stop to the boys' unmitigated sugar binge. Obviously, they had been taking advantage of Gabby's distracting phone conversation.

"I didn't even realize they could do that. Is that legal?" she continued and noticed Alyson watching the boys. When she turned her attention to them as well, she looked shocked and marched over to the counter herself, and gave Colten her frowny mom look as she shook her head in disapproval. With one quick swoop of her hand, Gabby took the box of cookies away. While she continued to listen on her phone, she pointed first at both boys, then toward the bathroom down the hall. "Go clean up," she hissed at them.

Alyson held her breath, certain that Andrew would balk or throw a fit at this unexpected disappointment, the loss of his sugary treasure. But to her great disbelief, Andrew simply furrowed his brow, slid off the chair, and shuffled to the bathroom with Colten to do as they were told.

Without one single complaint, whimper, or tear.

Alyson stared at Gabby as she continued to hold her phone to her ear, place the box of cookies back in the pantry, then run a sponge under the hot water.

As a mother, Gabby possessed a confidence and command that Alyson did not. Where Alyson hesitated and constantly second-guessed her every move as a parent, Gabby was decisive, swift, and never seemed to doubt that she could handle any situation that came her way.

Alyson watched as her friend wiped down the countertop, continued her phone conversation, and carefully inspected both boys' hands and faces when they returned from the bathroom. She pulled the phone away from her ear for half a second. "Okay, good job. Now go play in the basement," she whispered.

As Colten and Andrew fled toward the basement stairs, Gabby returned her phone to her ear. "Jessica…sorry but I'm going to have to call you back. Alyson just walked in…yes, I will…if I hear *anything*…yes, I *swear*…okay, bye," she finished.

She hung up her cell, placed it facedown on her counter, and leveled her eyes at Alyson. "Carl Wayland is being arrested."

Alyson blinked. "What?"

"That's what Jessica was just telling me." She pointed to her phone for emphasis. "Apparently there are three police cars out in front of his house, and he was escorted out his front door with his wrists zip-tied behind his back."

"Why?" Alyson asked as her mind raced to make sense of the news. She imagined some sort of white-collar crime: fraud, embezzlement, tax evasion, when another thought hit her. Her eyes grew wide, and she met Gabby's own stunned expression.

"Oh my God. You don't think…?"

Gabby must have understood exactly what Alyson was thinking, because she raised her shoulders several inches. "I don't know." Then she nodded. "But I guess it's possible," she said. "It's hard to imagine, but still possible."

CHAPTER TWENTY-ONE

Alyson crossed back over the street and up her driveway with Andrew in tow. She was so preoccupied with the news of Carl Wayland's arrest, she had completely forgotten about her miserable mother-in-law, sitting alone at their kitchen table with only a plain glass of water to occupy her.

She could tell, the moment she entered the kitchen, that Renee was annoyed that Alyson had been gone for so long. From the disapproving crease between her eyebrows to her down-turned lips, Alyson felt certain Renee had several snide remarks thought up and ready to fire the moment she was in earshot. Luckily, Andrew's exuberance over seeing his grandmother quickly redirected Renee's attention.

"Grandma!" he yelled as he ran through the family room and into the kitchen.

Renee's expression changed in an instant. A perfect, white-toothed smile and bright-eyed excitement swept away her sour face. She stood up from her chair, threw her arms wide, and bent low, ready and happy to take on the full force of Andrew's body hurtling toward her.

Alyson watched as Renee wrapped her arms possessively around him and lifted him up off the floor. She kissed his cheeks several times and cooed, "Oh, I've missed you so much." She closed her eyes and gave him another big squeeze before planting him back on the floor in front of her. She brushed his long hair away from his face and stood back up to face Alyson. "I just got off the phone with Justin," she said.

And as if on cue, the door to the garage opened. Surprised by the sound, Alyson turned and watched Justin walk into the house—hours before he normally would.

"Well, speak of the devil himself," Renee said, her current joy suddenly doubling down at the sight of her only son.

"Hey, Mom," Justin said. As he passed Alyson in the family room, he gave her a quick glance. "Alyson," he acknowledged on a fast exhale before continuing past her and into the kitchen. It was the first and only word she'd heard from him in days.

Andrew wrapped his arms around Justin's legs and gazed up at his father, who was leaning in to hug Renee and accept her kiss on his cheek.

Alyson stood still, watching the scene of reunion and love unfold from her spot in the living room. It didn't involve her, not even a little bit. The only person in the threesome before her who would have wanted to include her was only five, and he was too busy being sandwiched between his father and grandmother to notice his mother off to the side.

Justin tousled Andrew's hair, sending the long locks cascading back into his face. He turned toward Alyson. "Since you're not feeling well, I told Mom I'd take her and Andrew out to dinner," he said. "That way, we'll be out of your hair. And, you won't have to worry about cooking," he added. Without any further explanation, he turned back to his mom and Andrew and started to tell them about the restaurant downtown he was taking them to.

Justin's words stunned her. *She wasn't feeling well?* So that's how he was planning to get through this visit? With a lie?

On the one hand, she was genuinely relieved not to have to spend the next several hours placating Renee. Pretending to not notice either her backhanded compliments or the full-frontal insults.

On the other hand—who the hell did Justin think he was? They'd been fighting for days. Then he waltzed in tonight and announced the terms for their armistice from the safety of his mother's audience. As if Alyson could say a single word to contradict him while Renee stood by observing them.

Even as the three of them collected themselves and got ready to leave, Alyson could feel Renee's questioning gaze run between Justin and herself. Her mother-in-law was rude, but certainly not stupid. She suspected something was not quite right between them. After Justin's proclamation that Alyson was too sick to join them—when she neither looked it nor had said anything herself about not feeling well in the hours prior—Renee's radar would be up. Alyson knew her mother-in-law well enough. A connoisseur of other people's business and a master craftsman of gossip, she would carefully weigh their tone of voice, facial expressions, body language—all in an attempt to get to the bottom of a niggling suspicion.

Something was not right between her son and his wife.

The only question Alyson had was: *How would Renee feel about that?*

She had always felt like Renee disliked her and thought she wasn't good enough for Justin. But would she really be pleased to see their marriage hanging from the side of a cliff?

Especially considering how much Renee loved both Justin and Andrew. Did she really think divorce was the answer to her long-held animosity toward Alyson?

"Bye, Mom!" Andrew yelled as they headed out through the garage door while neither Justin nor Renee bothered to say a word to her.

The door slammed behind them.

"Bye," Alyson whispered into the empty house.

She was alone, and for the first time, she truly felt the weight of what life might be like if she and Justin continued on this way. It had only been six months, but so much had changed between them since moving to Colorado. She stood in the middle of their massive living room, surrounded by all their new furniture, and wondered if the effort they'd put into this new life was pointless.

If their marriage was ending, what would they do with this dream house positioned at the very edge of this dream neighborhood? Who would get it? What would they do with all this furniture and stuff they'd been filling it with? Stuff whose large dollar amount was still reflected on their monthly credit card bills.

She certainly couldn't afford this mortgage by herself.

Hell, she couldn't afford the utility bills. She was *unemployed.*

The swell of loneliness she had been feeling was quickly sucked out to sea by a much larger emotion gathering strength on the horizon of her awareness—fear.

She felt it out there, taking shape at the edges of her mind, growing larger and building momentum. It rushed toward her before she completely understood the nature of this sudden awareness; the full weight of it crashed over her just as she was able to articulate the danger.

What would she do?

Alyson looked around her house, taking a quick and now desperate mental inventory of it all. Every custom couch, chair, table. All the dishes, stemware, handmade rugs. How much had it all cost? And considering their credit card statements, how much of it did they even really own?

If Justin left her, he left with his job and income. His income that paid for all of this.

Her head started to throb, and she realized she had been holding her breath. She took a quick inhale and let the breath out fast between pursed lips, as if she could somehow blow away this new, terrifying dread that had taken up space under her sternum.

Under her current circumstances, she was powerless to hold on to anything she had been building here without Justin's help. And if Justin could now go days without even speaking to her, dismiss her from family dinners—lock her out of his life—the imbalance of power was far more than financial.

No longer able to stand still, Alyson headed for her kitchen and the half bottle of chardonnay waiting in her wine fridge. Burdened now with her new awareness, everything she touched—the knob of the custom cabinets, the stem of the Zalto Denk'Art crystal wineglass, the handle of the Viking wine fridge—only amplified the realization that she wouldn't have been able to pay for any of it on her own.

She had researched, shopped for, and picked everything—and Justin was still paying for it all.

Despite her growing panic, Alyson carefully placed the glass onto the marble countertop without a sound. She pulled the cork on the bottle and poured herself a full glass. She lifted the glass to her mouth, inhaled the buttery apple aroma, and willed herself to calm down before her first swallow.

Her body usually enjoyed this familiar routine. Delicious sips that led to a boozy loosening of muscles and release of tension. Today, her anxiety lessened by only a fraction of an inch. But after several large swallows, her panic had abated enough for slightly more helpful thoughts to find their way to her.

Alyson placed her glass back down onto the counter in front of her and stared into what was left of the rich yellow wine. Her marriage was in trouble. And if she wanted to get it out of trouble—and she did—she was going to have to first figure out precisely what was wrong with it. Then she would need to come up with a plan to fix it.

At the end of the counter, her phone buzzed with a text notification. Alyson reached for her phone as she took another large drink from her wineglass.

It was a group text from Courtney:

Have you guys seen the Enclave Facebook page? It's blowing up about Carl's arrest!

CHAPTER TWENTY-TWO

THE SPECULATION STARTED WITH A QUESTION:

Anyone know what's going on in the Highlands neighborhood? Was just walking my dog and three cop cars stopped in front of this house. Was waiting for my Bella to finish her business (yes, I picked it up!) and next thing I know, two of the officers are escorting a man from his home with his hands behind his back. I gotta say, I'm surprised to see this in this neighborhood! Always thought of The Enclave as an upstanding community. In the interest of keeping everyone informed of what's happening, I was able to quickly snap a picture with my phone—anyone have any information? Should we be concerned?

The poster's name was Steve Larson. Alyson wasn't sure, but she thought he might be the same neighbor whom Carl Wayland had called out months ago about letting his dog shit throughout the neighborhood and not bothering to pick it up. She'd go back through the previous posts and check later because, if that was the case, then she didn't believe for one second that Steve didn't know exactly who he had just publicly humiliated while being arrested.

It was simply too much of a coincidence to be an actual coincidence.

She imagined this as Steve Larson's ultimate social media revenge fantasy. She studied the photo carefully. Obviously, Steve had captured the picture from across the street; with the amount of grain in the photo, she figured he'd probably had to use the zoom feature on his phone to clearly capture exactly who the person was.

And because of that reason alone—Steve zoomed in so the subject could be identified—she knew Steve knew exactly what he was doing.

Because it was precisely what she had done to George Sloan when she tried to publicly shame him for speeding down her street.

Steve's post had only been live for sixteen minutes and already had one hundred and forty-seven "Wow," "Angry," "Sad Face," and "Thumbs Up" notifications. The number kept climbing steadily every second.

Alyson clicked on the twenty-seven comments and began reading.

That's Carl!

Carl Wayland

Carl Wayland

Reply: Who's Carl Wayland? I'm new to the neighborhood...am I missing something?

Reply: Loooooong story!

Reply: He's lived in the community FOREVER. Original owner, I think. Great guy, at least that's what I've always thought based on my interactions with him.

Reply: Not so great after all! LOL!

Reply: I have personally known Carl for over fifteen years. He's a respectable, upstanding, dedicated member of this community. We have no idea what is going on here and, quite frankly, I find it disgusting that a neighbor would post these pictures of him without having any facts about what may be actually going on. Remember people: We live in a country where our citizens are supposed to be considered INNOCENT before proven in a COURT OF LAW that they are guilty. Not a court of Facebook OPINION!!!

Reply: Well...he's obviously being arrested for something!

Reply: Just found this: http://www.9news.com/article/news/crime/adams-county-sheriffs-office-cold-case-arrest.

Alyson clicked on the link and was taken not to an article but a short 9News *Breaking!* update about a man in the Denver area who was recently arrested in connection with a decades-old cold case. There were no specific names, dates, or real information at all. 9News only suggested that "readers should check the 9News website for additional breaking news and updates as they become available." The picture they had in connection with their post was Steve's phone picture. The exact one he'd posted to the Enclave Facebook page.

Alyson couldn't help but wonder how it had all happened so fast. Did Steve call 9News with his photo and questions about what was happening? Did another neighbor? Alyson imagined the station had some sort of tip-line. Maybe they took whatever information they could find and then contacted local law enforcement agencies to see what details they could squeeze out of them? Either way, Carl Wayland's arrest was now a very public matter.

She was just swiping back to the Facebook page when another

text notification popped up on her screen. This time it was Gabby replying to the group text.

Oh my God, everyone is losing their minds over this.

Jessica replied: I know, so crazy. He was literally just at my house playing pinochle! Can you imagine? I can't believe it.

Courtney added: You saw what several people are saying now... right?

Alyson hadn't made it very far through the Facebook comments before getting sidetracked by the 9News blurb. She swiped back over to her Facebook app and scrolled down to where she'd left off in the comments, just below the news link.

Most of the comments were variations of each other. A few more people asking who Carl Wayland was. A few more people defending him as an upstanding citizen and successful Colorado businessman. A few links to his professional profile on LinkedIn that showed a younger version of him, maybe ten years ago, smiling in a suit and tie. His account listed all his many business accomplishments, executive leadership roles, and, more recently, board positions that he had held over his career.

One woman stated: I'm hardly surprised. I only met him once at the Adults-Night-Out three years ago. He gave me the creeps right away. You could practically feel something was off. I remember telling my husband that same night, it was like I had just shaken hands with a serial killer. The intense eye contact, his need to control the situation. He may have fooled lots of people throughout his life, most psychopaths can, but he didn't fool me. I'm very intuitive when it comes to people.

Two people offered up short defenses to her comment, calling her statements unfair. Slander, one man said. But on the whole, she opened the floodgates for what came next.

I can't be the only person putting two and two together here. It seems so obvious to me. This man, who was just arrested in connection with a cold case, which obviously means MURDER, lives steps away from a family who just lost one of their sons in an unsolved MURDER. It doesn't exactly take Sherlock Holmes to figure out that Carl Wayland is responsible for Elijah Sloan's death. Those of you defending this monster...wake the fuck up!

That was the moment any defenders of Carl Wayland had dropped off. From that declaration, there were another thirty or so comments, every one either condemning Carl Wayland or expressing relief:

At least that poor boy's killer has finally been caught.

Alyson read them all, feeling both bolder and more incensed with every comment and swallow of wine. As she finished reading the last remark, she refilled her glass with what wine was left in the bottle. She hadn't made a single peep on the community Facebook page since her cowardly post about George Sloan—she felt now it was time for her to both state what she believed and try to make some small amends with Bonnie. Alyson took another large swallow of wine, a deep breath, and started to type.

I, for one, will rest easy for the first time since Elijah Sloan's body was found the morning of October 1. I'm not sure it's possible, but I look forward to this neighborhood being the safe ENCLAVE it used to be. Where our children can play in the parks and walk along the sidewalks and their parents, and I, can once again have faith that this community is a safe place for them to live, grow, love, and experience life. There is so much catastrophe in this world—you only have to watch the news for five minutes to become inundated with it. I never wanted to see the horrors of the outside world inside the confines of our neighborhood. But October 1 changed everything I believed about where we chose to call home. It's a relief to know that justice will finally be served. I can only pray that it brings the Sloan family some comfort.

She read back over her words twice, carefully, checking for any misspellings or grammar mistakes that would both open her to judgment and detract from her message. She pressed Post and saw her picture, name, and declaration added to the community record.

Within seconds, her phone buzzed, and another text message slipped onto her screen. It was from Jessica, but not in the group text. She was texting Alyson directly.

I LOVE what you wrote! Absolutely perfect and also sums up exactly how I feel! Thank you for writing that—I had no idea you were so articulate. Eric's out for the night—want to come over for a sip?

A warm glow ignited inside Alyson as she read Jessica's words. It was her acknowledgment, the compliment, and the invitation to hang out—yes, all of this felt good. But it was also the fact that Jessica was identifying with her, her thoughts, the words she wrote and was actually brave enough, for once, to put out there into the world for everyone to see.

Jessica was endorsing her. Accepting her.

And inviting her to her house, just them, without book club or

Christmas Garage—just two friends sitting at her counter, drinking wine, and talking.

I'd love to. I'll bring a bottle. Red or white? Alyson texted back.

Oh lord, don't bother. We have a cellar full and overflowing with juice. Just bring yourself ASAP! And be forewarned, I'm in yoga pants, a sweatshirt, and my hair hasn't seen a brush all day. So nothing fancy! Jessica wrote.

Ha, ha. Not to worry. We must have the same stylist, and she's obviously on vacation, Alyson quipped.

She waited a few seconds for Jessica to reply. When she didn't, Alyson worried that maybe she'd overplayed her social hand, and a small flame of anxiety started to burn at her core. Annoyed with herself, for so many reasons, she slipped her phone in the back pocket of her jeans and finished off what was left in her wineglass.

She considered, for a moment, writing Justin a quick note just in case they came home before she did. But then she thought about the last few days—the last few months, really—and shrugged. "Fuck him," she said into her empty house. She slipped on the heather-gray Toms she'd left near the front door and headed outside. She left the door unlocked and felt confident, for the first time since October, in her choice to walk in her neighborhood, alone at night, the few blocks that separated her house from Jessica Hampton's.

CHAPTER TWENTY-THREE

For late November in Colorado, the days were unseasonably warm. But as soon as the sun dipped below the Rocky Mountains to the west, the temperatures slid with it. Alyson had remembered her coat and a scarf, but several gusts of wind caused her to stop halfway down her street, reach for the bottom of her parka, and zip it up.

All the yards were brown now. The bright petunias, delphiniums, and climbing clematis were long dead. Even the fall mums had turned from their soft yellow, orange, and maroon to brittle bushels of kindling. Only the dark greens of the evergreens and juniper bushes kept the neighborhood from falling into a complete landscaping despair.

Alyson hadn't been to Jessica's house since book club night in late September. The night before Elijah's body was found. Bonnie had been there too—but she hadn't stayed long.

The thought stopped Alyson on the corner of Jessica's street. *Why had Bonnie left early that night?* She wondered if Jessica knew.

She made her way up the Hamptons' beautiful brick walkway. It was impossible not to think about her own barren and unadorned front yard and entrance. Its utilitarian concrete path and six unremarkable rose bushes. Afterthoughts planted by the builder. Once again, Alyson was reminded that while she did indeed live in the same neighborhood as the Hamptons and Sloans, there was still a Grand Canyon of economic difference between them.

She would love to add landscape lighting, have a professional design, and plant her annuals, tastefully decorate both the inside and the front of her home for every holiday—but they couldn't afford it.

She thought again of their current credit card statement, maxed out with furniture, kitchenware, and things she had felt they were unable to live without. The size of the number now felt permanently lodged in her esophagus—she could neither swallow it nor force it back up.

She reached for Jessica's video doorbell, but a voice stopped her. "I seeeee you," Jessica laughed. "Just come in—it's open. I'm in the family room."

Alyson, aware that she was being watched, smiled big as she reached for the door handle. She mentally added a whole-home video surveillance system to her list of modern home accoutrements she and Justin could not afford.

She navigated Jessica's expansive entrance and main hall, passing the perfectly lit artwork and accent tables that meticulously displayed silver-framed family photos, decorative candles, and manicured potted plants. Jessica was exactly where she said she'd be, lounging on her custom cream leather sectional, a glass of red wine in hand, and her thin legs curled up beneath her. She had a light-gray chenille throw draped over her lap.

"Hello there," she greeted Alyson. She didn't bother to unfurl herself, but she did motion for Alyson to take a seat near her where another pale blue throw was folded and ready, should Alyson decide to use it. Alyson navigated around the long end of the sectional, slipped off her Toms, and sank back into the cushions that were neither too soft nor too firm. On the coffee table before her, Jessica had laid out both a bottle of cabernet and chardonnay along with the correct crystal stemware for each. There was also a small fruit and cheese plate, pâté, water crackers, and some rolled prosciutto. Jessica leaned forward, her hand hovering between the two wine bottles like a question.

"I'll have the cab," Alyson said and watched as Jessica poured her a glass. "Thank you," she added, taking hold of the glass as Jessica handed it to her. "This is quite the feast," Alyson said acknowledging Jessica's efforts. "I feel so special."

Jessica waved her off. "We had some of the junior partners from Eric's company over last night. These are just the leftovers."

Alyson kept her smile and tried to hide the fact that she had no idea if Jessica meant to insult her—*you're not that special, Alyson*—or was simply stating a fact.

She wanted Jessica to like her and hoped this would be the first of many individual invitations to hang out.

She missed her girlfriends from college. Now more than ever. She hoped the relationships she was building in The Enclave would be the beginning of having a group of close friends again. She needed it.

But as she took a sip from her wine and looked at Jessica across the couch from her, she wasn't one hundred percent sure Jessica, or Courtney and Gabby for that matter, could become those kinds of friends. Maybe it wasn't possible to forge those deep bonds later in life.

"So," Jessica said as she readjusted her blanket and settled herself deeper into the comfort of her couch. "You think he really did it?" Her perfect and tastefully manicured fingers held her glass near the base of the crystal stemware as she lifted the bowl to her lips. As she waited for the reply, she peered at Alyson from over the top of her wineglass and took a sip.

Alyson nodded. "I do, really. I mean, I know I hardly know the man. But it seems like, especially in situations like this...people are always surprised, aren't they? It seems like they never suspect. Well, maybe not never...but you hear that. *How could he? I've known him my whole life. He seemed so normal.* And then they start pulling bodies out of his basement and find thousands of hours of disturbing or violent or, God forbid, child porn videos on his computer—"

"You think Carl Wayland was into kids?" Jessica's eyes went wide with the very idea of it.

"Well...I mean, no. But I don't know. I guess that's the point, really. We don't know anything. Maybe he was. And if that's the case...well, I'm glad he was caught, and I hope he spends the rest of his life behind bars," Alyson finished. She leaned forward and reached for a piece of cheese and one of the rolled slices of prosciutto.

Alyson felt Jessica's eyes, following her hand as it collected the food and carried it back to Alyson's mouth. It was impossible to know what Jessica was thinking—she was very hard to read—but it kind of felt like Jessica was judging her. Her gaze slightly critical, like she was measuring Alyson's words and actions—sizing her up.

But for what? And why?

Alyson finished chewing her food and swallowed, feeling like she was a strange, eating performance artist. She noticed that Jessica had not touched any of the food on the table, and Alyson wondered if she had failed some sort of unknown test by taking the rolled meat bait.

Jessica was very thin, almost extremely so. Alyson wondered if Jessica was one of those women who were exacting experts on how to maintain a spindly, bird-like weight.

Was she sitting over there silently passing judgment because Alyson had dared to actually eat the appetizers Jessica had laid out for them? Correction, the appetizers she had leftover from the more important people she had originally prepared them for?

"Are you okay?" Jessica suddenly asked.

Alyson flinched. Surprised by Jessica's question, she felt like she'd been caught doing something she shouldn't, like Jessica had read her mind. "Me?" Alyson laughed, but it sounded fake even to her own ears. "Oh, yes. Totally." She shrugged and took a drink from her wineglass. It surprised her to see that it was almost empty.

The ever-gracious host, Jessica scooted forward from her seat, took hold of the cabernet bottle, and poured Alyson another glass before she had a chance to protest. Not that she would have—she did want another glass. But she mentally noted that she had already finished that leftover half-bottle of chardonnay before she even got here.

"Okay," Jessica said, giving her a smile that was meant to reassure. "It was, just then, a moment ago, you had a distraught expression on your face."

Alyson raised her eyebrows and blinked. "Really?" She shook her head and smiled. "That's weird." She shrugged. "I feel fine. I mean, I'm disturbed by the fact that someone like Carl Wayland,

and I mean someone you'd not suspect, turns out to be a killer." She wanted to turn the conversation away from her, what she was potentially thinking and feeling, and back to Carl. "And I guess maybe I was just thinking about that day we were all at Courtney's Christmas Garage." She turned her face toward Jessica and forced herself to hold her gaze. "And I think about Carl being there that day. Talking with everyone. He was *playing corn hole*. As if nothing at all was wrong or going on. I mean, our kids were there. And none of us had *any idea*." Alyson sighed. "So yeah, I guess I've been thinking about that, and it bothers me. How can we keep our kids safe if we can't even recognize the danger when it's walking among us?"

Jessica raised her glass to Alyson as if in toast. "How, indeed? Eric has been basically saying the same thing ever since Elijah was found. He hasn't let the kids do anything or go anywhere by themselves. Speaking of Christmas Garage, it was nice to meet Justin." Jessica smiled. "He's got to be easy to wake up to every morning," she said and gave Alyson a knowing look. "What's he think about all this? Has it made him as crazy protective as my nut job? It seems to me like this sort of thing hits home the hardest for men. Like it taps into that whole hardwired, keep-the-family-safe, primal thing."

"Um…" It was impossible for her not to think about how this was not at all the case with Justin. Not only was he *not* "crazy protective," but he also hadn't uttered a single word about Elijah's death except for when she brought it up. "I mean…" Alyson started before she had a chance to consider the impact her hesitation would have. "Yes, obviously." She tried to correct course, but her voice wavered over the words. "He's very worried." Alyson looked away from

Jessica's tilted head and questioning expression. "Just like everyone is, you know..."

Jessica nodded. But the way her eyes remained slightly narrowed, as if she were trying to clearly see an image that was barely out of focus, made Alyson feel vulnerable—like she was being studied.

Jessica took a sip from her wine, then placed her glass on the table in front of them. She looked like she was getting ready to speak but was weighing her words first. Finally, she inhaled through her nose, her chest rising, then let it out, the breath audible between them and setting the tone. "I know we don't know each other all that well, but I hope you know, if you ever need to talk..."

A tight ball of desperation formed at the back of Alyson's throat, and she could feel the rising tide of tears building pressure. Her lips held a smile, but her eyes stayed glued to the edge of the table in front of her. It was hard to lie, convincingly and outright.

"Alyson?" Jessica whispered and leaned forward. "You can talk to me."

Alyson swallowed, wondering if she had it in her to deliver a performance that would both prevent embarrassment and get them off the topic of Alyson's feelings.

Jessica sat back. "Is there something going on between you and Justin?" It was a question, but her tone was matter-of-fact, like she knew the answer already.

Alyson's eyes looked up to meet Jessica's just as several big tears broke loose and slid down her cheek. She didn't want to admit to Jessica that her marriage seemed to be falling apart, but she nodded once in admission anyway.

"Oh, honey," Jessica said. She got up from her place on the couch, sat next to Alyson, and pulled her into her arms.

With the unexpected embrace, and the outpouring of empathy, Alyson couldn't help but sob. With her chin over Jessica's shoulder, she hugged her back as her body expelled every pent-up frustration, worry, and fear she'd been shoving down for the last five months.

"It's okay," Jessica said as she rubbed Alyson's back the same way they all did when one of their kids got hurt. "Whatever it is, I'm sure it will be all right."

Alyson, released from the embrace, sat back and shook her head. "I'm not sure. It's so awful right now."

Jessica gave Alyson an appraising look, her mouth twisting to one side like she was thinking something over. "You know, I did notice something, but I didn't feel it was my place to say anything before. We really hadn't known each other that long."

Alyson froze, her breath stopped, and her eyes locked onto Jessica's as she waited to hear what she had to say. What could Jessica have noticed? Something about her? About Justin? Whatever it was, the fact that Jessica "noticed" *anything*—especially something she didn't feel she could share before—sent a wave of insecurity through Alyson.

"It was at Courtney's. I mean, obviously, it was at Courtney's—that was the only time I've ever seen Justin." She smiled quickly, then returned to her assessment. "I didn't think as much of it at the time, but now, hearing this, well, it made me remember that I thought it seemed like something was, I don't know, *off* between you two." Jessica lifted her wineglass to her lips and took a sip, but her eyes remained steadfast on Alyson's face. Clearly, she was watching and measuring Alyson's reaction to her words.

Alyson felt pinned under her gaze, exposed, and vulnerable. The insecurity she had been feeling gave way to the hot press of embarrassment. Her mind flipped back to that day. The who's who of the neighborhood decked out in their most outrageous and fun gaudy Christmas attire talked and laughed while both the drinks and socializing flowed under the red, green, and white lights strung from the ceiling.

And there stood Justin, in his black T-shirt and faded jeans. The neck of a half-drunk bottle of beer held loosely between his fingers all but completely forgotten at his side. His back was to the garage and everyone in it as he stared out at Andrew and a group of kids playing in the street. Aside from meeting Courtney and her husband when they greeted them on arrival, he had made no further effort at all to say hello or talk with anyone else. Not even her.

Alyson could see Jessica's concerned expression, and she could hear the empathy in her voice. She desperately missed the closeness and confidence of her girlfriends. She wanted to have those relationships in her life again—but sitting here, Alyson felt uncertain. She didn't know if Jessica was someone she could truly trust.

Seeming to sense Alyson's hesitation, Jessica sat back a few inches, and her expression morphed from extremely concerned to relaxed. "How long have you and Justin been married?"

"Seven years. We met in college, then lived together for a few years."

"You must have been young when you guys got married," Jessica said.

Alyson shrugged. "Sort of, I guess. We were both twenty-five. My parents were eighteen when they got married."

Jessica nodded. "Mine too. Right out of high school. Although they lived in a completely different world, if you ask me."

"Are your parents still married?" Alyson asked.

"Yes! We just celebrated their fortieth wedding anniversary in St. Thomas. It was gorgeous. The kids had a blast."

Alyson imagined Jessica and her perfect extended family on a Caribbean beach, a professional photographer capturing their bright white smiles as the sun sank over the horizon.

"How about your parents? Still married?"

Alyson shook her head. "No. They divorced when I was nine. My brother was twelve." Thinking of Paul, Alyson took a breath and exhaled. "It was probably hardest on my brother. He never really seemed the same after that, I think."

"Did your dad leave you?"

"No. I mean, he moved out of the house. But he rented a place only a couple of miles away. Paul and I split time between our parents' houses until we graduated and moved out. I don't really remember it being that big of a deal. Well, it was at first, but I got over the shock of them splitting up." Alyson shrugged. "I just had two bedrooms and had to be more aware of keeping track of what clothes were at what house. But Paul seemed to always be a little lost. Like he couldn't quite keep up with the change every week. His grades tanked and just seemed to get worse and worse every year." Alyson met Jessica's eyes. "He dropped out his senior year."

Jessica shook her head. "Divorce affects kids differently. Or, at least that's what I've read. Eric and I are in a good place right now... but it's not like we've gotten through the last eleven years completely unscathed."

"You've thought about divorce?"

Jessica nodded. "We've thrown the word around in the heat of the moment more times than I can count. We even printed up papers from the internet once." Jessica shook her head, then uncurled her legs from underneath herself, got up from the couch, and walked over to the bookshelves that flanked their large flat-screen television. "It's not easy," she said as she pulled an album from among the stacks of hardback books and silver framed photographs. "Not for anyone."

When she came back to the couch, she took the cushion right next to Alyson. She opened the large photo album across her lap, flipped past the first few pages, then pointed her pale-pink manicured finger to the five-by-seven picture in the center of the page. "There, take a look at that."

Alyson leaned forward. The picture was of Jessica and Eric on their wedding day. The couple leaned in toward each other, their eyes focused on the camera before them, their hands clasped between them. "You look so beautiful...and very happy, both of you."

Jessica smiled down at the memory in front of her and nodded. "We were. Really and truly, we had an amazing day. I know you shouldn't hope for a perfect wedding day—seriously, anything can go so wrong—but we really did have one. Everything happened like clockwork. The worst thing that happened was Eric's aunt Sarah got sick and threw up all over the bathroom floor—but honestly, I didn't even know about that until weeks after we got back from our honeymoon."

Alyson sighed and sat back in her seat; her own wedding day had been far less perfect, to say the least. "You're lucky."

The smile slipped from Jessica's face. "Not really." Jessica again pointed her finger, only this time she placed it squarely on the face of her younger self. "I was twenty-eight in this picture. I'm almost forty now. I've been married for eleven years, I'm in the middle of raising two kids, and at thirty I walked away from a career I'd spent my twenties getting really good at. You know what I see when I look at this picture?"

"What?" Alyson asked.

"A young woman who hasn't the faintest fucking clue how her life is about to get completely upended in every way she never even imagined it could. If I could talk to her, I'd tell her about how over the next decade she would compromise, sacrifice, roll over, bend, bleed, give up, and that by the time she turned forty, she'd basically transform herself into a woman that she would barely recognize. And I'd tell her she did it all for love. Love for her husband. Love for her children." Jessica reached over to the coffee table, picked up her wine, and took a drink. "And for the most part, she'll forget how much it hurt her, all that morphing into what everyone needed her to be." Jessica looked at Alyson. "But some days, she'll let herself remember who she used to be...and those days, those will be the hardest to bear."

Alyson watched Jessica give her a soulless grin and tried to think of something comforting to say—but Jessica's admission had left her speechless.

"So you see," Jessica said, closing the album with a slap, "that girl isn't really so lucky at all. She's just too stupid to see what's coming on the horizon of her *best day evah.*" Jessica tossed her wedding album onto the other side of the sectional. "And I tell you all of this because I want you to know, if you need to talk, you can talk to me. I implicitly understand how marriages can be non-working from time to time. And I know, from personal experience, it's helpful to have a few girlfriends in your corner to bitch, moan, and cry to when it gets bad."

"I do miss having girlfriends," Alyson confessed.

Jessica nodded. "It's hard to lose them," she said, then shrugged. "But people do change. Bonnie and I used to be thick as thieves. Now? We talk maybe once or twice a month."

Alyson's glass was empty again. She thought she probably shouldn't have any more, but with the conversation turning to Bonnie, she wanted to keep the flow going. "I knew you two were friends, but I didn't know you were that close," she said as she reached for the chardonnay since the red was now empty.

"*Were* being the key term in that sentence. Honestly, you probably know as much about what is happening with her as I do. Especially since everything with Elijah…" Jessica stopped her sentence and shook her head. Alyson wasn't sure, but she thought Jessica teared up for a moment before she quickly sighed and shook the emotion away. "But let's not talk about all that." Her voice cracked slightly. "I've had just enough to drink that if we open that box, I'll crawl into it for the next three days. I'm sick of talking about me. You said things were *awful* right now with Justin. What happened?"

Alyson bit the inside of her lip for a moment as she considered shrugging the whole thing off as nothing more than a stupid fight. But it wasn't just a stupid fight; whatever was going on with her and Justin had been dragging on for months. She had no idea what was wrong, and certainly not a clue as to how to make it right. She both wanted and needed help.

And she didn't know who else to talk to.

"Justin and I aren't exactly speaking to each other right now."

Jessica smiled and sat back in her seat. She waved her hand in front of her face as if to say, *Is that all? No worries.* "Eric and I have given each other the silent treatment countless—"

"He's been sleeping in the basement bedroom for weeks. And for months now, he spends all his free time down there." Alyson shook her head, as if now hearing herself out loud, even she could hardly believe how bad it had gotten. "He locks the door when he leaves, so I can't go in there."

The reassuring smile disappeared from Jessica's face, and she lowered her wineglass. Several seconds of silence passed between them as Jessica digested exactly what Alyson was telling her. "Wait… he locked you out of the room he's been staying in?"

Alyson nodded. "Actually, the whole basement," she whispered.

Jessica placed her glass on the table, her expression now a gathering storm. "What exactly…who the hell…I can't believe it! If Eric tried to lock *me* out of *any* room in my house—" She stopped mid-sentence, interrupted by a new thought. "What is he hiding in there?"

Alyson shook her head. "I don't know."

CHAPTER TWENTY-FOUR

The dark ripped away with a violence of light. It tore through the depths of stupor and pierced its way into the edge of her consciousness. And with the light, and the jarring flood of awareness, her head throbbed. Hard and painful, nerves throughout her skull sent a wildfire of pain rushing out over her brain.

"Alyson?" a voice questioned.

Alyson heard the person clearly but wasn't entirely sure who was calling out to her. Her face felt wet—no, not wet, cold. Her face was pressed up against something cold and hard. And there was also some vague sense of déjà vu.

She pulled her eyes open only to find that they didn't seem to be working at all. The image before her was a complete blur. It was white. Alyson reached out her hand and felt the cold, rounded edges of whatever was in front of her.

What was going on?

"My God, Alyson. You're drunk." No more questions—this was a declaration. And with the now accusing tone, Alyson could also place the source.

"Oh shit," she said, as understanding dawned, swift and

immediate. She was on the floor of their main floor bathroom, again. Only this time it wasn't Andrew and Justin finding her passed out and still drunk—it was Justin's mother, Renee.

Alyson closed her eyes and silently wished for death. But instead of death, a fast rush of nausea rose up her esophagus. She pushed herself up as fast as she could and managed to aim her head over the open bowl of the toilet just in time. The burning bile rushed out her mouth and filled her nose and sinuses.

"Jesus Christ, Alyson," Renee chastised her. But then Alyson felt Renee's hands sweep either side of her head, gathering Alyson's hair back and away from her face as she heaved the acidic contents of her stomach several more times into the toilet. When she was fairly certain she had nothing left, Alyson pushed herself away from the swirling mess before her and flushed the toilet.

Renee let go of her hair and ran the water in the sink. Moments later, she handed Alyson both a small glass of water and a wet washcloth. She accepted them and took several sips as she pressed the cool cloth to her eyes and forehead. It all came back to her. The wine she had when Justin, Renee, and Andrew left for dinner. The wine she had sitting on Jessica's couch. The talking, sharing, confessing—what exactly had she said to Jessica? And how many bottles had she and Jessica drunk? Now, along with the physical nausea and distinctly poisoned feeling, an unsettling grip of anxiety took hold.

What had she said?

And what did Jessica think about what she'd said?

And would Jessica tell anyone else what she'd said?

Alyson dragged the cold cloth down her face and dared to glance up at her mother-in-law, standing, hands on hips, glaring down at her. "Come on then," she hissed. "Let's get you up and out of here before Justin comes down and finds you this way."

Alyson sighed and resisted the urge to tell her that Justin had already found her once before in this *exact* condition and position. Furthermore, given their current marital circumstances, she wasn't entirely sure Justin would give two shits how or where he found her right now. But when Renee unexpectedly reached out her hand, Alyson took hold of it and accepted her help from off the floor.

Now standing, Alyson held on to the bathroom counter and waited out a fresh surge of nausea and a head-spinning moment of near fainting—she was never, ever drinking again.

"Are you okay?" Renee asked, and her expression actually looked sincere.

Alyson swallowed and nodded.

"Can you make it to the kitchen?"

Alyson nodded again and followed Renee out of the bright bathroom, through their dark family room, and into the kitchen. Renee pulled out one of the kitchen table chairs and gestured for Alyson to sit. As she lowered herself into the chair, Alyson watched Renee turn on the small light over the stove. It cast the kitchen into a soft, warm glow, allowing them to see while sparing Alyson any further grief from the brighter can lights overhead.

"I'm going to make you something to help with that hangover," Renee whispered. "Then I want us to talk about what is going on around here." Her tone was matter-of-fact, authoritative in a "we're-going-to-fix-this," but not unkind, way—which Alyson thought was strange. She and Renee did not have a good relationship. Certainly not the sort of camaraderie that would lead her to believe that Renee actually wanted to help her. If she didn't feel so utterly physically ill, she would have been on guard and suspicious of Renee's motives.

But given her current state, all Alyson could manage to do was lie her head on the table in front of her and surrender herself completely to Renee's plans. She listened to her mother-in-law open cabinets and drawers and shuffle through the contents of her kitchen, but Alyson couldn't muster the energy or will to care. She closed her eyes and waited.

Several minutes later, a glass was placed with a thud on the table in front of her face. Alyson opened her eyes and pushed herself upright.

"Here, you drink that while I make you some toast and a fried egg."

Alyson stared down at the brown liquid before her. She leaned forward and sniffed the drink, then recoiled. "What's in it?"

"Don't worry about what's in it. Just drink it. Your body needs it."

Alyson eyed Renee as she bent over and removed a frying pan from the cupboard next to the stove. Her kitchen island was littered with several bottles and containers that, if she chose to catalog them carefully, would likely tell the tale of what the brown mess of foul-smelling *cure* before her contained.

"It'll be easier if you hold your nose. Eighty percent of what we taste comes from our sense of smell," Renee advised as she turned, placed the pan over one of the six gas burners, and turned it on. "And once you start drinking, don't stop. Just chug it down."

Alyson took hold of the glass before her and steeled herself to do as she was told. She took a deep breath then held her nose, exactly like Andrew did every time he had to eat a single bite of broccoli. When she lifted the glass to her lips and saw the putrid-looking liquid sliding toward her mouth, she closed her eyes as well.

After the first gulp, she pushed past the urge to spit it out and forced herself to swallow, swallow, swallow. If smell made up for eighty percent of taste, then the shit in this glass must be truly horrifying at full strength. Even without scent, it tasted like the dank contents of a rotting compost heap.

With her eyes still closed, Alyson placed the now empty glass on the table in front of her and used her free hand to cover her mouth. When she opened her eyes a few seconds later, she wondered if she would need to race back to the bathroom at any second—Renee's cure might be just as bad, or worse, than Alyson's problem.

In front of the stove, Renee slid the contents from the frying pan onto a plate and pulled a single piece of dry, whole wheat bread from the toaster. She grabbed a fork and knife from the utensil drawer and placed the meal in front of Alyson as she took the seat directly across the table from her.

Alyson stared down at the rich yellow pool of yolk before her. "I'm not sure I can eat anything. I'm barely keeping that drink down."

"Eat it. You'll feel much better, much faster."

Alyson picked up the fork and knife, figuring a small cut of the dry bread was probably the safest place to start. She considered attempting to get through this meal in silence. Then she could figure out *how* to get through the rest of this night, and *where* since Justin was most likely already asleep in the master bedroom. But Renee's kindness, as stilted and standoffish as it was, was such an anomaly it was impossible to ignore. The woman had never, not even on her wedding day or on the day Andrew was born, shown Alyson even an ounce of goodwill. So why now?

"Why are you being so nice to me?" she asked, and placed the small piece of dry bread on her tongue.

Renee's mouth twitched.

Alyson chewed while she watched Renee. Renee wasn't like many of the Enclave women who—despite the many rumors they had listened to, created, or spread like an epidemic—wouldn't have missed a beat in a rush to negate the very idea that they held any sort of negative feelings toward anyone who dared to call them out like this. She also had never expressly stated her animosity toward Alyson outright either. No, Renee trafficked in backhanded compliments, disapproving glances, and insults that masqueraded as advice, but she was never fake. She never pretended to care more or put much effort, or any effort really, into acting as though she liked you when she so obviously didn't.

With her simple question, Alyson was laying all their relationship cards on the table. Acknowledging the never-spoken fact that Renee had never approved of or liked Alyson, while also questioning this uncharacteristic care.

But instead of answering Alyson's question, Renee countered with one of her own. "What exactly is going on around here?"

"What do you mean?" Alyson took a chance on a small piece of the fried egg white.

"I think you know exactly what I mean. Look, you and I…well, you know. And be that as it is, in the past seven years…I've never seen this. Whatever *this* is."

Alyson cut into the soft yolk dome and watched a rich yellow river run into her toast. She wondered what, exactly, Renee saw—or thought she saw.

Alyson skewered another small piece of toast and used it to sponge up some yolk. Alyson dodged the question. "I drank too much at a neighbor's house, and obviously I shouldn't have."

"That's not what I'm talking about. Well, it's probably a small part of what I'm talking about, but I think you know full well that what I'm asking is, what exactly is going on between you and Justin? Because I sure as hell can tell that *something* is wrong."

Now it was Alyson's turn to twist her mouth. *Had Justin said something to his mother?*

Alyson lowered her eyes to her plate. "I'm not sure what—"

"And don't try to bullshit me. You may be his wife, but I've been his mother for over thirty years. It's plain as the nose on his face that something isn't right." Renee tilted her head. "I have my guesses, but I'd rather just hear it straight from you."

Anger flared in her gut. Alyson narrowed her eyes. "You know him so well, why don't you ask Justin yourself? And actually, when you find out exactly what is going on around here, maybe you could do me the courtesy of filling me in as well." Alyson pushed her plate away and stood up from the table. "Because, to tell you the truth, I don't have any fucking idea what is going on around here, or what is wrong with Justin, or us. If you have so much *insight*, if you can *see* so much, then why don't you tell me what the hell you see here, because I don't know," she finished, shoved her chair hard enough to hit the table, and started to leave the kitchen.

Where she was going, she had no idea. Justin was in their bed. Renee had the spare room in the basement. She guessed she could go crawl into Andrew's double with him—although that would be a surefire path to endless questions from him in the morning.

Maybe she'd go sleep in her car.

"Alyson," Renee said. "Wait."

Alyson stopped halfway through the family room, but she didn't turn around. Behind her, she heard an exhausted sigh.

"Look, I know you and I have our differences."

At this, Alyson turned around and faced Renee head-on. She was just drunk enough, for once, to tell Renee precisely what she thought. "Differences?" Alyson shook her head. "You have been difficult, unwelcoming, critical…and horrible to me from day one. We don't have any differences beyond the singular fact that you have never liked me or thought I was good enough for your precious Justin. So, to be honest, I don't understand why you're all of a sudden so concerned about whatever the hell is wrong in my marriage. I should think you'd be absolutely thrilled that our lives are falling apart."

The words, they were out there now. Floating in the space between them, loose and unrestrained. Alyson felt the thrill of finally, *finally*, laying into Renee the way she had only dared to imagine in her head.

There was only one small corner of her mind that wondered if, just maybe, she'd regret this unbridled diatribe when she was both sober and rested in the morning.

Renee took a breath, and Alyson prepared to receive the clapback.

"You're not wrong," Renee admitted.

Alyson flinched. She must have heard wrong.

"You're not entirely right, either. But…some of what you said, yes, I know I've been difficult. And yes, I suppose, probably, I don't like you very much. But it isn't entirely about you, or who you are as a whole, I guess." Renee took another breath. "I've never thought you and Justin were a good match for each other."

"Because you don't think I'm good enough for him," Alyson clarified.

Renee shrugged. "Not exactly that. But I will admit that I have always thought you lacked a spine, Alyson. And if we're completely honest, I find you overly accommodating, and maybe even simpering, at times. And I guess, given my past, and Justin's past, those are two qualities in an individual that I find especially grating." Renee let out another sigh. "But, again, if I'm honest, the reason why is probably because I was very much an overly accommodating and simpering woman once upon a time—which, of course, led to no end of problems in my own life…in Justin's life. So I guess, when he met you and fell in love with you and ultimately decided to marry you…" Renee shook her head. "Well, it was like watching all the worst years of myself come back to haunt me."

Alyson sat down on the couch. She had misjudged this situation, and badly. Renee's words were no clapback—it was a psychological flaying of flesh. She stared at the decorative candleholder on the coffee table, unable to find any words at all. "Ouch" was all she could manage. All the fight she'd felt had completely drained away.

"You're not a bad person," Renee continued. "And you're right, I have been hard. Maybe even cruel at times. I will admit that, on occasion, I've wondered what it would be like if you and Justin separated. Imagined him and Andrew coming back to Nebraska to live."

This made Alyson look up, her eyebrows raised. "You seriously imagine I'd ever let Andrew go?"

Renee shrugged. "I mean, not seriously. I see how much you love that boy and how much he loves you. They were always just thoughts." Renee left her post in the kitchen and came into the family room. She took a seat, perched on the edge of the club chair across from Alyson. "But coming here now, seeing what is happening… I've never seen Justin this unhappy. Not since he was nine, and his father left us."

Alyson met Renee's gaze.

"So sure, maybe I once had stupid ideas about you two not making it. But I never, not for one second, wished or imagined him so unhappy. He seems so lost. So…abandoned. Again. And it's crushing, as a mother, to see that in him. I mean, imagine for one second Andrew feeling that alone."

Alyson could and had imagined that very thing. It was heartbreaking, as a mother, to see your child hurting and alone. Regardless of their toxic relationship, it wasn't impossible to empathize with Renee. But it felt impossible to fix what she could see was clearly broken.

Alyson shook her head. "I don't know what to tell you. Not

because I don't want to, but because I have no idea how we got here. I don't know what to do, where to go. I don't even know what's wrong. We don't speak, we don't sleep in the same room, we rarely acknowledge the other's existence anymore. We have all these symptoms, but I can't for the life of me figure out the cause."

Renee sat back in her chair, looking as helpless as Alyson felt.

A memory of Justin came to mind, one of the last times she could remember making eye contact with him. His expression full of contempt—for her. At that moment, it was easy to believe he actually hated her now.

"And even if I were to suddenly figure it out," Alyson said, "honestly, I think it might be too late."

CHAPTER TWENTY-FIVE

Bonnie sat at the edge of the pool, her bare legs dangling in the water. Gracie ran through the grass, onto the tile, and then took an enormous leap from the side of the pool and into the deep end. Her tiny body descended several feet below the now churned waters and resurfaced moments later. Her huge smile showed the gap from her recently lost two bottom baby teeth.

Bonnie watched her daughter, always so fearless, always so bold, as she kicked her legs and propelled herself back toward the pool's edge. Once both her hands were anchored on the ledge, Gracie turned her head to again face Bonnie.

"You jump," she commanded.

Bonnie gave a limp smile and shook her head. "I'll just watch you jump some more."

"But it's so fun."

"Then you should do it again," Bonnie replied, unmoved by Gracie's begging. It was nothing short of a miracle that she was here, suited up in last summer's Becca tankini, wholly sober and sitting upright. It had required every ounce of her will to get out of bed and move through the most basic functions of motherhood.

It was Thanksgiving break from school. Which meant Bonnie had to pull her shit together every day for the whole week. Gracie needed to be fed and entertained all day, not just the few hours after school prior to bedtime. In all the turmoil and upheaval since Elijah's death, Bonnie had neglected to schedule a pool closure date with Aqua Spas and Pools. It was beyond lucky that Colorado was having an unseasonably warm autumn—a broken water pipe was the last thing Bonnie could deal with right now. But having the pool heated and still open turned out to be a blessing this week. It both kept Gracie occupied and wore her out so much that she was back to taking an afternoon nap every day.

"Can I help make the turkey tomorrow?" Gracie called from her swan float in the middle of the pool.

Bonnie met her daughter's eyes. "We're not making one this year."

"Why?" Gracie whined.

"Well, George is busy, and Daddy is still out of town." Bonnie shrugged and tried to keep her facial expression light, but her mind thought the words anyway. *And Elijah was murdered.* "So it's just you and me this year, kid. I thought it might be fun to order a pizza instead. We could snuggle on the couch and watch a movie."

Gracie's expression perked up. "*Frozen 2*?" she asked.

Bonnie nodded. "Sure," she promised, knowing full well she would be asleep ten minutes after the movie started. Gracie, completely transfixed by a film she had already seen at least five times, would never even notice.

"And I want George to come too," Gracie demanded. "*Make* him come downstairs for pizza and the movie."

Bonnie nodded, *yes she would do that.* But their modified Thanksgiving would not go the way Gracie envisioned. Aside from her falling asleep on the couch, Bonnie was confident it would be nearly impossible to get George engaged. Ever since his brother's death. And with his high school football season over, every day, the moment school was out, George came right home, went straight upstairs, and sequestered himself behind his locked bedroom door. She wasn't one hundred percent sure, but she thought he might have even broken up with his girlfriend. Before Elijah's death, she rarely knew where he was and couldn't keep him home. Now, he never went anywhere with his friends.

Obviously, he was depressed. Clearly, she should intervene and get him some help. The thoughts made her miserable and anxious. She didn't have the energy necessary to run her own life from sunup to sundown; how could she possibly help George as well? She once considered herself to be a pretty good mother, but she definitely felt like a shitty one now. Thank God George had already been accepted to Yale—she couldn't imagine either of them trying to plot and plan for college admissions at this point. She didn't even know if he was still passing all his classes.

Gracie, both redirected and satisfied with Bonnie's lies, returned her short attention span to her bikini-clad Barbie doll pretending to sunbathe on the lounger next to her.

Bonnie's gaze shifted from her daughter to the scene out beyond their split rail fence, to the now halted Extreme Golf construction, and the snowcapped Rocky Mountains in the distance. It was seventy-seven degrees out, and the sun was shining over them, but she could see the clouds heavy with snow gathering over the mountains. She hadn't checked a single weather report in weeks, but she was fairly certain this would be one of their last days in the pool. She would look for all Gracie's snow gear later today—but she'd grown so much since last year, Bonnie doubted much of it would still fit. She would probably need to buy at least a new winter coat and boots.

The thought of spending money—and her and Bennet's inability to staunch the hemorrhage of funds draining from their accounts daily—made the muscles in her lower back tense. Every day the construction equipment out behind their house sat unmoving was another day Sloan Investment Group drifted further away from Bennet's last financial life preserver.

The Atlanta investors were losing faith in his ability to get the project up and running again. Which meant these strangers, at least, had a confidence in Bennet to lose. Bonnie had never believed Bennet would get all the ducks lined up, the t's all crossed. The investors had no idea how much Bennet had been banking on her connections, first as a city councilperson, and second, when she captured the state Senate seat.

And all of that had evaporated in the wake of Elijah's death—at least it had for her. Bennet, seemingly, had digested the news of his youngest son's death and processed it in record time. He'd made a heartfelt statement to the reporters, prepared by Shirley Evans, the public relations specialist for Bonnie's campaign. Attended the funeral, standing stoic between Bonnie and his mother. Then left for Atlanta two days later.

Bennet was desperate to hang on to the few straws remaining of his deceased father's once thriving empire.

But Bonnie knew the next financial breeze would blow those last straws away. And she couldn't manage to care enough to pull herself together and help try to prevent it. Part of her even wondered, as she lay in bed most days, if she actually wanted it all to fall apart. The business, their marriage—her career. Life, it would seem, had nothing but hard roads and insurmountable odds in store for the Sloans these days.

Bonnie often wondered if it was time to give up resisting—leave Bennet, sell the house, find a two-bedroom apartment for her and Gracie—and simply walk her path of grief in peace.

Her phone buzzed on the concrete next to her. She considered ignoring it, but she didn't actually receive much communication from the world beyond her own four walls these days. It was either Bennet, or Detective Crobin with his weekly update to let her know there were still no suspects.

She saw that it was actually a very long text from Jessica Hampton.

Hi Bon. I hope you and the family are doing well. I thought about calling, but I wasn't sure if that was right, or if you would be accepting calls anyway. I know I said it at the funeral, but I'm still just so very sorry for your loss. I wasn't sure if you really spend any time on social media these days, but I thought you should probably know, if you didn't already, about what is happening on the Enclave Facebook page. Sorry this is so long, and for bothering you...I probably should have just called.

Bonnie hadn't been on social media, or even the internet really, for weeks. She didn't want any reminders of the fact that normal life had the audacity to simply continue without Elijah in it. Her son had died, and people still posted selfies of themselves smiling—it was all too much for her to comprehend. Bonnie had been opting out of the outside world as much as she could.

So no, she had absolutely no idea what Jessica was going on about on the fucking neighborhood Facebook page. But given the fact that they had barely spoken a word since the funeral, for Jessica to bother sending her such an awkward text—

She closed out of her text app, opened Facebook, found the Enclave community page, and started scrolling through the latest posts. When she finished reading first about Carl's arrest and next about how many people in the neighborhood now assumed he was responsible for Elijah's death, she placed her phone back down on the concrete beside her.

Gracie had fallen asleep in the pool lounger, her tiny head tilted to the left, her small arms limp at her side.

Bonnie turned her head all the way to her right, gazed beyond her immediate neighbor's yard—their pool and spa properly shut down and covered for the season—and into Carl's. Her mind worked to digest the accusations her neighbors were making against this man who had lived two houses over from her family for the last twenty years.

Carl had his differences with her family. He had known from day one that it was Sloan Investment Group that had everything to gain from the Extreme Golf project going in on the parcel of land right behind their houses. But for twenty years, the Waylands had been—while not exactly friends—close neighbors. She and Bennet had attended the parties for both their kids' high school graduations. Over the years, there had been game-day barbecues, holiday parties, and the monthly mixers at the clubhouse. When Carol Wayland was still alive, she had attended Bonnie's baby shower when she was pregnant with George.

Carol, with all her warmth and wisdom, had been one of Bonnie's closest confidants in those early, most difficult school years with Elijah.

Carl was angry at her and Bennet right now—but she couldn't imagine him hurting any of her children.

There was movement in Carl's backyard. Bonnie pulled her legs from the pool, checked to make sure Gracie was still both asleep and safe in the center of the lounger, then walked closer to the split rail fence.

It was two uniformed, male police officers and one woman in a suit who Bonnie assumed, given the drab gray color paired with thick-heeled sensible shoes, was a detective. When the woman suddenly glanced up and made eye contact, Bonnie turned and walked back to her own poolside.

She lowered herself down to the deck and slipped her legs into the water. An icy chill ran over her and made her visibly shiver—it felt like their eyes were on her. Were they watching her right now? With her head tilted forward, Bonnie slid her eyes to the right and tried to see.

All three of them were standing at Carl's back fence, one of the uniformed officers pointing out to the stalled construction. Bonnie wished she could hear what they were saying.

Did the police also now believe that Carl was capable of murdering a child?

A shadow swept over the pool and yard, and the air temperature against her bare skin dropped several degrees. Bonnie looked up and out to the horizon. The clouds that had been collecting out over the mountains now blanketed the city and blocked out the sun.

Gracie stirred in her lounger, and Bonnie watched while her youngest woke up. For a moment, Gracie's expression was confused, almost scared when she didn't first know where she was, or why. Seconds later, remembrance and realization released the furrow between Gracie's eyebrows. "I fell asleep!" she called to Bonnie with a smile.

Bonnie smiled back. "I know, goose. I watched you."

Gracie pulled her knees up tight to her chest and wrapped her arms around them. "I'm cold now."

"The sun's gone." Bonnie slipped all the way into the pool and waded across to the deep end until she could reach Gracie's lounger and pull her to the steps. "Let's head inside and get warmed up."

Gracie nodded. "Can we have grilled cheese for dinner?"

"That sounds perfect," Bonnie said and found that she actually meant it. "And some tomato soup." Bonnie lifted Gracie off the float and felt her small legs and arms wrap tight around her waist and neck. Bonnie turned her nose toward her daughter's hair, catching the scent of her strawberry shampoo and sun lotion.

When he was little, how many times had she carried Elijah in from the pool? His wet body soaking her. His smiling face tan from the summer sun.

They were halfway across the patio when Gracie asked, "Who are those people?"

Bonnie stopped. She knew who Gracie was asking about, but the question was instinctual. "What people, silly?"

Gracie shot out her left arm and pointed directly at Carl Wayland's backyard.

Bonnie gave a quick glance and saw that both of the cops and the detective were now standing right at Carl's side fence—looking directly at Bonnie as she carried her daughter into the house.

Bonnie turned away from them and kept walking. "They must be friends of Mr. Wayland," she said, her tone light—dismissive.

But she felt their eyes on her, all the way to the patio door. They watched her slide it open and then disappear into her own home. And with the attention came an awareness; these people knew things. Things about Carl. About her. It was only a matter of time before they knocked on her door to tell her.

Tell her exactly what they think had happened to her Elijah that night.

CHAPTER TWENTY-SIX

Alyson stared at her bedroom ceiling. The early morning light streamed through the window, brightened the room by degrees, and signaled her body to get up.

But she didn't move. Next to her, rolled onto his side and facing away, Justin still slept. The familiar rhythm of his breath was the only sound in the room. She wanted to stay here, next to him, close enough to touch him—she wanted to touch him.

Reach across the expanse of mattress between them, feel the warmth of his arm beneath her palm. Alyson turned her head and watched his broad shoulders rise and fall beneath the sheet. Right now, lying beside him, watching him sleep—she missed him. She missed his warmth, his smile, the feel of his arms around her.

She missed believing that he loved her.

With her palm flat against the bed beside her, she slid her hand toward him until, only inches from his back, she could feel the heat radiating from his body. She stopped, not daring to move any closer and risk waking him up. It was the most intimate connection she'd experienced with him in months.

If he woke up now, she felt there was a good chance he'd recoil from her. And she wanted to stay here, next to him, remembering as best she could what it felt like to be close to him, for as long as possible.

His alarm was set to go off in just a few minutes—it was the last day of Renee's visit, and he was getting up early to take her to the airport. Alyson was surprised to find she dreaded Renee's departure. It wasn't that they were close, now that Renee had held Alyson's hair back while she retched and mothered her through a hangover. No, they did not schedule a mother-daughter mani-pedi appointment.

The bold and harsh words she and Renee had shared that first night were not revisited. Still, they had irrevocably altered the foundation between them. For years, her relationship with her mother-in-law had been an exercise in enduring veiled slights and backhanded compliments. The conversation between them had changed that. They had both said what they needed to and survived their respective blows. Renee seemed to no longer need to chip away at Alyson. The full-frontal verbal assault had cured that, apparently. And as a result, Alyson now felt she understood the complex lay of the land between them. So the week had been, if not exactly a pleasure, at least a welcomed interruption to her and Justin's constant conflict.

With Renee here, both she and Justin did their best to behave like adults toward each other. They spoke to each other in full sentences and with measured tones. It was a stilted version of their normal family life. Only made more bearable by Andrew's incessant chatter and oblivious excitement that left no space for awkward silence to stretch. And with Renee in the guest bedroom, Justin didn't really have any other choice but to sleep in their bed beside her.

Alyson watched the back of his head now, his hair untidy and in need of a cut. She wanted to move her hand from the bed and run her fingers through his messy locks. He would roll over, his expression soft with sleep, and reach for her body. Pull her hips toward him. Fold his arms around her, draw her into him until her face pressed against his neck, and she could feel the press of him, hard and wanting her, against her thigh.

She couldn't remember the last time they had made love. It had been months. They had never gone this long without sex before. Over the years, and even when there'd been arguments and minor battles, Justin had always still wanted it. Wanted her.

If she touched him now, slid her hand down his back, ran her palm over his cock, let him know she wanted him now…would he take her?

Or would he look at her, his expression hard and distant, and pull away. Throw back the covers, his back to her, and get out of bed. Reject her without needing to say a word.

That possibility, and all it would mean about the salvageability of their marriage, terrified her. So she kept still in the bed beside him. Silently wondering if the distance between them was now too great for them to go back to the way they were. Fearing the leap of vulnerability she knew she'd have to make if there was any chance of healing.

Because what if moving forward meant moving forward alone? What if she pushed against the already loose seams of their marriage, and sat down with Justin to *really talk*, as Jessica had suggested—what if she forced the curtains between them aside and found that it was too late? What if Justin was already gone?

Involuntarily, her hand slipped a fraction of an inch closer, and she thought she could now feel the barest brush of his skin. She held her breath, waited for some sign that she'd woken him. But other than the continued rise and fall of his rib cage with his breath, he didn't move at all.

And she didn't dare move more.

All week, woven between the cooking, keeping Andrew entertained, and pretending her marriage was fine, Renee's personal critique came back to her again and again. *I have always thought you lacked a spine, Alyson.* It hurt to hear those words. She found it hard to toss them aside and let them go, explaining them away as yet another unwarranted insult she had endured from Renee over the years.

Time and again, she found herself returning to the statement, holding it up against the evidence of her life. Part of her wished she could ask Renee, "But why?" And she realized, not as a defense, not as an objection to Renee's assessment, but rather because she wanted to know, "What do you see in me that is spineless? Specifically, what do I do, or not do, that led you to this conclusion?"

Because Alyson couldn't plainly see the evidence herself. Examining her own lived life often felt like trying to perform surgery on herself. But now, lying here next to her sleeping husband, too afraid to move toward him and begin to break down the walls between them, she was unable to dismiss Renee's observation. Because even if she didn't want to *think* she was spineless, she felt it.

On the other side of Justin, blocked from her view by the mound of his stacked shoulders, the alarm pierced the tenuous silence of their bedroom. Even though she had expected it, the rapid-fire beeping startled her.

Justin, however, didn't move. The noise continued for several seconds before he reached his arm out and pressed the button to silence it. Alyson noticed that the rest of his body remained still, which seemed odd. Generally, when either of them was jarred from the depths of sleep by the alarm's shrill wail, their bodies responded with a jolt of confusion and the immediate annoyance that rode in on the wave of adrenaline.

She continued to watch him, his back still to her, not move. He was awake, but he didn't sit up, throw his legs over the side, scratch his head, and flex his feet before planting them onto the pale-gray rug beneath their bed. He lay there. Silent.

As she continued to study his back, she wondered if he had, in fact, been awake for some time. Like her, lying in silence, waiting on the alarm.

Had he felt her timid trespass across the vacant lot of mattress between them?

Seconds later, he did push himself up from his pillow, his movements both slow and careful, like he was trying to not disturb her. It reminded her of when Andrew was a baby. The many nights they'd struggled to get him to sleep and the way they would exit his nursery like it was a minefield.

Justin stood next to their bed and paused again for several seconds before turning to look back at her over his shoulder. His eyes met hers, held her gaze for several seconds, and then dropped the connection by looking away.

"Sorry for waking you so early," he said and started toward their master bathroom.

"It's fine," she said. "I was already awake. Andrew will want to say goodbye to your mom. I'll get him up."

With this, he stopped at the door to their bathroom and nodded once. "Thank you," he said without turning around. "She'll like that." Then he passed through the door and shut it carefully behind him.

As she listened to the sounds on the other side of the closed bathroom door—first the flush of their toilet, then the rush of water from their shower—Alyson lay flat on her back again, staring up at their bedroom ceiling. They had spoken to each other. The sentences were careful but complete. Devoid of any audience other than themselves. She rested her palms on the hollow of her chest and pressed into the bubble of hope their small kindnesses had blown into her heart. She would get up herself in a moment, rouse their sleeping son from the tangle of his Spider-Man sheets. Just as soon as the tears that ran hot from the corner of her eyes, across her temples, and into each ear stopped, and she felt confident of being able to hold a convincing smile.

CHAPTER TWENTY-SEVEN

Alyson pushed the extra-wide shopping cart down one of the many aisles packed with Christmas decorations in Costco. It had been only a week since Renee returned home to Nebraska, the Sunday after Thanksgiving. Still, she felt the press of time slipping away as Christmas rushed up on her calendar. Typically, she would have had presents for both Andrew and Justin purchased, wrapped, and hidden away by now. But this year, with only three short weeks left, she hadn't yet even started shopping.

But there had been a lot going on—for months now.

So as she made a right-hand turn down one of the four, jam-packed toy aisles, she reasoned that she should give herself a break and took a sip of the Starbucks white chocolate mocha she'd treated herself to. Still, it was hard to quell the rising panic she'd been feeling ever since waking up that morning and seeing the "helpful" Days Till Christmas counter one of her neighbors had posted on the Enclave Facebook page.

19 Days Left! it proclaimed above a scrolling, bomb-like digital timer that counted the hours, minutes, and even seconds that remained.

"Nineteen?" she'd questioned out loud. Obviously, she knew Christmas followed right after Thanksgiving, but how were there really only nineteen days left? Sure, she'd seen the exterior lights going up on all the houses throughout the neighborhood. She'd even considered gently encouraging Justin to go buy some multi-colored strands for their own home. Although she'd stopped herself. Since Thanksgiving, things between them had been just this side of good, and she hoped to keep them heading back toward the life and marriage they used to have. She wanted it so much, she had even started to simply ignore the amount of time he still spent in the basement—or at least, she pretended to ignore it. The point was that when it came to choosing her battles, prodding Justin to drag the ladder out of the garage rafters and risk life and limb to hang a few festive lights on their concrete-tiled roof wasn't high on her list.

This new awareness—nineteen days—suddenly shifted her whole day on its axis. She had snapped her laptop shut and began plotting and planning on what and how much she would be able to accomplish on her own, and what and how much should be saved and performed with the intent of *shared family experiences.*

She grabbed the notepad with the magnetic strip that she kept attached to the refrigerator door and started her divided lists: Me and Us.

Me: Drag all the Christmas items they had from the basement upstairs.

Us: Decorate the tree.

Me: SHOP FOR GIFTS!!!

This was as far as she got when a fresh, previously unrecognized reason for terror gripped her. Ever since Halloween, Andrew had been begging for a very specific Spider-Man action toy. What was it called? She racked her brains to remember even though Andrew had been talking about the toy nonstop since watching an unboxing episode on his favorite YouTube channel, Ryan's World. The Spider-Man was tall, at least eighteen inches, she thought. With complex joints, moving limbs, and a removable, latex-looking mask—that she did remember. But the qualities that sent Andrew into the realm of stratospheric desire were the fact that this Spider-Man not only talked but he also crouched and posed in a variety of positions and possessed the ability to shoot fabric-like webs from his hands.

Any time he'd been asked, "What do you want for Christmas?" this had been his only response. When she was in town, he had even made Renee open YouTube on her phone, so he could show her exactly which Spider-Man he wanted.

She opened her laptop back up, wondering how popular this toy could be, but she really already knew the answer to that. It had been featured on Ryan's World, after all. What were the chances of this "best Spider-Man action figure EVER" being at the top of the list for only a handful of elementary school kids? Zero.

"Shit, shit, shit," she said as she grabbed her purse, keys, and sunglasses and headed for her car in the garage. She had barely raked her hair into a messy ponytail for morning drop-off, and she was still in her baggy sweatshirt and most comfortable, and shabby, yoga pants—no need to get dressed for drop-off when she no longer got out of the car anymore.

Normally, she would have been sure to change her clothes and apply at least concealer and mascara before heading out of her house and into stores, but there was simply no time for vanity. She was in emergency mode.

That had been three hours and five stores ago. After discovering the second Target closest to her house was also all sold out of *the best Spider-Man action figure EVER*, it occurred to her to check the online retailers. Sitting in her car in the parking lot, she'd experienced a moment of elation to see that Amazon had them.

She clicked the *Buy* button immediately, barely even registering the toy's price tag of $89.00. She felt like she'd won the lottery just finding one! It wasn't until the app on her phone directed her to the online shopping cart that she completely deflated.

This item will be available to ship on January 6.

Her finger, which had been about to strike her phone screen and complete the order like a starving viper, recoiled. *January 6?*

Her mind quickly ran through the pros and cons of acquiring Andrew's most feverish Christmas wish, even if it wouldn't show up until well into the new year, versus not being able to get it at all.

Goddammit, why, why, why hadn't she bought this weeks ago? Maybe there was still a chance she'd be able to find it in one of the stores a little further away from their house? Yes, she would still try, but the *I'm so sorry* facial expressions of the toy department sales associates she'd already begged for help were not encouraging.

She sighed and clicked the *Buy* button on her phone. This was the worst-case scenario, five-year-old Andrew's Christmas present being delivered weeks late—but maybe she could make it work? Somehow. Maybe there was something else she could find that would still be as fun and exciting to open Christmas morning.

And so, she continued to scan the Costco shelves. Already knowing they wouldn't have this year's "must have" toy, but they certainly had shelves and shelves of other items that could potentially blow Andrew's current gift aspirations out of the water.

The trick, she realized, was finding something he hadn't thought of that was even better than *the best Spider-Man action figure EVER.* Something even Ryan's World hadn't considered.

For God's sake, there was a powered four-seater Jeep that had a working radio. A workbench with plastic power tools, screws, and nails. A three-foot-wide Millennium Falcon from *Star Wars—actually, that might not be a bad gift for Justin*, she thought as she considered adding it to her cart.

And those were only a fraction of the over-the-top toys that fit under that stereotypical "boys' toys" umbrella. Never mind the stainless steel mini kitchenettes, American Girl Doll knockoffs, and oh, the pink powered four-seater Jeep.

It was all amazing, but she needed a showstopper capable of making him forget.

After she'd exhausted the toy aisles—this problem required more thought and planning than an expensive impulse buy, she decided—and resigned herself to only purchasing the Millennium Falcon for Justin and one of the real pine Christmas wreaths, she steered her cart toward the lines of other shoppers waiting to check out.

When she saw them, a small gasp escaped her, and she stopped. Away from the toys in the center of the central aisle that led to the checkout, large cardboard boxes were stacked six deep and five high. She knew, immediately, that this was her Christmas showstopper.

This was precisely the right thing, and the vision came to her all at once.

Andrew would rip through his lesser gifts—whatever Renee had found at one of those holiday craft fairs she loved so much. His hope of finding that *best Spider-Man action figure EVER* painfully obvious on his face. And, eventually, every last present under the tree would have been exhausted, their crumpled red and green papers shredded and strewn across the floor. The realization that he had not, in fact, been gifted the item he had been feverishly begging for, for months, would only begin to dawn in his five-year-old mind.

Not even Santa, he might think.

"Andrew," she would say, "I think Santa left you one more present. But he had to put it in the backyard."

His budding disappointment would suddenly shift. First to curiosity, and then hope. Did Santa leave *the best Spider-Man action figure EVER* in their backyard? Still sitting in the middle of all their Christmas trash, he would look at her with a question in his eyes before getting to his feet and rushing to the back door.

And there, in the middle of their backyard, would be one of these items currently stacked in cardboard before her. Fully erected by her and Justin on Christmas Eve the moment they were confident Andrew had at last fallen asleep. A present Andrew would use for his entire childhood, years after *the best Spider-Man action figure EVER* had been relegated to, and forgotten at, the bottom of his toy bin.

A trampoline.

It was absolutely the most perfect solution. Andrew would lose his mind when he saw it.

As other shoppers streamed around her, her mind considered the size and probable weight of the box compared to her shopping cart—she needed a flatbed trolley, for sure. But those were all the way back at the very front of the store.

She pivoted her cart back the way she'd come, rushing as much as was possible down the congested aisles and toward the door.

At the front of the store, she had just finished transferring the Millennium Falcon and her Christmas wreath from her cart to a flatbed trolley when she felt her purse, slung over her arm and pressed between her arm and breast, vibrate. Now alerted, with the second ring, she could now also hear the faint sound of her phone's trill ring from the depths of her bag. *Damn it, why now?*

With her left hand, she fished into her purse while her right hand continued to try to steer the unwieldy flatbed through the throngs of shoppers and carts. Without both her hands, she miscalculated a turn and clipped a display stack of two-pack insulated thermoses. She cringed and held her breath, glancing around to see if anyone had witnessed her reckless driving before pulling her phone out and checking the screen.

The number displayed made her pull the flatbed to a complete stop. "Shit," she said and swiped to answer the call.

"Hello, this is Alyson," she said, bracing herself for whatever this was about.

"Hello, Ms. Tinsdale?"

"Yes," she replied, noting the clipped tone of annoyance in her own voice. The person on the other end was not the voice she had been expecting. She propped the phone up to her ear with her shoulder and continued through Costco toward the trampolines.

"Hello, this is Principal Judy Evans from The Enclave Academy. I'm calling because there has been an incident today. It involves your son, Andrew, and another student in his class."

Alyson digested this news as she pulled her trolley to a stop next to the stacked boxes of trampolines. The principal? Her heart pumped double time as she considered the very limited reasons she would be getting this call.

What had Andrew done now? she thought, then immediately hated that this was her first assumption. It was completely possible that it was the *other* child who had done something to her son—wasn't it? Why had she allowed this school to plant a negative knee-jerk response in her about her own kid?

Alyson took a breath and framed her next words deliberately. "What happened to Andrew? Is he okay? I told his teacher, weeks ago, that he is being bullied and excluded by the other kids."

The other end of the line was silent for several seconds, and Alyson wondered if her phone had maybe dropped the call. Her cell reception was notoriously bad the farther into any store she went. But then, she heard Principal Evans clear her throat on the other end of the line. "I'm sorry to hear that Andrew has been having some difficulties with peers in his class, and I will be sure to follow up with Mrs. Sinclair about your concerns. However, I don't believe that today's incident is related."

Alyson inhaled deeply and felt every hair on her body stand up as an electric current of frustration coursed through her. "Andrew has been *repeatedly*—"

"Ms. Tinsdale," Principal Evans cut her off. Her tone was now sharp and without any of the conciliatory olive branches she had affected before. "The facts today are this. Andrew is currently in my office and will remain in my office until either you or Mr. Tinsdale arrives to pick him up. He is being suspended for the rest of today and the next two days for aggressive and violent behavior toward another student that resulted in bodily harm, and for aggressive and violent behavior toward a staff member not resulting in bodily harm."

"What could he have—" Alyson tried to interject, but Principal Evans kept talking, a verbal freight train that had no intention of stopping.

"Today, at approximately 10:37, Mrs. Sinclair's class was outside for their morning recess. Andrew was playing with several other students beneath the climbing structure when he became emotionally escalated and then proceeded to bite another student on the forearm. The bite was severe in nature in that it both broke the skin and drew blood."

And just like that, all the mother-bear fight drained out of Alyson in a single instant. She held her phone to her ear, her arm suddenly weak as disbelief and shame collided head-on with her desire to be her son's greatest advocate.

"Are you able to come to the school, Ms. Tinsdale, or should I call Andrew's father?"

Alyson shook her head. "Yes," she managed to whisper. "I'm coming."

"Very well," Principal Evans said. "Then I look forward to meeting you shortly," she finished. Not sounding even remotely like this meeting was something she really *looked forward to*, and hung up.

Alyson slid her phone from her ear and dropped it into her

purse, still wedged under her arm. The image of what Andrew had done came to her clearly. It wasn't at all hard to envision him angry and out of control, so far beyond reason that he lashed out at another kid in the most horrible way possible.

She stared at the boxes of trampolines, confused about what should be her next move. Two other people were now pulling at the boxes and adding them to their own Christmas purchases.

Overwhelmed and frustrated, she felt powerless to hold back the tears that rose up and began running down her face without warning. Alyson fished around in her purse until she found her sunglasses and shoved them onto her face, hoping to at least disguise her disappointment and grief as she deliberated.

No matter how shocked she felt, she couldn't just stand here all day. She checked the time on her phone—she needed to get going—and had just about decided to forget buying the only present she could think of that could beat out *the best Spider-Man action figure EVER*. At the present moment, she was so angry with him that she didn't give a shit how disappointed Andrew would be Christmas morning.

She *hoped* he was disappointed.

He *deserved* to be disappointed.

That was how she felt—at the present moment. But she knew, come Christmas morning, she would feel differently.

So when yet another person arrived and selected one of the trampolines for themselves, she bent over and began dragging one of the boxes onto her own flatbed as well.

CHAPTER TWENTY-EIGHT

When Alyson arrived at the school, it was nearly forty-five minutes after Principal Evans's initial phone call. She rolled into the lot of The Enclave Academy a little too fast and parked among all the Hyundai Tucsons and Honda CRVs that seemed to be the teachers' vehicles of choice. She snatched her purse off the passenger seat and hurried across the parking lot, already formulating the excuse she would give for why it took her so long to get here.

She certainly would not be sharing the fact that it had taken her much longer than she expected to buy Andrew his fantastic Christmas present *before* picking him up to begin his three-day suspension from school. She was just crossing from the parking lot to the school's entrance when she saw it—Bonnie Sloan's Porsche Cayenne.

Alyson stopped where she was and stared at Bonnie's car. The sight of it created a fresh wave of dread. Why was Bonnie here? Alyson took another deep breath and blew it out as she pressed the security buzzer next to the main entrance door.

The office manager, Sharon, asked over the speaker, "Hello, can I help you?"

Alyson leaned in close to the box on the wall. "Yes. I'm Alyson Tinsdale. I'm here to see Principal Evans."

"*Oh, yes*," she said with a knowing tone of accusation that was impossible to miss. Then the buzzer sounded to indicate the door was unlocked.

Alyson opened the door that led to the vestibule and then took a right turn toward the second door that led to the front office. As she entered the space and faced the two women who worked behind the long, counter-height desk—Sharon and Debra, the administrative assistant—she felt both guilty and ashamed. Like *she* was the one reporting to the office to be reprimanded by the principal for bad behavior.

"Hello, Ms. Tinsdale," Sharon greeted her with a limp smile. "Please log in to the system and have a seat. I'll let Ms. Evans know you're here."

Alyson swallowed and nodded as she pulled her wallet and driver's license from her purse. When she'd slid her ID into the computer system mounted on the counter, she waited while it scanned some criminal database to determine if she was a child abuser. When it spit out a visitor name-tag sticker with her picture, she peeled the back off, stuck it to her sweatshirt, and then realized she still looked like absolute shit.

Oh, God. Why was today the day, of all days, that she'd rushed from her house in her crappiest yoga pants and a baggy sweatshirt? Her hair still in the messy ponytail from morning drop-off. Not one drop of makeup on her face. She took a seat, two chairs away from a sullen boy who looked to be about ten or eleven years old. Clearly, he was also in some sort of trouble today. Alyson resisted the sudden urge she had to lean over to him and ask, "And what are you in for?"

Back behind the long countertop, there were two doors with windows in their centers. The one on the left was stenciled with the word "Principal." The one on the right, "Vice Principal." Alyson remembered Principal Evans telling her on the phone that Andrew would remain in her office until Alyson arrived to pick him up—was he in there now? Sitting, sullen and unhappy like this boy beside her, regretting his terrible behavior and wishing he could take it back?

The thought revived some of her protective instincts. He was her son, after all. And yes, Principal Evans was in charge of her school, but what exactly was being said to Andrew on the other side of that door? How was he being made to feel about this situation? About himself?

She glanced up at the standard-issue school clock mounted to the wall between the doors. It felt like she'd been sitting here waiting for longer than necessary. She eyed the window in the principal's door, trying to get a look at what was happening inside. Whether he deserved it or not, it felt like she was being kept from Andrew while he was most likely suffering. It ignited an instinctual drive to get to him—she needed to see that he was okay.

A door to her left, which led to the school's interior hallways and classrooms, opened. When Alyson glanced up, she saw Bonnie Sloan move through the door carrying her daughter, Gracie. The little girl's arms and legs were fastened tight around her mother, like a starfish to a rock. Her face was buried in Bonnie's neck.

A sickening realization dawned at the periphery of Alyson's awareness, but there wasn't time to connect all the dots.

Bonnie didn't take a seat in one of the empty chairs lining the wall beside Alyson. No. Bonnie Sloan moved through the office space like she owned it. Carrying Gracie right around the backside of the long countertop to the principal's closed door, which she opened herself, and entered. A second later, Principal Evans appeared in the open doorway herself.

"Ms. Tinsdale," she called as she made eye contact with Alyson hunched in her chair, "we're ready for you now."

Alyson stood, her legs watery with fear. Andrew was in trouble, big trouble. And Alyson felt every pound of the responsibility for him and his actions weighing on her.

Principal Evans, a woman who looked like she was somewhere in her midsixties, was small, probably just over five feet tall. She kept her blonde hair short and her athletic body draped in a fitted women's suit—sensible flats on her feet. And while she took up very little physical space in the world, and Alyson had never heard her raise her voice above a conversational tone, her presence was commanding. A captain at the helm of her ship.

Principal Evans held the door as Alyson passed through it. Once inside, her eyes immediately found Andrew, sitting at the table at the center of the room, a box of markers and a coloring book before him. "Hey, Andrew," she said, her voice barely above a whisper.

But Andrew didn't look at her. He kept his eyes glued to the half-colored page in front of him, the green marker in his hand scribbling over the same spot.

She stood, arms limp at her sides, uncertain of what she should do next. She could feel Bonnie's and Principal Evans's eyes on her, measuring her parenting moves in this moment. "Andrew?" she tried again, her voice a little louder. When he continued to ignore her, and hunched even closer to the page before him, her already overtaxed nervous system flooded in embarrassment.

"I think maybe," Principal Evans interjected as she pulled a chair out from the table for herself, "it might be best if we all have a seat, and then we can discuss what happened today and next steps for moving forward."

Alyson nodded once and pulled out a chair for herself next to Andrew. As she and Principal Evans took their seats, she noticed that Bonnie wasn't taking a seat herself. She continued to stand while Gracie clung to her. Gracie now had her hands on Bonnie's shoulders, and Alyson could clearly see the white gauze wrapped around her left wrist.

This, she knew without being told, was where Andrew had bitten her. When Bonnie met Alyson's gaze, the shame and mortification she felt over what he had done were too much to bear. Alyson dropped her own eyes to Andrew's coloring page as well.

"I won't be taking a seat," Bonnie announced. "I have already made my feelings and my intentions for next steps perfectly clear while we waited for Ms. Tinsdale to find the time to join us here. I am taking my daughter to her pediatrician and then home so she can rest and try to recover from this assault." Bonnie then turned her attention directly toward Alyson. "Furthermore, after we have been to the doctor and have thoroughly documented the extent of Gracie's injury, I will be filing a report with the police department and getting a restraining order against your son." She then swung her gaze back to Principal Evans. "And once I have that order in place, I fully expect him to be removed from my daughter's class. At the very *least*. Quite frankly, a child like that should be expelled from this school."

Without another word, Bonnie turned away, opened the door, and left Principal Evans's office.

Alyson processed everything Bonnie had just said, her mouth dry and her hands shaking. She looked first to Principal Evans, wanting to ask so many questions but unable to form any words. But then she heard a small sob, and when she looked, she could see that Andrew was now crying. Large wet tears ran down his cheeks, their salty splats bleeding the marker colors where they landed on his pages.

Alyson took a deep breath and tried her best to hold back her own tears as she placed her hand on Andrew's back. "Honey," she whispered.

In one quick movement, Andrew climbed out of his chair and into her arms. His face was planted between her breasts, but she could still hear his muffled cry. "The police are going to arrest me."

Alyson pulled him all the way into her lap and pressed his head to her chest. "No," she tried to reassure him. "That's not going to happen."

"Yes, it is!" he screamed. "The police…are going…to put me… in jail." His sobs were now hysterical as his hands grabbed handfuls of flesh painfully at her waist.

"Andrew," she tried again. "Andrew, please." But it was no use. He couldn't even hear her over his own loud wails.

At the head of the table, Principal Evans took a deep breath and got up from her seat. Alyson watched as the woman circled the table, then knelt down beside them until she was eye to eye with Andrew.

"Andrew," she said, her voice kind but firm.

At first, Andrew didn't seem to hear her, but when the woman touched his arm, then slid her hand down to grasp his own, Andrew's continuous sobs broke into gasping breaths. "Andrew, I want you to listen to my voice. Can you hear me?"

He nodded against Alyson's chest.

"Good. Now listen carefully. I want you to try to take some deep breaths. Okay?"

He nodded again.

"Good. Now." Her voice was soft, and Andrew quieted his sobs in order to hear her better. Alyson realized the woman was purposefully lowering her voice and tone, like a tool she was using to help calm Andrew down. Alyson never would have thought of this and felt, yet again, like the least qualified person in the room to manage her own son. "The police are not going to put you in jail. Can you look at me? Andrew, give Ms. Evans your eyes…there you go. Now, did you hear what I said? The police are not going to put you in jail. I promise, and you know, Ms. Evans never makes…" she trailed off with an expectant tone.

"A promise she can't keep," Andrew mumbled.

Alyson sat holding her son, thankful that this woman seemed to know how to help him, but paralyzed by the realization that Andrew could finish her sentences. If she had been asked, Alyson would have said that Andrew didn't even know who the principal at his school was. Now, she was learning for the first time, he seemed to have a relationship with her.

Principal Evans took a deep breath and let it out with a loud sigh and a smile. "That's right." She stood up and took the seat right beside them. "So, I promise the police will not arrest you, Andrew. But what's the other thing I always say? At every morning assembly and over the intercom after the pledge and announcements, what's Ms. Evans's number one job at our school?"

Andrew took a second, and for a moment Alyson didn't think he'd be able to answer her, but then he lifted his head and said, "To keep students safe."

Ms. Evans gave him a big smile as a reward and sat back in her chair with a satisfied expression as she nodded. "That's exactly right. So," she said, her tone shifting ever so slightly. Now that Andrew was calm, it was back to the business at hand. "Knowing that my number one job is to keep students safe…do you think your behavior at recess today was safe?"

Andrew shook his head, and Principal Evans nodded.

"And, given your behavior, do you think Gracie was being kept safe today?"

Andrew paused before answering this time, then shook his head again.

"No, she wasn't. And now, she's been injured by you. Very badly. And when Mrs. Sinclair and Ms. Gibs tried to help Gracie and to get you to come inside…do you remember what happened then?"

Andrew nodded.

"Can you tell your mom in your own words?"

Alyson felt Andrew's body tense in her arms, and she thought he probably wouldn't admit to whatever other offense he had committed, but then he said, "I hit Mrs. Sinclair."

Principal Evans nodded. "And what else?"

Andrew sunk farther into Alyson's embrace. "I called her…a bad word."

"*What?*" Alyson asked, unable to help blurting out disbelief. "What did you call her?"

Now that she was questioning him, Andrew shut down, shook his head, and refused to answer.

Principal Evans picked up one of the markers from the table in front of them and flipped over one of Andrew's earlier and now discarded pictures. She wrote something on the back and then turned it so Alyson could read what it said.

In a neat, blue script, she had written the word "bitch."

And whatever reserve energy Alyson had been hanging on to to get through the rest of this nightmare of a morning drained away from her.

CHAPTER TWENTY-NINE

Alyson buckled Andrew into his booster seat in the back of her car without speaking or looking at him. Her hands shook, and tears she couldn't control ran down her cheeks. Once she was confident the seat belt was properly threaded and clicked in, she stood up, slammed the back door shut, and opened the driver's door.

As she sat behind the wheel, her entire body trembled as she grabbed her own seat belt and started the car.

"Mom, can we—"

Alyson whipped around in her seat. "Shut up," she commanded, her voice a low growl that she barely recognized. "Don't you dare ask me for anything right now. Do you think for even one second that you deserve *anything* right now? After what you *did* today? You *bit* Gracie! You *hit* your teacher! You called a grownup the *B-word*! Do you have any idea how much trouble you are in? How much you've embarrassed me? When we get home, you're going to get out of this car, march straight upstairs to your room, and spend the rest of the day there until your father gets home. And then! Then, you can tell him yourself exactly how horrible you've behaved today."

She watched his small face darken and collapse into anguish and then tears. She had never spoken to him so harshly, and now, seeing his reaction, a swift dose of guilt took up residence in her chest right next to all that anger. Alyson sighed, closed her eyes, and shook her head in exasperation as she shifted the car into reverse. She placed both her hands on the steering wheel and backed out of the parking space.

For the entire two-minute drive back to their house, she took measured deep breaths and tried her best to ignore Andrew's loud sobs behind her. She couldn't even begin to think about what any of this would mean for Andrew's future at The Enclave Academy. He was only suspended for now, and that was bad enough, but what if Bonnie was true to her word and kept pushing for his expulsion? The Sloans and their family practically *were* the Enclave neighborhood. And was Bonnie seriously going to get a restraining order? Against a five-year-old?

By the time Alyson pulled onto their street, she was beginning to wonder if she would need to preemptively pull Andrew from the school. He was already labeled "The Bad Kid" in his class. What would his life there be like after the Sloans took legal actions against him? God, how had parenting gotten so fucking hard?

She pulled into the driveway too fast, and the tires hit the curb hard enough to bounce the large box in the back of her car. The box slammed with a heavy thump against the side of the cargo space. Until that moment, she had forgotten entirely about the trampoline back there.

"What was that?" Andrew asked, alarmed.

"It's nothing," she snapped and pulled the car all the way into the garage. "Don't you worry about it."

But the second the car stopped, she heard the click of Andrew's seat belt release. In the rearview mirror, she saw him jump up from his seat and turn to face the back in a flash.

"Andrew!" she shouted. "No!"

But it was too late. He was now kneeling on his booster seat and peering in the cargo trunk of the SUV.

Before she could get the car turned off, Andrew had registered and processed the meaning of the picture on the large box—a color photo of two ecstatically happy children bouncing high in the summer sun. "A trampoline!" he shouted. Any remorse for his actions today at school was utterly forgotten.

In her rush to get him away from his Christmas present—that he didn't deserve!—Alyson fumbled with her seat belt for several seconds longer than it should have taken. "I said no," she repeated and finally managed to unlock the belt and get out her own door. By the time she made it to the back door and opened it, Andrew was bouncing on his knees and staring happily at the box in the back of the car. No longer bothering with words, she grabbed him around the waist and pulled him from the car.

Rage. Sharp claws intent on destruction pulled at her breastbones, pulsed adrenaline through her arms and legs, and hammered all patience and reason from her head. Andrew's surprised wail at being yanked from the backseat of the car fell on her now deaf ears. All Alyson could understand was the thunderous rush of her own blood pounding through her veins.

"Mom!" he cried as Alyson carried him like a large sack of potatoes up the garage stairs that led to the mudroom. With her free hand, she hit the button to close the rolling garage door behind them and opened the interior door to the house.

There was no plan, only momentum that drove her past the washer and dryer, through the family room, past the basement stairs, then up, up, up to the second floor. Even burdened with Andrew's weight, and his squirming attempts to escape her raptor-like grasp, her legs pumped like two powerful pistons.

She had heard that fear could fuel a mother's strength in times of desperate need.

Apparently, so could fury.

With her free hand, she opened his bedroom door, took three steps to the edge of his bed, then dropped him into the middle of the mattress. His small body bounced once before he fell onto his back and stared up at her with confused, but still angry, eyes.

She stared into his belligerent little face and felt her hands flex into fists. For one brief, sharp moment, the urge to lash out at him, physically hit him, swelled up inside her.

Immediately, she thought of her own mother. Belt in hand, unleashing a torrent of blows onto both Alyson and her older brother, Paul. Their mother hadn't used it often—maybe five times that Alyson could distinctly recall—but she vividly remembered every beating. Her mother wild with outrage, her clenched fists driven by exasperation.

This. Every overtaxed cell in Alyson's body that was begging her for a physical release, this was how her mother had felt when she'd lunged for Alyson or Paul, then dragged them somewhere in the house where she could release her own rage onto their bodies.

Andrew continued to stare up at Alyson, his angry expression now gone and replaced by something altogether different. Confusion. Whatever her son saw in his mother right now, he didn't recognize it. She had broken out in a cold sweat, and a shiver ran through her body as she forcefully flexed her hands open at her sides.

Alyson took a breath and pointed her finger at him. "You are staying in this room for the rest of the day. There is no TV, no video games, no iPad, no anything. Do you understand me?" she asked but didn't wait for a response. "What you did today, to Gracie...I cannot believe it! It was disgusting. I am disgusted with your behavior. What were you thinking? You bit someone! What on earth makes you think it's okay to *hurt* another person?" Alyson dropped her pointed finger and shook her head instead. "And now you're suspended from school! For three days! So, you should probably just plan on spending all that time here in this room doing nothing but thinking about what you've done and what you're going to do to make it better."

Her tirade had returned Andrew's remorseful expression—good.

She turned to leave, but before she could make it out the door—

"Mom?"

"What?" she snapped.

"Are you going to put the trampoline up today?"

She turned and stared at him, both her hands pressed flat into her thighs at her side. "Are you kidding me? Do you think for one second that you deserve a trampoline?" Alyson turned back to the door and opened it. "As soon as your father gets home, I'm taking the trampoline back to the store!"

She didn't turn around to look at him, but she could hear him start crying again. Without another word, she stepped out of his room and slammed the door behind her. She was both ashamed at her outburst and relieved that she had walked away. As she stood in the hall, her body shook from the tornado of confusing thoughts and emotions still flying inside her. It was horrifying to know how close she was to replaying her childhood traumas onto her own child. It was sickening to think that Andrew didn't really care about hurting Gracie. She felt powerless in this moment to teach her child anything meaningful when she herself didn't feel completely capable of solving today's multitude of conflicts without inciting new and far worse problems.

She moved away from his door and the sound of his sobs. Walking away was the only completely right thing to do right now. At least she did know this. She needed to do more than shake her finger at Andrew and take away all of his favorite screens—greater lessons should be imparted. But right now, not fully in control of her own emotions and barely hanging on to her behavior, she was not the person for that job.

She could only settle on being satisfied that Andrew was now, at least, again feeling sad that he had behaved badly instead of ecstatic at the thought of getting a trampoline.

Honestly, what the hell? She knew he was only five, but still. How could he even begin to think she was going to give him a goddamn trampoline after what had happened today?

Alyson took the stairs back down to the first floor, her every step a heavy fall that echoed through the now quiet house. The surge of adrenaline that had driven her up the stairs had now receded and left her limp. When she reached the last step, she stood with one hand braced on the banister for support. She looked up and caught sight of herself in the entryway mirror. Several large chunks of hair had broken loose from her now lopsided ponytail. The sweatshirt she was wearing had a stain down the front she hadn't noticed before. And the dark circles under her eyes and flushed and sweaty-looking complexion weren't doing her any favors either. Jesus Christ, she looked like absolute shit. And, aside from the impact from hauling Andrew up to his room, this was probably pretty close to what she'd looked like while collecting him at the school.

She could easily imagine what Bonnie had thought when she saw her this morning.

It was bad enough having to go to the school and listen to the laundry list of infractions your kid had perpetrated. At the very least, you'd like to at least appear to have your shit together enough to dress in clean clothes and run a brush through your hair. Alyson turned from her own image in disgust and pulled her wild hair into a new ponytail while she headed for the kitchen and tried to wrap her head around what had happened, and what she was going to do about it.

The entire morning had been chaos, one shit show after the next. She needed quiet and space to think through it all. She would need to call Justin, obviously. Figure out what to do about Bonnie. Should she try calling her? And of course, she was not done dealing with Andrew. A day spent in his room was hardly going to solve his seemingly increasing behavior concerns.

Should she pull him from school? Should she take him to his pediatrician? Maybe Andrew really did have ADHD? Had Mrs.

Sinclair been right all along? Was Alyson just being stupid and blind to Andrew's needs?

It was all too much. Coffee, she needed more coffee; that was for sure. She would drink her coffee, think, make a list, and tackle one goddamn emergency at a time.

Alyson began her typical coffee ritual, hoping it would calm her. But with her shaking hands and jittery nervous system, she felt more like an addict prepping her next hit. She took her favorite blue-and-white coffee mug from the cupboard, selected a Kona Nespresso pod from the carousel, and pressed the start button on the top of the coffee machine.

Her phone rang. It was at the bottom of her purse in the middle of the family room floor where she'd dropped it while hauling Andrew into the house. Cream-colored coffee streamed from the machine and filled the kitchen with the rich, smoky aroma. The phone rang again, increasing her already sky-high anxiety; she considered ignoring it. She didn't have any idea who it might be, but she felt certain, given the disastrous course today was taking, it couldn't possibly be good news or anything she might want to hear.

Best-case scenario: it was a telemarketer trying to sell her on a timeshare presentation in Florida.

Worst-case: it was the police trying to inform her that Bonnie had been true to her word and had gotten a restraining order against Andrew.

It rang again, the shrill clanging of phone bells rattling her already shot nervous system. "Shit," she whispered to herself and jogged through the kitchen to catch it before it rolled over to voicemail. She dumped all her purse contents out onto the couch and snatched up her phone the moment she saw it. She glanced at the caller ID as her thumb swiped the screen to answer—it was Gabby.

"Hello?" she asked, her brain processing the small relief she felt knowing it was a friend on the other end. This was a good thing—Gabby was exactly who she needed right now. Gabby would know exactly what to do about the school, Bonnie, Andrew—all of it.

"Alyson, it's Gabby." She sounded frantic herself. "Did you hear?"

The machine in the kitchen was now hissing and spitting the last few drops of coffee into her mug. Alyson pressed the phone to her ear, made her way back to the refrigerator and the assortment of flavored creamers lining the shelf in the door. "Hi, Gabby. Hear what?" she asked, unable to imagine how there could possibly be anything happening that was more significant or "Did you hear?" more worthy than what was going on in her own life right now.

"It's Carl Wayland," Gabby said, sounding breathless. "They're *not* charging him with Elijah's murder."

Alyson stopped halfway to her fridge. "What?" This news both surprised her and managed to knock her beyond the borders of her own crumbling universe for the moment. "Why not? I don't understand."

"Apparently, he was never even a suspect. His arrest for that cold case and Elijah's murder…completely unrelated. Also, he has an alibi. He was out of state staying with his daughter and her family in San Francisco."

"So what? They just let him go?"

"No, no, not even close. He's still been charged with the murder of that woman down in Colorado Springs from twenty years ago," she ended in a whisper.

The coffee machine gave one final hiss, reminding Alyson of her drink and prompting her to open the fridge. "I don't understand. Everyone was so sure it was him. What with his history and all the drama between him and the Sloans. If it's not him, then who *do* the police think killed Elijah? Have they made any other arrests?"

"No one else has been charged," Gabby said. "I don't think they have any other leads."

As Alyson reached for the French vanilla creamer, her hand stopped and rested on the rounded red cap. "But then...that means whoever killed Elijah is still out there."

CHAPTER THIRTY

Bonnie picked Gracie up, sat her on the black marble counter in their downstairs bathroom, and pulled the first aid kit from the cupboard beneath the sink. "Let's take another look and see if we need to add some more Neosporin," Bonnie explained, even though she had seen the bite in the nurse's office when she first arrived at the school. What she really planned on doing was taking several pictures on her phone as evidence, before going to the pediatrician for official medical documentation, and then to the police department to file the restraining order.

If Alyson Tinsdale, that smug, self-righteous bitch, thought she was doing her *civic duty* when she posted that picture of George's Jeep on Facebook, well, wait until she found herself on the receiving end of goddamn Bonnie Sloan's *civic* response. By the time she was through, Alyson was going to wish she'd never even heard of The Enclave.

Bonnie grabbed the flat-sided bandage scissors from the kit and took Gracie's thin arm in her hand. While Gracie watched, Bonnie snipped the white fabric tape holding the wad of gauze in place over the wound. When she pulled it away, she could see the twelve tiny tooth marks, six on each side of Gracie's left forearm. The angry, red-hot little holes were only just beginning to scab over. Seeing them again sent another rush of anger through Bonnie.

That little shit.

She pulled her phone from her back pocket and pulled up the camera app. She snapped several pictures, first of the entire bite, then close-ups.

"Are you going to put the Sporin on it?" Gracie asked.

"Just a second," Bonnie said. She was trying to get a good close-up that really showed how bad the bite was, but she was having a hard time getting the stupid camera app to focus. "Mommy needs to get some good pictures." The problem was that the light in this fucking cave of a bathroom sucked. With the dark marble, mahogany cabinets, and forest-green and gold paisley wallpaper, the bathroom was a black hole that sucked light into nonexistence. The thought reminded her of just how horrifically dated their entire multimillion-dollar house was. An antithesis of every *Elle Decor* magazine littering her office, with their bright home photo spreads with high ceilings, pale-gray furniture, and white pile rugs. Their own home was heavy by comparison and would cost a fortune to remodel if they wanted to price it competitively for sale.

As it was, she and Bennet were going to take a hit putting it on the market now. Every realtor she'd interviewed had let her know that buyers would take the cost of a gut renovation off their asking price.

"Goddammit!" Bonnie said, scrolling through the pictures she'd captured on her phone. Each one more out of focus and unusable than the last. She swept Gracie up with one arm and carried her out of the bathroom.

"Where are we going?"

"We need to go outside. Mommy needs a *good* picture."

"But what about the Band-Aids?" Gracie whined and squirmed.

"We'll get them in a minute. This will only take a second. I just need—stop squirming." Bonnie lost her grip on her daughter's writhing body, and Gracie slid down her hip and to the floor.

Once free, Gracie inspected her own arm, her fingers probing the tender flesh.

"Come on," Bonnie commanded and grabbed Gracie's uninjured wrist. She pulled her to her feet and started toward the back door. "We need better light for the pictures."

"But why do we need pictures?" Gracie asked.

Bonnie opened the back door and guided Gracie to a sunny spot on the patio. "Because we need to document the injury." She dropped Gracie's good arm and carefully lifted the injured one up so she could take the picture.

"But why?" Gracie asked.

Bonnie sucked her breath and reminded herself that Gracie, no matter how annoying right now, was also just a very curious child who needed answers for practically everything—all the time. "Because." Bonnie held her phone over the bite and lifted it up and down, trying to focus as close to the marks as she could. "It's evidence. We might need this to show the police. Or our attorney. You should always take photos when something bad happens. That way, you have proof. Especially when someone has hurt you."

Bonnie shifted her phone another centimeter, and the focus square lit up with the perfect shot of Andrew's teeth marks. Bonnie snapped the picture quickly, then took several more, before Gracie moved and ruined it. "There," Bonnie said as she scrolled through the various shots she'd gotten. As she inspected each one, she realized that photos didn't accurately capture how bad the bite really was. Yes, she could see that there was a bite on Gracie's arm, but the photos failed to convey the vibrancy of the injury. It looked less severe than it really was, and she wondered if she should contact a professional photographer, with better equipment and the skill to document an accurate account.

Gracie cradled her hurt arm, staring down at the bite with a wrinkled brow. When Bonnie slid her phone back into her pocket, deciding that, yes, she should probably get some professional shots as well, Gracie looked up at her. "Did you take pictures of Elijah when George hurt him?"

Bonnie's breath stopped in her chest. Her eyes found Gracie's and held her questioning gaze. Bonnie didn't answer her daughter—she couldn't because of the constriction in her throat. She had clearly heard her daughter's words, but her brain was still processing it. Untangling the syllables, dissecting each vowel, trying to parse meaning from this question. On the one hand, what did Gracie mean asking it? On the other hand, Bonnie already knew exactly what she meant.

"Mommy?"

"Yes," she whispered.

Gracie wrinkled her brow again and tilted her head, clearly waiting for her answer.

Bonnie took a breath. "George and Elijah…that was different. George didn't mean to hurt Elijah. They're *brothers* and had a disagreement. It was…an accident, sweetheart. That is completely different from what Andrew Tinsdale did to you. What Andrew did was an assault, and on a little girl who was not his sister. Do you understand the difference?"

Gracie returned her gaze to her injured arm, cradled against her. The intensity behind her dark-brown eyes hinted at the lengths her mind was going to in order to understand and discern the difference.

"Look," Bonnie said, hoping to change the subject, "I have a few calls to make before we head over to the doctor and the police station. And it's almost lunchtime now. How about we go inside, I'll make you some macaroni and cheese, you can eat, and you can watch one episode of *Doc McStuffins* before we leave." Bonnie held out her hand and shook it once, prompting Gracie to take hold.

Gracie looked at her mother's hand but ignored it. She shifted her eyes up to Bonnie's face instead. "Andrew didn't *mean* to hurt me either. We had a disagreement too."

Bonnie was afraid of this. "No," she said, squatting down, so she was eye to eye with her daughter. "This is not the same." She pointed to the bite marks on Gracie's arm for emphasis. "It is never okay for a boy to hurt a girl. Do you understand me? It doesn't matter if you had a disagreement or not."

Behind her, the back door opened. When Bonnie turned around, she saw it was George. She stood up and faced him. "What are you doing home from school so early?" She regretted her clipped and annoyed tone as soon as she saw the stunned expression on his face.

"It's an early release day," he shot back. "Teacher In-Service. But I can turn around and leave again if that would make you happier."

Bonnie took a breath and dropped her shoulders. "No, I'm sorry," she said, registering her oldest son's unkempt appearance. From his limp and stained clothing to his overgrown and greasy hair, George stood before her, looking almost nothing like the son she knew. Two sharp, dark hollows ran the length of his cheekbones—he'd lost so much weight—and the circles beneath his eyes told her he wasn't sleeping. When was the last time she'd really thought to check in with George? On instinct, Bonnie took a step toward him, her hand reaching for his face.

He recoiled, his expression darkening.

Bonnie stopped and dropped her hand back to her side. Getting George back wasn't going to be easy. "I'm sorry," she repeated. "You just caught me off guard in the middle of a day that already had me spinning from another emergency." Bonnie stepped to the side so George could get a clear view of his little sister.

At the sight of her, looking sad, confused, and holding her arm, George took three quick steps and crouched down in front of her. "What happened?" he asked her.

When Gracie didn't answer him, he gently reached for her arm and carefully repositioned it so that he could see what she had been hiding beneath her right hand. "Someone bit you?" he asked, his voice rising in proportion to the anger that was blooming inside him.

Instead of answering, Gracie covered the bite back up and rolled both her lips between her teeth.

Seeing he wouldn't get a response from his little sister, George turned on Bonnie. "Someone bit her?"

Bonnie nodded. "A boy in her class. During recess."

George turned back to his sister and grabbed her arm. "What?" he said, taking a closer look at the bite marks. "That little shit broke the skin."

"George!" Bonnie chastised. "Language—not in front of her."

George dropped Gracie's arm, stood back up, and faced his mother. "I'm sorry, but Jesus Christ. He broke the skin like a fucking animal. Is the school going to do anything about it?" George stormed toward the back door. "What's the kid's name?"

"George, honestly," Bonnie said, following after him and into the house. "I'm handling it. And what on earth do you think you're going to do about it? Beat up a five-year-old?"

The sound of the front door closing echoed down the hall toward them. Bennet must be home.

Just past the kitchen counter, George stopped. Whether it was because of the rationality of her words, or the realization that his father was home, Bonnie didn't know. But the sound of Bennet's leather-soled shoes crossing the travertine-tiled floors could be heard, and seconds later, he was standing before them both. Bennet looked up from his phone and seemed surprised to see them standing in the kitchen. His eyes shifted from Bonnie to George, and his furrowed expression morphed into concern. "What's going on? What's wrong?" he asked.

"Nothing," Bonnie answered like a knee-jerk, her tone clipped and annoyed.

Bennet focused on her directly, his expression pissed off. "Don't do that," he commanded.

Hearing his anger, Bonnie couldn't help the volcanic rise of her own temper. "Do what?" she shot back.

"You know exactly what. Tell me *nothing* is going on when clearly there is something. George is my son too. You like to keep your little secrets, but I have a *right* to know what the hell goes on in this house!"

Bonnie squared her shoulders and narrowed her eyes. "What the hell is that supposed to mean?"

"You know exactly what it means. Whenever there is something going on with one of the kids, you've always tried to keep it from me or go behind my back or sweep it under the rug. You have lied to me about our kids, our life, what happens in this fucking house, for years."

Bonnie gasped. "How dare you—maybe if you spent one goddamn second in this house—maybe if when you were in this house, you didn't have your fucking nose buried—"

"I work, Bonnie! I have to provide for all of this!" He threw his arms wide to encapsulate their whole world. "Money's not fucking magic, and you don't make it by puttering away on the PTA or listening to community bullshit on a fucking city council."

"You work?" Bonnie asked, her head snapping back in surprise. "Is that what you call pissing away your father's fortunes, and your family's future, on a never-ending series of bad deals and shitty business decisions? You call that work? Because from where I stand, I'd call that fucking gambling, *and* being supremely shitty at it."

Bennet glanced at George then took four fast strides toward her. His hand shot up and grabbed hold of her face, his fingers and thumb digging into her cheek. "Don't you ever fucking say that again."

Bonnie jutted her chin, pushing her face deeper into his hand, daring him to do more. "Or. What. Thanks to all your *hard work*, Sloan Investment is on the brink of bankruptcy, and so are we."

Bennet's eyes bore into hers, his scowl working hard to communicate a power they both knew he didn't have.

"Glare at me all you want, Bennet," Bonnie said and yanked her face from his hands. "You want to come around now and complain about being in the dark when it comes to our kids. You were never there. Not for me, not for Gracie…not for Elijah." Her voice broke on his name.

"Stop it," George whispered into the room.

"No," Bonnie said. "I won't stop. Not anymore." Bonnie straightened her spine. "It's your fault he's dead, Bennet. It's your fault my son is gone." She shook her head, her eyes never leaving his. "I could have forgiven your shitty business practices. Hell, I was even willing, once upon a time, to commit fraud and try to help you dig your way out of them." Bonnie swallowed hard. "But I will never forgive you for Elijah's death. I will never forgive your temper, inflexibility, and complete unwillingness to even try to acknowledge or understand his condition." Her anger gave way to the ever-present grief. That sorrow rose up her throat and lodged there as she struggled to get her last words out. "It's your fucking fault that my son is dead. And I'm done trying to pretend it's not. It's over, Bennet. Sloan Investment is over. This family is over. Our marriage is over."

"What are you saying?" Bennet asked. Bonnie could see that he had real fear in his eyes now.

She took another deep breath. "I'm leaving you. We should put the house on the market and try to get whatever we can for it before it's too late."

"You can't just *leave*, Bonnie. This is a rough time, but we'll get through this."

"The very fact that you can even say those words to me proves that you have no idea how far beyond a *rough time* we are. You don't even mourn him. If I'm completely honest, I think you might even be relieved that he's gone."

"Stop it!" George suddenly shouted from the kitchen. Bonnie turned and saw that he wasn't silently standing by watching his parents fight. George was curled into a ball on the floor with his hands over his ears. "Please, just fucking stop." He looked up at both of them, tears running down his face.

Bonnie was shocked at the sight of him. Her eldest son, always so cocksure and confident. Now cowering on their kitchen floor.

His eyes focused on the tiles in front of him. "I can't take this anymore," he said. "Elijah's death. All the fighting." He shook his head once. "I wish it were me who had died instead." He looked up at both his parents. "I wish I were dead. Every day. I wish I were dead."

Bonnie and Bennet stood still and watched tears run down George's face. Neither one moved or said a word.

"George," a small voice, Gracie's, cut the silence from the back door.

"Oh, God," Bonnie whispered. She'd completely forgotten about Gracie. They all turned toward her. She stood, stock-still, with the bite on her left arm cradled beneath her right hand.

Gracie saw them all, suddenly seeing her, and she started to cry as well. "I don't want George to die too."

CHAPTER THIRTY-ONE

Alyson sat at their kitchen counter, waiting for Justin to walk in the door after work. She had made lasagna, his favorite, then pulled a bottle of Meiomi Pinot Noir off her wine rack in the dining room and uncorked it so it could breathe before dinner.

Not that Justin wold know the difference; whether it was decanted or not, he would undoubtedly prefer the 90 Shilling amber ale from the fridge. But even if Justin didn't care about the wine, she hoped that the scent of Italian bread warming in the oven coupled with the sight of his favorite dinner, ready and waiting on the table, would put him in a good mood before she told him about the nightmare that had happened today.

She felt nervous and hated that she did. God, how had her life gotten so fucking retro? It reminded her of her mother, how she would cater and kowtow to Alyson's father's every angry whim or expectation. Dinner would be ready and waiting, the house would be clean, the children's homework completed—all of this was her mother's domain, and *only* her mother's domain. This was the price of staying home. Alyson had come to register this fact around the age of eight when, one night, her father arrived home to find the house in a slight disarray and a note on the fridge for her father to heat up some leftovers for himself. Her mother had been invited to attend a Pampered Chef party down the street.

And her mother had had the audacity to actually go.

Alyson watched her father crumple that note in one hand and knew, instinctively, that her mother was in big trouble when she got home. It wasn't until she was in high school that Alyson registered, and began to examine, the fact that her mother had hardly any more power in their family than she and her brother. And it wouldn't be until college, in her Introduction to Women's Studies class when they read *The Meaning of Wife*, that all the pieces of her mother's existence began to formulate into a recognizable picture of domestic servitude with paltry benefits.

At nineteen, Alyson vowed to herself that her life would be different. Her husband would be different. *She* would be different.

So why then was she sitting here, waiting for Justin with food meant to appease, with her stomach in nervous knots and a bead of sweat running down her back?

Renee's words came back to her for the hundredth time since she'd spoken them aloud. *I have always thought you lacked a spine, Alyson.* And even though she and Renee had parted ways in a better place than they had ever been, that memory still galled her.

Mostly because, deep down, she wondered if Renee was right. Was she *simpering* and *eager to please*? Justin wasn't anything like Alyson's own father had been. On the rare occasion she didn't make dinner, or keep the house clean, or get his laundry done, Justin never really said anything about it. At most, he'd simply ask, "Should I make something tonight?" But she always understood, from his indifferent tone, that this was only a question about the necessity of food production—not the subversive judgment proclamation that her father would have issued before the full-frontal tirade followed.

No, Justin was not her father.

But was she turning into her mother anyway?

Alyson slipped off her chair and plucked her wineglass from the table setting. She grabbed the open bottle of Meiomi and poured herself a generous glass. She needed to stop overthinking right now. Andrew was their son, both Alyson and Justin's responsibility. Anything they needed to deal with, whether it was his behavior, a potential diagnosis, or a fucking restraining order from Bonnie Sloan, they would handle it together.

The way families *should* handle things.

It was while taking her third large swallow of wine that she heard the door to the garage first open, and then shut—Justin was home. When he emerged from the mudroom into the family room, he met her gaze and gave her a careful smile. Things had gotten better between them since Renee's visit, but they were still a long way from the couple they used to be.

Justin let his computer bag slide from his shoulder and land on the couch. "Hey there," he said as he crossed into the kitchen and gave her cheek a kiss. "It smells delicious in here." He inspected the already set table and the covered lasagna at the center. "Is it a special occasion I've forgotten?" He gave her a smile, then surprised her by grabbing his own wineglass off the table and pouring himself a glass to match hers.

"No. No special occasion. I just know how much you like lasagna, and I realized I hadn't made it in a while."

Justin took a drink from his glass while his eyes held hers

over the rim. Did she imagine it, or was he weighing her words? Measuring them for the lie that they were. It made her consider not telling him about what happened today, because now she wondered if he would think the dinner, wine, and warm bread were all setting the stage for her careful manipulation of his response.

Which, of course, they were.

"Well, I'm starving. I ended up skipping lunch, so this is perfect. Where's Andrew?"

And just like that, the opportunity to not tell Justin evaporated. How could she otherwise explain that their son had been banished to his room all day? Never mind the fact that Andrew would certainly sell himself down the river the moment he saw Justin. There wasn't any way that wasn't the first thing he said to his dad.

Alyson took a deep and audible breath through her nose, priming Justin to know that unpleasantness was coming, then sighed it out. "He's in his room, and he has to stay there. But before I tell you why, let's sit down."

Justin placed his glass of wine on the counter as his semi-relaxed demeanor vanished. "Why? What happened?"

"I'll tell you, but first, let's sit down," Alyson said as she pulled out her own chair and sat down herself, hoping he'd follow her lead.

Instead, Justin turned around and started out of the kitchen. "If you're not going to tell me, I'll go up there myself."

Goddammit. "Fine!" she said in order to stop him from leaving and hearing from Andrew first. "He bit another kid at school. He's suspended for three days. Oh, and the parent of the other kid has threatened to get a restraining order against him and insists that he be moved to a different class…he also called his teacher a bitch," she finished with a whisper.

Justin stopped in his tracks. A second later, he turned back around and came to stand beside the table. "What?" He shook his head in confusion as he worked to process all she had just said.

Instead of listing it all out again, Alyson took a drink of her wine and pulled the foil covering off the lasagna while waiting for him to catch up.

Justin stared at her, the crease between his eyes deeper than she had ever seen before. She reached for his plate and began dishing noodles, meat, and melted cheeses onto it. When she put his plate back on its placemat, Justin looked down at it like he couldn't quite understand what was happening, but he pulled out his chair and sat down anyway.

"He bit another kid? That doesn't sound like him. Are they sure it was him? You said yourself that his teacher hates him. She could be targeting him. I'm not sure he even knows the word 'bitch.'"

Alyson took another deep breath and let it out. "He did it. They even have it on camera. It was during recess, and it was another teacher that was first on the scene. Plus, he didn't even try to deny it."

"Why?" he asked.

"I don't know," Alyson said, realizing that she had been so angry with Andrew she hadn't even thought to ask him. "Maybe he'll tell you when you speak with him."

Justin picked up his fork and held it over his plate, his gaze centered on a spot behind Alyson's left shoulder. She watched him and waited while she used her own fork to cut a corner from the lasagna on her plate.

A minute later, Justin put down his fork and picked up his wine. He took a large swallow and refocused his eyes on her. "A restraining order? Seriously? They're in kindergarten."

Alyson nodded. "I know."

"Who is it?"

Alyson hesitated for a few seconds, but there wasn't any way to not tell him. She could safely assume the information would be on the documents from the police anyway. "It's the Sloans. Well, Bonnie Sloan, in particular. I don't know if her husband knows about her plans. I'm hoping that if and when he finds out, he'll be more reasonable and talk her out of it."

"The Sloans. As in, Elijah Sloan's parents. The kid who was killed by the lake?" he asked, his tone incredulous.

Alyson nodded. "The very same."

"Jesus Christ," Justin said. "Of all the kids in Andrew's class… he bit *their* kid?"

Alyson assumed this was more of a rhetorical, why us-why them, question at this point. But, all in all, this seemed to be going better than she'd imagined. Maybe the lasagna and wine were helping more than she had dared to hope they would.

Justin, still processing but at least starting to wrap his head around what had happened, finally picked his fork back up and cut himself a large bite. "Well, I'd be surprised if someone at the police department allowed them to file a restraining order against a five-year-old. That's just bullshit. Entitled, rich-bitch bullshit. The cops will see that for what it is."

"Maybe," Alyson said. Justin's aggressive tone had caught her by surprise. Obviously, he had reasons to be upset, but the venom was out of character. "They do have a lot of influence...the Sloans."

"Over the police?" Justin snapped.

Alyson shrugged. She felt herself getting smaller in direct proportion to Justin's growing anger. "I mean, I'm not sure. It's just a guess. I imagine they have political connections. Bonnie was going to run for the state Senate. Until Elijah...well. Then she dropped out of the race."

She wondered if she'd prematurely overestimated Justin's response. It now seemed like the more he thought about it and talked about it, the angrier he got.

Justin sat across the table from her fuming and taking one large bite after another. He paused only to tear a chunk off the loaf of bread between them, soaking it in the shared dish of oil and seasonings. A nervous disquiet settled in her stomach, robbing her of her appetite and making her nauseous. Justin was obviously mad at the Sloans, and at the situation in general, but on some level, it felt like he was also angry with her.

"I'll tell you this much," he declared around the half-chewed noodles and cheese still in his mouth. He took half a second to finish his swallow, then continued. "If that bitch thinks she's getting Andrew kicked out of his class, well, she can think again. He has just as much right to be there as her kid. And frankly, I don't believe Andrew would hurt another kid for no reason at all. Know what I mean?" He gave Alyson a knowing look. "I can almost guarantee *their* son had a part to play as well."

"Their daughter," Alyson corrected him.

"What?"

"Their kid. It's a girl, not a boy. Her name is Gracie."

This information, in contrast to whatever boy-on-boy conflict Justin had been forming in his mind, deepened the crease between his eyes. "Andrew bit a girl?"

Alyson nodded. She completely abandoned the idea of eating any more food and took a sip from her wine instead.

"Well…" Justin tried to continue, but he was obviously having a hard time with the new scenario this constructed in his own head. "Still. They're both five years old. It's not like Andrew is a grown man hurting a woman."

"I'm not sure Bonnie saw it that way."

"Well, you know what?" Justin dropped his fork onto his plate. The loud clank and clash of metal against china ruptured any chance of them returning to the pretense of a relaxed evening meal. "I don't give two shits what Bonnie sees. Or what she thinks. Or who she knows. Just because that woman has money does not mean she gets to hold court over this entire fucking neighborhood and everyone who lives in it." He pushed himself away from the table so fast, his chair teetered on its back two legs, then tipped and crashed to the tile behind him. "I knew we never should have moved into this goddamn neighborhood. It's been nothing but a nightmare since we got here. Filled with fake assholes obsessed with money, titles, and social status. Jesus, and after attending that stupid fucking pre, pre, pre-Christmas party? I mean, what the fuck was that, anyway? You know what I saw? A bunch of dickheads who smile at each other, then the moment their backs are turned, they do nothing but talk shit about each other. People who sit on their asses all day, with no real aspirations or direction, so bored by their meaningless existences that they drink themselves into stupors. They probably can't even stand themselves!" He snatched his wine off the table and finished it in one long gulp.

Stunned and feeling attacked for some reason, Alyson sat in abject silence, staring at the uneaten wedge of food in front of her. Justin was mad about Andrew, yes. And railing against Bonnie and the other neighbors like her, yes.

But it also felt like this speech was kind of aimed at Alyson as well. In fact, she was practically sure that it was. And the realization ignited her own flame of fury. "I get that you're pissed off, but to be fair, you don't even know any of them."

At this, Justin turned his glare on her. And there it was, in his eyes, the proof that it wasn't just these current circumstances or the location of their house—Justin was mad at her too. "And you think *you* know them?" His tone was laced with sarcasm.

"Yes. I do know them. I have taken the time to get to know them…unlike you. And some of those *dickheads* have become my friends."

"Wait." Justin took a step backward in exaggerated disbelief. "You think Bonnie Sloan is your *friend*?"

"Now who's being the dickhead?" she asked as she picked up her plate—dinner was over—and stood up from the table. "No, Justin. *Obviously*, Bonnie is not my friend, and you know damn well I wasn't talking about her." Alyson walked her plate over to the counter, opened the slide-out garbage can, and made a dramatic show of dumping her practically untouched food into it. She dropped her plate into the sink, misjudging the height and force, and was startled to see it break into four irregular-sized pieces inside the deep, farmhouse styled basin.

"That's fantastic," Justin commented. "What did that cost me? Thirty? Forty bucks?" He reached for the bottle of pinot still in the middle of the table and poured himself another full glass.

Actually, their dinner plates had cost around fifty-two dollars apiece, but she wasn't going to mention that right now. "Cost *you*? Not *us*? Well, that's interesting to know."

Justin didn't even bother to correct himself. He flatlined his lips and gave the smallest of shrugs as if to say, *Yes, that's exactly what I meant.*

"Wow. Okay, I get it. So basically, because you're the only one working right now, all the money is yours. I provide essentially no value because I don't currently contribute a resource as tangible as fucking money."

"You think I don't see what's going on with you lately, but I see it. You're the one who wanted this fucking house that we can't afford. You're the one who has filled it with all this shit that we can't afford. You're the one who swore, '*Oh Justin, of course, I'll get a job,*' to help offset the cost of living above our means. And yet, now you're the one who every fucking day sits on her ass not getting a job, pretending that we have the same financial circumstances as your goddamn book club bitches."

"Don't you fucking *dare* talk about them like that. Don't you fucking talk to *me* like that."

Justin finished off his second glass of wine and threw his free hand in the air. "My God, Alyson. Open your eyes. Bonnie Sloan and her husband are practically criminals, and Gabby Lawrence leads her brain-dead husband around by the nose. You think these women are your friends. Fine. But you don't really know shit about them. So I'm going to help you out and share some information that might change your perspective. At that Christmas party, that one filled with all your super great new friends? Jessica Hampton followed me into the house when I went to use the bathroom and came on to me. She chatted me up, leaned in real close, pressed her body up to me, and basically let me know that if I ever wanted to see the inside of her bedroom...well then, she was almost always home. The door would be open for me."

Alyson stared at him, looking smug and right and so goddamn self-satisfied. "You're lying," she said.

Justin snorted and gave her a look of pity. "Why would I? Think about it." Then he poured himself the last glass from the bottle and left the kitchen. She figured he'd probably go down to his basement hideaway, but a second later, she heard his footsteps heading upstairs. He was going to speak with Andrew in his room.

As she stood alone in the kitchen, Alyson's mind reeled through everything Justin had just said while tears of anger and frustration pooled beneath her lids.

CHAPTER THIRTY-TWO

"Wonderful. Well, I think that is all we need at this point. I want to thank you both for coming in this morning. I know you must have very busy schedules," Principal Evans said.

Next to Alyson, Justin twisted his head as if attempting to pop his neck. She read this body language as: *Yes, he had a busy schedule. But Alyson, well, Alyson*—how had he put it again? Oh yes—*Alyson sat on her ass all day*. It had been two days since their argument in the kitchen, and they had spoken no more than a handful of only absolutely necessary words to each other.

When neither Alyson nor Justin responded, Principal Evans continued. "We are very happy to be welcoming Andrew back to school today. And we are quite certain that this will be a good day." She turned her head to Andrew, who was seated directly to her left and across the table from Alyson and Justin. "Isn't that right, Andrew?"

Andrew stared at Principal Evans, and Alyson could see he was neither following the conversation nor knew what was expected of him at that moment. "Tell her yes," Alyson prompted.

Beside her, Justin stiffened.

"Yes," Andrew parroted.

"Are we done here?" Justin asked. His tone was neither conciliatory nor respectful, and Alyson hated to imagine what Principal

Evans was thinking of them at this moment. Or what would be said about them after they left.

Of course, Justin didn't "give a shit" about any of this and felt a reentry meeting with the parents present was "a bullshit power play" on the part of the school trying to "railroad us into submission."

All this was expressed as they were heading out the door for the meeting, and they were the most words he had directed at her in days. For her part, Alyson had remained silent. Largely because Andrew had, in fact, committed a terrible wrong toward Gracie—regardless of who her mother was.

"Well, that's about it," Principal Evans finished and stood up to signal the end of the meeting. "We'll make sure he gets to class, and I'll be checking in on him throughout the day." She turned again to Andrew. "Mrs. Sinclair is out sick today, so you have a substitute."

Andrew stared at Principal Evans and blinked. Alyson suppressed a sigh; she knew he was confused by the statement because he had no idea what a substitute was. "Thank you," Alyson said, and extended her hand to Principal Evans.

"Of course," Principal Evans said and shook Alyson's hand.

"We're looking into some alternative school options for Andrew," Justin said. "Is there anything we need to know, or paperwork we would have to fill out?"

Alyson couldn't help herself; she turned to Justin in utter shock.

Principal Evans, however, didn't miss a beat. "Well, I am sorry to hear that" is what she said, but Alyson would have sworn her facial expression actually perked up an infinitesimal degree at this unexpected news. "But it's a fairly simple and straightforward matter.

In fact, if you already have the new school lined up, I'm sure Sharon out front can get the paperwork started for you today."

What was happening? In less than two seconds, they had gone from getting Andrew settled back in his class at one of the best schools in the state to withdrawing him with absolutely zero good alternatives lined up.

What the hell was Justin doing?

"Well," Justin said, "we're still exploring our options at this point. But given the circumstances...we're probably going to pull him after Christmas."

Principal Evans gave Justin a bored smile. "Of course," she said, her tone flat and uninterested. "Just let us know what you decide and when you're ready." Then she ushered them out of her private office and into the waiting area where the secretary and office manager sat behind their long, counter-height desks. "Andrew," she instructed, "you can head down to your classroom now." Then, she turned back into her office and shut the door.

They both gave Andrew a hug and a kiss and watched him join in with the herd of other kids heading into the school. Once he disappeared through his classroom door, they turned and exited through the double doors.

When they were in the parking lot, and safely out of earshot from anyone else, Alyson asked, "What the hell was that about? We're going to pull him from school?"

"Yes. We might. At the very least, *she* should realize that we are unhappy with what is happening and that there are other options we are considering."

Alyson stopped in the space between where their two cars were parked. "And do you have any idea what the *other options* are? Because I do, and none of them are anywhere I would want our son to go."

Justin shook his head and shrugged. "I was just trying to make a point."

"No, you were just trying to get her to beg us not to leave. And what you don't understand is that this school has a waiting list five miles long. She wouldn't care, not at all, if we pulled him. In fact, given what happened and the Sloans' legal threats, it'd probably make her life a whole lot easier." Alyson opened her car door and lowered herself onto the driver's seat. "So maybe, next time, make sure you understand what side of the power dynamic you're actually on before you start spouting off idle threats." She didn't bother to wait for his response. She slammed her door, started her car, and pulled out of her space before Justin had even unlocked his.

"Jesus Christ," she said aloud to herself as she pulled out of the school lot and onto Martin Street. What the hell was he trying to do? "Jesus Christ!" she shouted this time, her voice reverberating off the interior of her car. Justin could be so frustrating. So idiotic at times. So—

Jessica Hampton's silver Volvo XC90 was stopped and waiting to turn left at the cross street. She was behind the wheel, and as Alyson approached, Jessica smiled, raised her hand off the steering wheel, and waved.

Alyson ignored her and kept her eyes trained to the road right in front of her.

Justin's admission about Jessica's advances was an image she couldn't get out of her head. Had Jessica really done that? Or was Justin lying to make a point and unsettle Alyson with her new *friends*? Given the current and ever-widening rift between her and Justin, Alyson didn't know what to think or believe anymore.

She needed to talk to someone. Someone who knew Jessica well and would have some insight into the potentiality of Justin's account being true. Courtney was closest to Jessica and would probably know for sure if Jessica was the type of woman to hit on another woman's husband. But it was exactly because they were so close that Alyson couldn't go to her. Courtney's loyalty would be to Jessica. They seemed ride-or-die tight, which probably included keeping extramarital secrets.

Gabby was the only woman she both knew well enough and trusted to keep *her* questions confidential. Still, she would have to find a way to ask Gabby about what she thought without coming right out and confessing what Justin had told her.

Especially if it wasn't true.

Alyson pulled her car into the garage, shut off the engine, and pushed the programmed button between the sun visors to close the large door behind her. In the cocoon of her vehicle, she let her head fall back against the headrest and closed her eyes. She felt loose. Untethered from her life. She didn't understand what had become of the key markers she used to identify herself. What was her marriage now? What was she doing as a parent? What sort of woman had she become?

She opened her eyes and stared out the windshield in front of her. All morning she'd managed the ever-constant anxiety that kept her on edge. Now, a real sense of terror was seething at her neck. She didn't know what was happening. Once, she had felt certain of Justin's love, felt confident in herself as a mother, and thought she knew her own son better than anyone else on the planet—none of that was true anymore.

And maybe all of her self-assured certainty had always been a facade made only of beliefs. Beliefs that had never before stood up against any real-life challenges. Once upon a time, life with Justin had been easy. When it was just the two of them, a one-bedroom apartment, and a social life that consisted of only their friends from their college town. They had fallen in love with each other when life was simple.

She wondered if they had what it took to stay in love now that life was both complex and hard.

The light from the electric garage door opener went off and left her in the dark. And still, Alyson didn't want to get out of her car. It felt safe here. Or at least safer. It reminded her of when she was little and would create a nest of blankets and pillows in the corner of her closet, and surround herself with every stuffed animal she owned.

She had been only a year or two older than Andrew was now.

Alyson took a deep breath, grabbed her purse off the passenger seat, and opened the door.

Alone inside their house, she glanced into the kitchen at the disarray of open cereal boxes and bowls half-filled with warming milk and bloated, uneaten scraps of sugary oats. They had been in such a rush to get out the door, not wanting to be late for Andrew's reentry meeting, she hadn't had time to clean up first. As Alyson navigated the mind-numbing task of dumping the bowls and loading the dishwasher, it occurred to her how quickly she and Justin had slipped back into not speaking.

Since Renee's visit, it had seemed like they were finding their way back to each other. After months of disjointed communication and Justin spending most nights in the basement, they were actually having whole conversations. Smiling, even laughing together once or twice. And all of it was undone by a short fifteen-minute argument about Andrew's behavior at school.

Well, not exactly about Andrew's behavior. The conversation had started there, but then evolved, devolved, and finally ended in an argument that was about all of the usually unspoken wedges between.

Alyson dropped the sponge in the sink and dried her hands on the dish towel. Ever since the fight, Justin had returned to sleeping in the basement. He had also returned to spending all of his free time down there.

And Alyson had returned to wondering what on earth he spent so much time doing in the basement.

She dropped the dish towel on the counter and headed for the basement stairs. She hadn't been down there since after Renee's visit, when she stripped the bed to wash the linens and clean the bathroom. She turned the handle and shoved open the now unlockable door. Once inside, she gave a quick look around the living room space and bar area—nothing seemed changed—then continued on to Justin's office.

They had never gotten around to replacing the handle Alyson

had removed in frustration, so this door also remained unlockable. In fact, without the latch from the handle, it barely stayed shut at all. Alyson pressed the door lightly with the very tips of her fingers, and it swung wide open. She flicked on the light and headed for his desk.

When she'd broken in before, she'd been both relieved and annoyed to discover that there hadn't been anything obviously incriminating, but maybe she hadn't looked hard enough. The wood surface was barren. Only his computer monitor took up any space. The keyboard and mouse lived on the pullout drawer underneath. There were no pictures, pens or sticky notes, no stacks of paper waiting for his attention. The entire space appeared to have never even been used, like an office in a model home. But this wasn't surprising to Alyson. Justin had always abhorred clutter of any kind. Even back in their college days, Justin was never one to leave towels on the floor, or his shoes outside a closet. She imagined the desk at his work looked exactly the same.

She took a seat in his high-backed leather chair and considered where she might begin her search. For what, she didn't know. But he spent so much time down here—there must be some sort of evidence as to why.

She started with the drawers. First, the larger filing cabinet to her left. She found only what she'd seen before, hanging files with plastic tabs and alphabetized labels for most of their family documents. The closing documents for their house, the appraisal paperwork on her engagement ring—it wasn't even their most important documents; those were kept in the small fireproof safe under their bed. Alyson rifled through and between a few hanging files, just in case he was trying to hide something in plain sight, but found nothing and let the drawer roll shut.

She swirled around in the chair, stood up, and opened the cabinet doors behind her. Like the rest of the office, the shelves were filled mostly with books, but they were orderly. And on closer inspection, she realized they were even alphabetized by title. She recognized most of these; they had been on the bookshelf in the family room of the small home they had rented in Nebraska before moving here. But a few of the titles were new, and while their topics surprised her, they didn't alarm her or seem *that* unusual. She closed the cabinet doors.

Next, she checked all the other drawers and found nothing more interesting than a mechanical pencil and his sticky notes arranged according to size. It wasn't until she opened the last and smallest cupboard, the one tucked underneath the desk, the one she had to get on her knees to open, that Alyson found something that she couldn't really place or understand what it was for. She pulled it out and placed it on the desk. She had a feeling, because of the way it seemed to be so specifically hidden, that this item meant something. It was some sort of clue, but she still had no idea as to what.

She had waited to check his computer last, both thinking that if she was going to find something problematic, that's probably exactly where she'd find it, and fearing that this instinct was right. She pulled out the sliding platform with the keyboard and shook the mouse, but nothing happened on the monitor, and she realized Justin wasn't the kind of person who just left his computer on.

She reached beneath the desk again and pressed the power button. A few seconds later, the monitor came to life and prompted her for a password, which thankfully she was fairly certain she knew. Justin believed, religiously, in complex passwords. But she had always known that the chink in his cybersecurity fence was the fact that he used the very same complex password for everything. And had done so for years.

She typed his fifteen-character password in and watched as the computer verified it as correct, of course, and seconds later, his desktop opened to her.

She took hold of the mouse and started investigating the different and still well organized desktop icons. She clicked through several that turned out to be nothing. Files for work. Old files from college. Past tax returns. And then she opened one that wasn't a file but a program. When she realized what it was, the item that Justin had been hiding in the cupboard suddenly made perfect sense to her. The dashboard and the program were unfamiliar to her, but after a few minutes, she was able to locate its history feature. When she opened it, she was able to view the exact dates and times that Justin had logged on to the system. She was also able to see the hundreds and hundreds of hours he had spent on it.

Well, she had her answer about what he was doing down here all the time. Now the question was: Why was he hiding it from her?

Alyson closed out the program and was planning on taking the item from the cupboard back upstairs with her so that she could ask Justin about it directly when he got home. No more being spineless. No more not saying what she thought, wanted, and needed out loud. If things between her and Justin were ever going to get better, then communication was the first item on the improvement list.

She leaned over and placed her finger on the power button but stopped short of pressing it when one particular file on the desktop caught her attention. It was titled *Neighbors*. She didn't even hesitate—she sat back up in his chair and opened the file.

It was a tabbed Excel spreadsheet. And each page at the bottom was titled with the name of one of their neighbors. In alphabetical order, of course. There were separate pages for Bennet and Bonnie Sloan. Carl Wayland, Dennis and Gabby Lawrence, George Sloan, and Jessica Hampton.

What the hell was this?

Alyson clicked through each tab, and what she read left her speechless. First, because she could hardly believe all of the terrible things she was reading. Second, because she realized it was her husband who had written it all.

Justin had been researching their neighbors. Public records, major business dealings, and even background checks. He had been digging into their lives, learning their secrets… Was this what he meant when he said she didn't *know* these people?

She went through each tab, reading everything that was documented. When her phone buzzed in her back pocket, she had no idea how long she'd been down here reading, but her neck and back muscles were tight from being hunched over for hours. Alyson was still trying to digest what she was reading on Gabby's sheet, wondering if it could possibly be true, as she pulled her phone from her pocket. When she lifted it to see who was calling, a flash flood of dread washed through her.

The Enclave Academy.

CHAPTER THIRTY-THREE

"Hello?" Alyson asked as she stood up from Justin's desk and headed for the door, already sure that whatever fresh hell this call was about would require her to head back to the school.

"Ms. Tinsdale, this is Principal Evans. We need you and your husband to come to the school right now."

"What? Why?" Alyson asked as she hurried out of the basement. She took the stairs two at a time, her heart beating hard from the exertion and the fear of what Principal Evans would tell her Andrew had done now.

She heard the principal take a sharp inhale of breath. Alyson clutched her phone to her ear and gripped the banister at the top of the stairs for support.

"Andrew is missing," she said. "Multiple staff members have been scouring the school. And we've made announcements throughout the school. He isn't responding, and no other students seem to know where he is."

Alyson felt lightheaded; black dots swam in her vision. She was afraid she might pass out, so she sat down on the top step. "You can't find him?" she asked. "What are you saying? I don't...how is that possible?"

"Ms. Tinsdale, I know this is extremely upsetting for you. And I will share everything we know up to this point as soon as you and your husband arrive. But right now, it's imperative that you get here right away. We've called the police, and they're doing what they can to help. But they need to speak to you as well. They are very concerned because...well, because several hours had already passed between when he was last seen and when his disappearance was noted."

Alyson's throat clutched as Principal Evans's words sank in and comprehension gave way to a dawning panic. This wasn't happening. No. No, no, no. This wasn't possible. "I'm coming right now," she choked into her phone and got to her feet.

For several agonizing moments, she didn't know what to do next. She looked down at her feet—shoes, she'd need them. And her car keys—hanging in the mudroom. Her purse—on the couch in the family room. Gripping her phone, she started to move. She snatched up her purse as she passed it and her keys from the hook in the mudroom. Her boots she'd left on the mat next to the door leading out to the garage. She didn't want to waste any seconds; she just held it all in her arms and headed out the door in her socks to her car.

Alyson dumped everything onto the passenger seat and started her car. As she backed down her driveway too fast and without looking, she wondered if the school had also called Justin. Once she was heading down their street, she grabbed her phone, pulled up her recent calls, and hit Justin's number. The phone rang once.

"Are you there yet? I'm on my way right now," he said immediately. Alyson could tell he was trying to stay calm, straining to keep his voice even. But the terror she felt, she heard it in him too.

"I'll be there in three minutes," she said.

"Call me as soon as you get there so I can listen to what the police say. Traffic won't be bad at this time, but it'll still take me at least twenty minutes to get there."

"I will," she said, and for the first time since the principal called, tears rose up and spilled onto her face. "Justin?" she whispered, her voice cracking on the word.

"Alyson," he said, his voice forceful, "he's okay. Do you hear me? This is going to turn out just fine. He's hiding in a closet, or behind a bookshelf. Okay?" He was trying to keep her calm, convince her not to panic. But she knew they were both thinking the same thing.

Elijah Sloan's murder had not been solved.

"Yes," she forced herself to say. "I'm pulling into the parking lot right now. I'll call you back once I'm inside."

"He's fine," Justin said again, and Alyson knew, this time, he was trying to convince himself.

Parked in the Hug-N-Go lane directly in front of the school, three police cruisers were lined up one behind the next. At the sight of them, Alyson experienced a confusion of relief and dread. They were here to help find her son—who was only five years old and missing.

She slammed the door behind her and ran to the front door. There was no need to push the intercom button and announce herself—the secretary who usually sat behind the counter had been waiting for her in the breezeway and opened the door. "They're all in Ms. Evans's office," she said as she led Alyson through the secondary door and into the main office.

As she rounded the counter, Alyson could see the principal's door was closed, but two uniformed police were visible through the glass window. She didn't knock or wait to be let in. Alyson grabbed the door handle and walked right in. "Have you found him?" she asked.

Both officers and Principal Evans turned at the same time to face her. "Ms. Tinsdale," the principal began, but she seemed to lose her way and didn't seem to know what to say next. Alyson could hear the tremor of fear in her voice, and whatever hope she'd been hanging on to that Andrew would have been found before she arrived vanished.

"How did this happen? What's been done now? Why are we just standing here?" Her last question was almost a scream. Andrew was out there, all alone, with God knows who, enduring…no, she couldn't allow herself to imagine the absolute worst; otherwise she would lose her fucking mind right now.

"Ms. Tinsdale. Alyson. May I call you Alyson?" one of the officers asked as he stepped toward her. "I'm Officer Ben Reed. This is Officer Carson Brown." He extended his hand.

She stared first at his outstretched hand, then up at him. Were they really wasting time with introductions and pleasantries? On autopilot, she reached out and shook his hand. "Yes, Alyson is fine. My husband, Justin, is on his way." Which reminded her, she was supposed to call him. She pulled out her phone, pushed his contact, and put him on speaker. "My husband wants to hear everything," she explained as Justin answered.

"Hello, I'm here. What's happening?" he asked.

"I'm at the school. There are two police officers, and everyone was just about to tell me what's going on," Alyson said as she made direct eye contact with Principal Evans.

"Hello, Mr. Tinsdale. Officer Reed here. We have a team working this and are actively recruiting volunteers. Right now, we've started a more extensive search of the school and surrounding areas. Some members of our team have already started searching the neighborhood. At this time, we are very confident that Andrew will be found shortly. There isn't anything at this point to suggest this is any more serious than a runaway situation. As soon as you get here, we'd like to enlist you and your wife directly in the search efforts. If he is hiding, it's far more likely that he'd come out for you instead of strangers."

"Yes, of course, we'll do anything and everything to find him," Justin said over the phone. "But I still haven't heard how this happened in the first place. And why did it take so long for anyone to notice he was missing?"

Alyson could tell from the edge in his voice that Justin's fear was giving way to anger.

"Mr. Tinsdale? This is Principal Evans. I can speak to that—at least, this is what I know at this point. After our meeting this morning, Andrew headed down to his classroom. His new classroom. Which...well, it just so happened that his new teacher is out sick today. So he had a substitute. And while we've physically switched Andrew's class assignment, I'm afraid the computer system still has him listed in his old classroom. Unfortunately, this means, the best I've been able to guess, is that when his class returned from morning recess with the other two kindergarten classes, and Andrew wasn't present, the substitute had no way of knowing since she is isn't familiar with all the kids in the class and Andrew's name wasn't yet a part of the class roster. And, since Andrew is new to this class today, none of the other kids realized he was missing either. It really is just the most unfortunate turn of events, and I'm very sorry to tell you this has happened. We take safety very seriously," she finished.

As Alyson stood processing this new information, she couldn't help but notice how silent Justin was on the other end of the phone. She might've thought that the call dropped, except for the sounds of road noise still piping through the speaker.

"So what you're telling me," Justin finally said, "is that because you went ahead and did exactly what I said I didn't want to happen, and you did a shitty job of it by not documenting the change in classroom, you now have no fucking idea where my son is."

Even though he wasn't in the room, Justin's rage hung in the air of Principal Evans's office.

"Mr. Tinsdale—"

"No, I've heard enough from you," Justin interrupted her. "I'm five minutes away. All I want to know now is how you and that entire school are going to be moving heaven and earth until Andrew is found." Justin's voice broke at the end.

And when he hung up on them, they all knew it was because he was crying.

CHAPTER THIRTY-FOUR

They first tried having Alyson make a plea to Andrew over the announcement system to please, if he was hiding somewhere in the building, please come out and let someone know he was okay. She did this twice, with promises that he would not be in trouble, and assurances that nobody was angry with him. She even said that if he let someone know where he was right away, he could come home right now, and Mom and Dad would also take him to Dave & Buster's for dinner.

But the only response was from an Andrew in first grade. At first, he was confused, but then very excited when he thought it was his own mother making promises to leave school early for an evening of burgers and video games. Alyson's own Andrew was not in the building. By the time Justin exploded through the school's front doors, she was certain of that.

Now, in her coat and boots, she was sweeping her way back and forth in an ever-widening arc away from the school. Calling Andrew's name. Begging him to please come to her. Taxing every fiber in her being to hold herself together. To not fall to her knees in the middle of the baseball field. To not curl into a ball while every one of her worst-case-scenario fears plucked at the few strands of sanity she had left.

"Andrew!" she yelled with her hands cupped around her mouth. "Andrew! Please, please, Andrew, let Mommy know where you are!" She kept shouting. She kept moving. She kept praying from her chest that any moment she would see him erupt from some tall grass, or from behind a large tree, his arms spread wide as he ran toward her.

She would never want anything again. She would never take anything, not ever, for granted again. *Just God, please, please, please let Andrew be okay.*

Nothing in her life had prepared her for this.

This sense of loss, this all-consuming fear. Her body was a runaway vehicle careening at breakneck speeds down a steep decline with no breaks. She had never felt so utterly out of control. She had never been so terrified of every second that passed in which Andrew didn't reappear. Empty moments carrying her further and further away from the last time she saw her boy safe.

What if that was the last time she ever saw him?

Had Bonnie Sloan thought that same thing? That last day, that last moment, the very last second she'd seen her own son alive?

Of course, she did. It was probably all she ever thought about.

"Stop it," Alyson told herself out loud. "Stop it right now." But a cascade of tears fueled by fear was pouring down her cheeks. "Andrew!" she screamed. "Andrew! Please!" She could hear her own hysterics ricochet back off the neighboring houses. But when it stopped, her ears felt stuffed with silence.

She stopped walking and checked her phone. It was three thirty now. The rest of the school was out, and parents were learning from Principal Evans's carefully crafted email that a search was being conducted for a missing student. Volunteers were needed. Any information would be appreciated. If anyone was to see Andrew Tinsdale, school picture attached, they should please contact the police at this number immediately.

She considered calling Justin, who was searching on foot in the opposite direction from her, to see if he had any news. But she already knew he didn't—he would have called her the moment he found their son. She slid her phone back into her coat pocket and kept walking, back and forth, her voice already feeling strained from screaming her son's name.

By four o'clock, she could hear other people shouting Andrew's name as well. The closest was a man's voice to her left. She stopped walking and looked. In the distance, she saw him. He wore a large blue parka and snow boots. His gloved hands cupped around his mouth as he called Andrew's name, his breath exhaling as a vapor into the cold, late-afternoon air. She didn't recognize this man who was helping her, but she raised her hand when he saw her, saying, *Thank you.*

He waved back but didn't stop. He ventured farther left, focusing his arc away from hers.

It was December in Colorado, and the sun was going down. Alyson had her winter coat on, but beneath it, she was dressed in daytime temperature clothing. In just her jeans and a long-sleeved T-shirt, she could already feel the rapidly dropping temperature working its chill over her body. It had been forty-five degrees in the middle of the afternoon; it was likely closer to thirty now. Andrew would be getting cold. Before she and Justin had started their search, along with the police driving the neighborhood, they figured out that Andrew was wearing his coat and boots. Both were missing from his coat hook in the classroom.

With the playground half covered in snow for weeks, all the kids were required to bring snow boots to school if they wanted to venture past the shoveled surfaces. So thankfully, if there was anything to be thankful for, at least Andrew was wearing something more protective than his Spider-Man tennis shoes.

Alyson kept walking. If she stayed out here much longer, though, she'd need to see about getting hold of some better gloves and thicker layers beneath her coat.

When she realized where she was, she stopped and stared out at the scene before her. She had reached the lake.

She hadn't been to the neighborhood lake since the summer. When the trees were still filled with leaves, and the temperatures soared past ninety. In July, the water glittered in the afternoon sun, and many people used the kayaks and SUP boards that could be rented from the boathouse on the south side near the pool.

Today, the water was frozen and white. And all along the shore, the once lush, green cattails, where geese and ducks nested and raised their young through the warm summer months, were now brown and broken, like trampled straw.

How many days had she and Andrew spent walking this shore? How many times had they counted the groups of goslings and ducklings?

The wind picked up and blew back her hair. Her ears were getting cold and painful. Did Andrew have his hood on? Would he think to pull it up if he was cold?

Alyson walked over a stretch of grass that, in the summer, was watered and mowed and ran the length of the concrete path that separated the wilder shore growth from the manicured lawn. The brown and frozen grass was only visible in the patches where the snow had melted.

Her earlier searching had been more random. Now, she felt the pull of this specific destination—the lake. When she'd set off from the school, she and Justin had agreed to go in opposite directions and attempt to cover as much ground as they could between them. And if she'd been asked then, she wouldn't have consciously known she would choose to go south on purpose. She likely wouldn't have even thought about searching specifically around the lake at all.

But standing here now, on some level, she realized this was where she'd been heading all along. Because as much as the thought of finding him here terrified her, discarded on the shores the way Elijah Sloan had been, she also couldn't imagine not looking. Whether she wanted to admit it or not, from the very moment she had digested the fact that Andrew was missing, she'd been thinking about Elijah Sloan.

And those thoughts had drawn her here.

She crossed over the concrete path and made her way to where the firmer earth gave way to the marshy edge. The perimeter of the lake was just over one mile, a fact appreciated by many of the runners and walkers who used the concrete path as an outside track when it wasn't covered in snow. Alyson intended to walk all the way around right now. Before she lost any more light. She needed to mark this place off her list. She needed to know for sure, and then forget it and put it behind her.

As she walked, her boots tromping through icy mud, she scanned the broken cattail reeds for any sign of Andrew. A discarded mitten. A lost boot. What it would mean to find any of these items removed from their small owner, she couldn't allow herself to imagine. But she looked anyway.

After five minutes, she'd reached the end of this stretch of boggy wild. This part of the lake, and the next quarter-mile round, was where the wild grass was generally kept short. It was a favorite spot for many fishermen to plant their lounge chairs and Igloo coolers during the summer months.

About one hundred yards to her right was the parking lot where she and Andrew had seen the fire trucks and police cars parked the morning Elijah Sloan's body was found. She didn't know precisely where, but she knew she must be very close to the spot.

In the sky above, dark clouds had rolled in fast from over the Rocky Mountains to the west. Blanketing the sun as it descended, the clouds accelerated the disappearing light and the drop in temperature. She could smell the approaching snow in the air and knew that fresh flakes would be falling within the hour.

She pulled her phone from her pocket again, her thin mittens doing little to protect her stinging fingers from the cold. There was still no message from Justin or the police. Andrew still hadn't been found. She slipped her thumb from the knitted mitten, scrolled to the flashlight app, turned it on, and directed the beam along the ground ahead of her as she continued to call out Andrew's name.

She had just about reached the end of the prime fishing area when her phone buzzed in her hand and the shrill ring of the incoming call fractured the silence. The caller ID popped up—it was Justin.

She slid the answer bar and held the phone to her ear. "Please tell me—"

"We found him!" Justin shouted. "They have him, the police. He's okay. It's okay. He's safe."

"Oh my God," Alyson whispered, the stress of the afternoon finally dropping her to her knees. Her hand reached for the cold ground to hold herself up. "He's okay? They're sure? Nothing's wrong?"

"No. He's fine. A woman found him. They're taking him back to our house. Where are you? I'm running back to my car right now—I'll come pick you up."

Alyson nodded her head. Her sobs of relief made it difficult to speak. "The lake. I'm near the parking lot on the south side of the lake."

"I'll be there in five minutes," he said and hung up.

Alyson dropped her phone and sat in the snow. She placed both her hands over her eyes and cried as her body rocked back and forth.

She was so afraid she'd lost him.

So afraid she'd never see him again.

"He's safe. Thank you, God," she whispered as she tilted her head up to the sky. "Thank you, thank you, thank you."

Never had she been so terrified.

The butt and knees of her jeans were now soaked. Between the flood of relief, her wet clothes, and the cold air, Alyson began to shiver. She pushed herself to standing, picked up her phone, and started toward the parking lot where Justin would be arriving at any moment.

She noticed light bouncing along with her steps and realized the flashlight on the back of her phone was still on. When she reached the three-foot-high rock wall that separated the parking lot from the lake area, she stopped to turn it off before she passed through the break in the wall that led to the lot.

As she swiped to get back to the flashlight app, the light caught something at the base of the wall that reflected back at her. She crouched down and held the light closer, trying to get a better look at what it was.

It was barely visible, mostly covered in snow and mud. Alyson pulled off her left mitten and used her fingers to dig away some of the dirt. She worked her fingers around the object, and a second later, she was able to free it from the ice. She held it in the palm of her hand and used her thumb to rub away more of the grime.

She recognized it, distinctly remembered seeing it before—but where?

Headlights arced across her field of vision, and when she looked up, she saw Justin's car. Alyson stood, slipped the item into her coat pocket, and ran to go see her son.

CHAPTER THIRTY-FIVE

When they pulled into their driveway, Justin had barely shifted into park when they both exploded out of either side of the car and rushed to the police cruiser parked in front of their mailbox. The officer behind the wheel got out of the car and opened the back door. Alyson recognized him from the school, Ben Reed.

Alyson ran toward him and immediately saw Andrew sitting in the back seat. He looked scared and like he'd been crying. "Oh, thank God," she said as she leaned into the car and gathered him into her arms. She pulled him out and stood up, squeezing his small body tight against her own while Justin brushed the hair from his face then pulled both her and Andrew into his arms.

Officer Reed sighed. "All's well that ends well. I had a gut feeling this was a runaway situation. I'm glad to see this little guy back safe and sound."

Justin released Alyson from his arms and turned toward the officer. "Where exactly was he found? And who found him?"

"Well, he got pretty far on those two little legs." Officer Reed raised his eyebrows and ran his hand through his hair. "He was walking down Clear River Parkway, if you can believe that. A little over two miles away."

"What?" Alyson asked in disbelief. Clear River Parkway was a major four-lane road. With a speed limit of fifty miles per hour, it was one of the major commuting routes for cars exiting I-25. She couldn't even imagine Andrew walking down that road all by himself.

"Lucky, a Mrs. DeeDee Walters spotted him and thought it seemed pretty suspicious for someone so little to be wandering down such a busy road all alone. Apparently, she's a grandmother herself—fifteen grandkids!" He shook his head in disbelief. "Anyway, she said she just knew something was off, so she pulled into the Radisson parking lot, just past where she'd seen him, and called the police. She was afraid that if she approached him, he might spook and run into the road, so she just followed behind him until an officer arrived."

Justin stood beside Alyson, his arms limp at his sides, staring at Officer Reed as he finished his story. "I don't know how to thank you," he said.

Officer Reed smiled at them and nodded. "It's not necessary. Honestly, I really am just relieved to see him in one piece and home." He opened his car door. "I've got two kids myself, both girls. Believe me when I say I know exactly how scared you both were today." He slid back into his cruiser. "And speaking of that, think I'll head home and give them both a big hug too."

"Thank you," Alyson said. "For everything."

Officer Reed raised his hand in goodbye, closed his door, then pulled away from the curb and down the street. Once he was out of sight, Alyson turned to face Justin. Their eyes met and held, silently communicating all the shock, horror, and cataclysmic relief they'd both experienced today. Justin shook his head once and lowered his gaze as several tears slipped down his face. He cleared his throat and said, "Let's get him inside."

Together they fed Andrew his favorite dinner, dinosaur chicken nuggets with Kraft macaroni and cheese, and canned corn. They gave him his bath, together. Then dressed him in his favorite Spider-Man pajamas, together. Neither one yet ready to leave his side for even a second. When Andrew crawled into his double bed, Alyson and Justin climbed in on either side of him.

They lay there for several seconds, staring at the ceiling as Andrew's rotating nightlight spun and cast star-, moon-, and planet-shaped light up the wall and over their heads. Justin took a breath.

"Hey, buddy, about today."

"Maybe we should wait until the morning," Alyson whispered, even though Andrew could clearly hear her.

Justin hesitated, like he was considering her concerns, but continued on. "I just need to know." His voice was soft. "How come you left school today? Did something happen?"

Between them, Andrew lay silent and unmoving. For a moment, Alyson wondered if he'd fallen asleep. But when she turned to look at his face, she could see that his eyes were still wide and staring at the ceiling above.

"Andrew?" Justin prodded. "Hey, buddy, you're not going to be in trouble or anything like that. Mom and I, well, we just really need to know why you'd do something like that."

Andrew inhaled, hesitated for a second more, then said, "I didn't mean to."

"Didn't mean to what?" Justin asked. "Leave the school?"

Andrew shook his head. "I didn't mean to be by Gracie. I forgot I wasn't supposed to, and at recess, I was next to her."

"Oh, well," Alyson chimed in. "It was an accident. I'm sure the teachers would have understood. But is that why you left?" It didn't make sense to Alyson. Then again, if motherhood had taught her anything, the fact that five-year-olds didn't always make the most rational decisions was undoubtedly one of the lessons.

Andrew shook his head. "Gracie saw me. She said I was going to get in trouble. I didn't want to get into trouble again, so I ran to the bushes by the baseball field and hid inside them."

"You hid in the bushes?" Alyson asked. "How long were you there?"

Andrew shrugged. "I only stayed there until everyone went back inside. Then I came out and walked around for a little bit. But then the police came. I saw their cars in the parking lot. I thought Gracie had told on me for being close to her, and her mom had called the police. I thought they were going to arrest me. So, I ran away."

"But where were you going?" Justin asked.

"I don't know," Andrew said. "But I didn't want to go to jail."

Alyson heard Justin give a frustrated sigh on the other side of the bed. "Buddy, there isn't any way that would ever happen. Okay? And Gracie's mom may have been mad at you for what you did, but she never should have said that you'd be in trouble with the police for that. Because it's just not true. Okay?"

Andrew nodded several times, then rolled toward Justin and wrapped his arms around his dad. Justin bent his head so his lips connected with the top of Andrew's head. "Mom and I love you more than anything in the whole world. You've got to promise us you'll never do something like that again. Okay?"

Andrew nodded his head against Justin's chest.

"Promise?" Alyson asked.

"I promise," Andrew said.

After they both kissed him good-night and gave him extra hugs, Alyson and Justin stood outside Andrew's closed bedroom door.

"What do you think we should do?" Justin asked her.

"I'm not sure. But I can't even imagine sending him back to that school tomorrow." She looked up and met her husband's eyes. "I think maybe you were right. I think we have to pull him from there and find another school."

Justin nodded in total agreement. Then he looked into Alyson's eyes. "Yes, but also," he added, "Alyson, I'm sorry, but we need to sell this house and move."

CHAPTER THIRTY-SIX

Bonnie sat behind her massive desk and opened the first of the two emails from the school. The subject line captured her attention right away: Missing Child. The body of the email went on to explain how one of The Enclave Academy's kindergarteners, Andrew Tinsdale, had been missing from the school since approximately ten thirty this morning. His parents had been contacted and had given permission for the school to share any relevant information that may help the community locate Andrew.

His class picture was included in the email, and they were requesting parents to be on the lookout for Andrew. If anybody spotted him, they should please contact the police department at the number provided.

Bonnie stood up from her desk and shouted, "Gracie!" She waited for her daughter, who was down the hall and in the family room, presumably watching television, to respond. After several seconds went by and Gracie neither appeared at her door nor shouted back, Bonnie tried again as she opened the second email. "Gracie!"

"What?" her daughter shouted back from the family room.

Bonnie began reading the second email. "Come here, please!" This one had been sent fifteen minutes ago—Andrew had been found. Bonnie exhaled and sat back down in her chair. "Jesus Christ," she whispered right as Gracie appeared in her doorway.

"You're not supposed to say that," Gracie said, with one hand on her hip.

Bonnie ignored her daughter's sass. "Did you see Andrew Tinsdale at school today?"

Gracie stood up straight, and both her arms went limp at her side. She stared back at her mother but didn't say a word.

"Gracie, answer me. Did you see Andrew today?"

"Yes."

"When did you see him? He's not in your class anymore," Bonnie prompted.

"He didn't mean to. It was an accident."

Bonnie narrowed her eyes slightly, trying to decipher her daughter's cryptic five-year-old reasoning. "What do you mean? What was an accident?"

Gracie gave a loud, exasperated sigh. "It was at recess. I was playing with Asher. But Asher was also playing with Andrew. He didn't come near me on purpose. But I told him he should go away or else he was gonna get in trouble."

Bonnie stared at her daughter; the three-day-old bite mark on her arm was now only a series of small scabs. "What do you mean, you told him to go away?"

Gracie shrugged. "I don't know. Just go away. If the teacher saw him, he would get in trouble, and they would tell you and George. I didn't want George to get mad again and hurt Andrew." Gracie put both her hands on her hips. "It was just an accident."

It occurred to Bonnie all at once: Gracie was trying to protect Andrew Tinsdale. Both from getting into any more trouble at school, and from her own family. Andrew, obviously, had listened to Gracie. He had listened to her so well that not only did he go away from her, he went away from the entire school. "Did you know that Andrew went missing today?" Bonnie asked.

"No," Gracie answered, her tone matter-of-fact, like a missing child was neither particularly interesting nor a big deal. For all Gracie's precociousness, at the end of the day, she was still only five years old.

"Well, he did. And none of the teachers could find him. And none of the other students knew where he went. And they called his parents and the police, and they even had volunteers out looking all over the whole neighborhood. And no one could find him."

"Did they look under the bush for him?" Gracie asked. "When he ran across the field at recess, I saw him go into the bushes to hide."

Bonnie stared at her daughter for several seconds. "You knew where he was?"

"Yes."

"Why didn't you tell your teacher? Why didn't you go tell Principal Evans?"

Gracie seemed to consider these questions, then shrugged again. "He was going to get in trouble. I didn't want to tattletale on him."

Bonnie stood silent and thinking, wondering what, if anything, all this meant. "You can go back and watch TV now."

Gracie smiled, turned around, and skipped down the hall back to the Disney Channel. Bonnie sat back in her chair and looked around her office, feeling exhausted and ashamed. She had once thought of it as her command center. It was where she planned and strategized, scheduled and organized; it was where she launched her ships—both the public and the private ones.

Now, nothing happened here. She hadn't planned or given anything much forethought in almost three months. Her drive had died, and with it, all her downstream plans had simply floated away. And most days, it was hard to tell if she even cared. It suddenly seemed to not matter at all anymore.

Her eyes lifted to the doorway into the hallway beyond. Her ears could clearly hear the sounds of Gracie's television program from the family room.

Maybe she couldn't care anymore about dropping out of the Senate race. Maybe it didn't matter that she was about to lose her seat on the city council. And maybe she didn't even really care that Sloan Investment had finally hit its iceberg.

But she knew for a fact that she still gave a shit about her kids. Elijah was gone. And he wasn't coming back. She'd never accept it, but she was going to have to learn how to live with it. Because she couldn't give up on everything. She still needed to show up and be a mother. Gracie still needed her.

"And she's not the only one," Bonnie whispered and stood up from behind her desk.

Upstairs, she stood outside her son's door and knocked gently before turning the doorknob. It gave easily beneath her hand. It was unlocked, and this surprised her. For years, ever since he turned twelve, George had worked hard to assert his independence and privacy by keeping his door locked. It seemed strange to now enter his world without incessant knocking that gave way to banging when he couldn't hear her through his gaming headphones.

She pushed the door slowly and poked her head in. Her go-to image was George at his desk, seated in his elaborate gaming chair, oblivious to the outside world. So when she instead saw him with his back to her, sitting in the chair beside his window staring out, it caught her off guard. "George?" she asked.

"Yes?" he answered.

"Can I come in?" she asked.

"It's your house."

She decided to take this as a yes and carefully crept into his space and closed the door behind her. He didn't turn around or say anything—he just continued to sit and stare at his window. Bonnie approached, and as she did, she couldn't help but notice how clean his room was. For most of his life, she'd had to ask, beg, cajole, and finally resort to simply picking up all his dirty clothes and used dishes herself. And that was just so that the housekeeper could get to the surfaces to actually clean.

But Bonnie had let the housekeeper go a month ago; it was one of the many luxuries they could no longer afford. So to see that George, of his own volition, had not only tidied his room but also dusted and vacuumed as well—it was unusual. She stood over his right shoulder and noticed the way the bone jutted beneath his T-shirt in a way it never had before. When he finally turned to face her, she saw there was a hard line to his jaw, a gauntness beneath his cheek. George had lost weight. And by the looks of it, it was probably a lot. The circles beneath his eyes were a clear indication that he'd also not been sleeping.

In his hands, he held a picture, and it was one she knew well. In it, George and Elijah stood together on Kaanapali Beach in Maui. They were so young, and their little bodies were so tan from their week of vacation. With their windblown hair, brightly colored swim trunks, and sand-covered shins, her two boys had stood still long enough for her to capture this moment. George grinned directly at the camera, while Elijah was in profile. He stared up at his older brother, his adoration evident. "I think that was probably one of my favorite days, ever," Bonnie said. "What are you doing with it?"

George returned his gaze to the window. "I was just sitting here thinking about what a shitty brother I was. About how, when I really think about it, all Elijah ever really wanted was to hang out with me. Spend time with me." He shook his head. "And what did I do? Tore him down. Made him feel like shit. Or worse." His voice broke as he started to cry. "Push him into one of his episodes. Why would I do that? I mean it's not like I didn't know, exactly, how to get him going. And I would. I'd say something, or do something just so he would lose it and then I could be the asshole that called him a freak."

"George—"

"No, don't do that. Don't try to make me feel better. I don't deserve it. And I didn't deserve him."

"All brothers—"

"It's my fault he's dead." He stood up from his chair and faced her. "I've been too afraid to say it. And Dad said telling you was pointless, and that it would only upset you more. That it wouldn't bring Elijah back anyway. But I can't live with myself anymore. It's killing me, and I deserve that. But you should know too… it's my fault he's dead."

CHAPTER THIRTY-SEVEN

"Sell the house? We've barely lived in it for six months," Alyson said.

Justin put his finger to his lips, pointed to Andrew's closed bedroom door, and motioned for her to follow him into their bedroom. He closed the door behind them, then went and sat on the edge of their bed. "Look, maybe right now isn't the best time to talk about this. Or I don't know; maybe with everything that happened today, it's exactly the right time. I know we've been through a lot today in a very short amount of time, but I really feel like there are some things I need to talk to you about."

Alyson sat on the chaise lounge beneath their bay windows. This felt monumental, and like it had been a long time coming—it felt like they were finally going to speak the truth. She wasn't sure if she was ready.

"Okay," she said. "What's on your mind?" She was both dreading and longing for whatever came next. This day had ripped off whatever Band-Aids were holding their marriage together. For better or worse, she was going to learn what was going on with Justin. Why so much had changed between them. And—scariest of all—if too much had changed for them to go back.

Justin took a deep breath and began. "We can't afford to live here." He looked her in the eye, like he was waiting for her response. "It kills me to say that to you. I know how much you wanted this house. How much you wanted to live in this kind of neighborhood. For Andrew to go to this particular school… Although I gotta say, right now, I feel like walking away from that school is the best decision we'll ever make as parents. But aside from that, facts are facts, Alyson. I don't make enough money. Between the mortgage payment, the credit card debt we have, and every month it feels like our bills have ballooned beyond anything we've ever come close to planning for. If we stay here another four months… we'll be in foreclosure."

Alyson blinked. *What? Foreclosure?* She realized they were living somewhat beyond their means, but she had no idea it was this bad. "I don't know what to say."

She watched the worried shadows as they drifted across his expression. "Alyson," he said, hanging his head. "I'm so sorry."

He was sorry. *Justin* was sorry. What was happening? Because from where she was standing, this entire mess looked like it was pretty much her fault. "What are you sorry for? Honestly, Justin… Oh my God, I'm such an asshole."

He looked at her and shook his head. "I wish, I *really* wish, I could give you this life. In a house like this, in a neighborhood like this—"

"Please stop," she said and held up her hand. "Please, I can't bear for you to think…" She dropped her head back and took several breaths. "Yes." She looked at him. "I wanted all this. And the furniture. And the appliances. And the fucking dishware. But none of it is even enjoyable at this point because I've been so terrified that our entire marriage was crumbling around my head, and I had no idea why. You've seemed angry and distant. And I feel like you never want to spend any time with Andrew and me. And I even actually thought that maybe you had met someone else. Someone from work—I don't know, maybe that sounds stupid to you. But I feel like I don't even know how to talk to you anymore. And that's so weird because you used to be my best friend. It wasn't until I found that joystick in your office, and saw all the hours you've been logging on your Microsoft Flight Simulator, that I realized that's why you've been spending so much time down there. I guess I've always thought of your flying as just a hobby."

Justin held her gaze and took a breath. "I really want to fly, Alyson. Not just for fun, or as a hobby. I want to become a pilot, as a career. It's what I've really wanted ever since I was a kid."

"I also found your spreadsheet. The one about the neighbors? I'm sorry for snooping, but I didn't know what else to do. What is all that for?"

He sighed and closed his eyes for a moment then shook his head. "Honestly, I don't know. I mean, yeah, I know, but I guess it just sounds stupid to me now. It started when Carl Wayland was arrested. I mean, this guy lived in this neighborhood for years, and nobody knew or suspected anything? It kind of freaked me out. I couldn't stop thinking, well, what else don't we know about these people? And then at that Christmas party, and Jessica, who was supposedly one of your new best friends, and she comes on to me like that…it just made me realize that these people were becoming a part of our lives and we don't really know anything about them. At all. I felt like I was losing you, and my son honestly, into a world of people that I didn't trust. I guess I thought maybe if I could find out more about them, I wouldn't be so worried. But then I started actually finding out all this shady shit. And at some point I started documenting everything I found because I thought I might need it to prove to you that these people, this life, weren't everything you had made them out to be." He paused and seemed to be gauging her reaction to his confession. "I'm sorry," he finished.

Alyson shook her head. "For what?"

"Because I know how important this kind of life is to you. And I feel like me wanting something else, *somewhere* else, means you can't—"

"Stop. Please stop. Because I don't want any of this if it means we're not both happy."

Justin stood up from the bed, crossed the room, and pulled her into his arms. "I've known from the day we looked at this house that we couldn't afford it, not on what I make alone. But I didn't want to disappoint you, and I guess I was hoping that it would somehow work out. That you would be able to find a job, and that would help."

She leaned her forehead against his chest and closed her eyes. "This is my fault, Justin. Not yours. I pushed and pushed until I got my way." She tilted her head back and looked up into his eyes. "It's not like I didn't know. I can't even say what the hell I've been thinking. I was just so blinded by wanting to have that life that I always idealized as a kid and never had. And I thought it was important to give that to Andrew. But nothing has been like I imagined it would be. And then today happened… I'm the one who's sorry, Justin."

She felt his lips on the top of her head as he hugged her tight. Alyson wrapped her arms all the way around him and turned her head so that her ear rested against his chest. She could hear the sound of his heart hammering.

When was the last time they'd touched like this? Embraced and come together as one? She had missed this so much, the assuredness of him and his love for her. She had been so afraid, for months now, that this part of her life, this marriage, was ending.

She pulled away, just enough to look up into his eyes. "I don't care if we sell this house. I don't care where we live as long as we're all together."

She saw the relief in his eyes. And when he leaned down to kiss her, she reached up and pulled him closer.

CHAPTER THIRTY-EIGHT

Bonnie looked at George sitting in front of her and clearly saw the anguish he was going through. "What are you saying?" she asked. "Of course, it's not your fault Elijah's dead. Don't say—"

"That night," he interrupted her. "You were out, and Dad had taken Gracie to get ice cream or something. Elijah and I got into a fight." George started to cry.

"George—"

"No. Please just listen. I have to say it. All of it."

Bonnie stopped and bit both her lips. She wasn't sure she wanted to hear what George had to say. The confession he felt he needed to bear. Because what if what he said was something she wouldn't be able to forgive him for? What if she had already lost her Elijah and was now on the brink of losing her other son too?

George stood up, the picture of him and Elijah still in his hand. "And it was my fault. Elijah was in the kitchen, and I walked in, and I could tell right away that he was upset about something. You know how he got when he was breathing heavy and getting ready to have a meltdown." George shook his head, the tears coming faster and putting a strain on his words. "And I just had to make it worse,

I guess. And I don't know why, but it was just so frustrating to see him like that. Part of me just wanted to scream at him to cut it out, or grow up. I think maybe it just embarrassed me." He looked into Bonnie's eyes. "And I'm so sorry for that, Mom. It was so stupid, and selfish, and I just can't help but think that if I had just walked into the kitchen and kept my goddamn mouth shut… Elijah would still be alive."

"What did you say?" Bonnie couldn't see where this was going. How on earth George could possibly think he was responsible.

"I was so mean to him. I called him…horrible things. And every name just made him more and more upset. And the more upset he got, the more frustrated I got. So by the time Elijah finally broke, and he rushed me from across the kitchen, I think I was just as ready to fight as he was. I wanted him to start something; I goaded him into it. And then when he did…"

Bonnie waited several seconds, hoping George wasn't about to say what she feared the most. "What?"

George's eyes dropped to the ground between them. "I beat the shit out of him, Mom. We wrestled at first, but Elijah…"

"Was never a fair match against you." Bonnie finished the sentence George couldn't. "What happened. Exactly," she asked, fearing that George was right. Had her oldest son beaten his brother to death? Was he capable of something so horrific?

George took a shaky breath. "I had him down. Straddling his chest, with his…with his arms pinned under my knees so he couldn't hit back. And I just kept…" George sobbed, choked by the awful memory of what he had done. "I just kept punching him."

Bonnie stared at George. She felt frozen, numb with shock. Everything George was saying stunned her. But it did not surprise her. After all, she'd seen it before. The difference was, that night, she hadn't been home to stop it.

"And then I felt his nose, I heard it crack. And that's what stopped me. I knew I'd broken it. And then the blood started. Pouring down his face and all over his shirt. It scared me, and I knew it had gone—I had gone—too far. So I got up off of him. And at first, he didn't do anything. He just lay there, blood everywhere, and stared up at me. And I could see how afraid of me he was. It was like…it was like he didn't even know me. Like he'd just been attacked by some monster, and now he was too afraid to even move."

Bonnie's whole body felt limp. She took the tiniest sips of air, while her mind worked to digest everything George had just said. "But he was alive," she clarified.

George nodded. "Yes. But when he finally did get up, he just ran. He was running away from me. He was beaten and so scared, and as soon as the shock wore off, he was up and running away from me as fast as he could. He went out to the garage and got on his bike." George's voice was now a wail. "And that was the last time I ever saw him. That was the last thing my brother ever knew of me. And he ran away that night because of me. And if I'd just left him the fuck alone, he never would have done that, and he'd still be alive, and it's all my fault, Mom. It's all my fault. It's all my fault. It's my fault he's dead."

Bonnie stepped forward and pulled George into her arms while he heaved and sobbed with the secret regrets he'd been carrying for months. She didn't say anything, only held him and let him wear himself out. After several minutes, she lifted his face from her neck and held his cheeks between her hands. She wiped his tears with her thumbs and breathed, hoping he would too.

"George," she whispered, "you fought with your brother." She closed her eyes, never more grateful for any words than she was for the ones she would speak next. "But he was alive when he left here." She shook her head. "You didn't kill Elijah," she said.

"But he never would have—"

"I understand that. And I know how easy it is to blame yourself, given what happened. But you didn't kill him. You had a terrible fight. But you didn't kill him."

Bonnie could see the torment George had been inflicting upon himself in the sharp lines on his face. She pulled him back into her arms, and while she hugged him, she could feel it in the way his body had atrophied over the past few months. "I understand feeling responsible, and we're going to work through this. I'm going to help you. But George, I swear to God, this tragedy is not your fault. And God willing, the person who *is* responsible will be found soon, and justice will be served, and maybe then…maybe we can all start to heal and stop blaming ourselves every day."

CHAPTER THIRTY-NINE

Alyson sat beside Justin on the couch in their family room with her legs curled beneath her. She held a steaming cup of white chocolate mocha in one hand while the other aimed her camera phone at Andrew tearing into gifts beside the Christmas tree.

"Do you think he'll be disappointed?" Justin whispered as he leaned into her.

Alyson raised her eyebrows and tilted her head. "Maybe? Although honestly, we've ended up getting him so many other things… If he's disappointed, I might be a little disappointed in him." She smiled. "It will be his first lesson in not always getting exactly what you want."

Justin kissed her cheek and gave her a half-smile. "I know," he sighed. "And it's probably for the best. But it's hard to watch him be so excited knowing that what he's hoping for isn't under there."

Alyson shrugged and took another sip of her coffee. "Well then, just focus on how thrilled he's going to be when he goes into the backyard."

Even as angry as she'd been with Andrew all those weeks ago when she picked him up from school and found out about him biting Gracie Sloan, Alyson never actually got around to returning the trampoline. She had tried twice during his suspension days, when her anger was still ripe. But both times she'd shown up to Costco, the customer service lines had been out the door, and her resolve had withered. She vowed to find a time when not every person in Denver and their grandmother was shopping.

But then Andrew had returned to school and gone missing that same day; the trampoline and her plans for it had been forgotten entirely.

"Let's hope so," Justin said. "It took us long enough to set the damn thing up. And I'm pretty sure my fingers got frostbite in the process."

The moment Andrew had fallen asleep, and they were sure he was asleep, she and Justin had hauled the enormous box to the backyard and began setting the trampoline up in the dark with only two flashlights to guide them. It galled them both to think they would only be again taking the contraption down in about three weeks when they moved to the new house. But neither one could stand the idea of Andrew not having his main gift on Christmas morning.

Especially since that main gift wasn't *the best Spider-Man action figure EVER*.

Surrounded in mountains of ripped paper, discarded bows, and half-torn boxes, there were only a couple of gifts left. Andrew pulled one from deep beneath the tree. The wrapping paper, silver with bright-white snowflakes, was different from the red, green, and gold paper she and Justin had used for all their presents. "That one's from Grandma Renee," Alyson said.

Andrew inspected the tag. His reading had improved somewhat since the parent-teacher conferences, and he now often tried to read things himself. "No," Andrew said, "it's from Santa."

Alyson squinted. She knew it was from Renee, she recognized the paper as the same that wrapped her own gift from her mother-in-law: teardrop aquamarine earrings, her birthstone. She stood up and over Andrew to peer at the tag. Renee had signed the tag from Santa, but why?

As Andrew ripped into the package, Alyson sat beside Justin to watch. Moments later, Andrew's eyes went wide as coins, and he stood straight up. "He remembered!" Andrew shouted as he looked at his parents and turned the box in his hands around for them to see. "It's the Spider-Man I wanted. The one that shoots real webs! He remembered!" Andrew shouted as he jumped up and down among all their Christmas debris.

Alyson and Justin glanced at each other and back at their son. "That's so awesome!" Justin said.

"I can't believe it!" Alyson said.

Andrew ripped into the box and began struggling against all the plastic zip ties anchoring the Spider-Man to his cardboard display. Completely surprised, but very relieved, Alyson leaned into Justin and whispered in his ear, "I never in a million years would have guessed that she would have nailed this…but we owe your mom big-time."

Justin smiled and nodded, then got up to help Andrew free his Spider-Man.

With Spider-Man in hand, and the last of the presents under the tree opened, it was finally time to show Andrew his last gift. "Hey, buddy," Justin said, "I think there might be one last gift from Santa in the backyard. Let's get our boots and coats on and go check it out."

Andrew looked up from his Spider-Man with a confused

expression—*an outside gift?*—but jumped up and ran to the closet anyway. While he sat on the floor and shoved his pajama feet into his snow boots, Alyson and Justin reached into the closet for their own coats. With his boots on, Andrew jumped up and raced to the back door.

"Hey," Justin said. "Wait for us."

She and Justin hurried after him, not wanting Andrew to see his gift without them. Alyson pulled the camera up on her phone and got ready to record Andrew's expression as he waited for them on bouncing feet by the back door.

"Ready?" Justin asked him, his eyes wide and his eyebrows arched.

"Yes!" Andrew yelled.

Justin opened the back door while Alyson worked to capture everything on video. As the cold morning air rushed into the house, Andrew bolted into the yard. Alyson lost sight of him in the viewfinder for a few seconds but managed to refocus on him right as he stopped in his tracks and processed the site of the contraption, taking up a quarter of their yard.

He turned around and faced his parents, hysterical with excitement. "A trampoline!" he yelled out, disrupting the early morning silence.

Alyson cringed, hoping their neighbors would understand their five-year-old's excitement.

"I thought you took it back because I was bad!" Andrew shouted.

Crap, Alyson should've figured he'd remember that. "Shhh." She mentioned with her free hand for him to keep his voice down. "I did," she said quietly and moved closer so Andrew could hear her, and they wouldn't have to yell into the morning. "But I guess Santa thought you should have one anyway."

Andrew considered her for a moment. And she could tell from the expression on his face that the wheels were turning in his mind. Working to decide how true her explanation was. She worried she'd overplayed her hand. Andrew was still only five; it would be nice if he could hang on to his belief of Santa for at least a couple more years. But half a second later, he let it go—much to her relief. "Can I go on it?"

"Yes," Justin said as he moved toward Andrew and got ready to help him up and through the opening in the safety netting. "But only if I get to jump too," he added.

It was absolutely freezing, but Alyson didn't care. She stood in the snow, filming her family, her heart near to bursting with gratitude. With all they'd been through these past six months—the problems between her and Justin, Andrew's struggles in school, and then thinking they'd lost him, even if it was only for a few hours—Alyson wasn't sure if she'd ever felt as happy as she did in that very moment. For the first time, it was very clear to her exactly what she wanted, the order of her priorities, and the knowledge that she already had it all.

She had agreed with Justin that they should sell the house, and the very next day, they called the real estate agent who had helped them buy this house only six months ago. Alyson had worried, with it being Christmas and the middle of winter, that they wouldn't be able to sell the house fast enough. After Justin sat her down and really explained the dire position their financials were in after all the spending, Alyson completely understood why Justin had been so stressed for months. She only wished he had shared it with her sooner. Or better, she had thought to dial in and pay attention to it herself.

But the past was the past, now all the cards were on the table, and they both knew how important it was to sell the house quickly. When they spoke with the real estate agent, Justin and Alyson had both been ready to price it low. They were terrified of what even a couple more months would mean for them financially.

But their real estate agent had different advice. "Look, I understand what you're telling me and how vitally important this is to you. All I'm asking is that you give me one week at the price I'm suggesting. I know this market, and I know the demand for this neighborhood. I think you're going to be surprised."

And she was right.

Houses in The Enclave sold themselves. Within the first twenty-four hours of listing, they had five offers on the table, all of them above the asking price their real estate agent had set. "I told you when you bought this place, people want into this neighborhood. Especially at these entry home prices."

And so in less than forty-eight hours from them making the decision to move, Alyson's *dream* home in her *dream* neighborhood was under contract. They would need to be out two weeks after Christmas.

As she watched Justin and Andrew jumping and laughing in the early morning light, she realized she had regrets. But selling the house wasn't one of them. Insisting they buy it in the first place, that was one. Allowing her marriage to teeter toward the brink of collapse, that was another. Losing sight of what was most important to her, that was the biggest.

Her hand holding the phone was cold and stiff, so she switched it to her other hand and plunged the frozen one into her coat pocket.

They would all need to go back inside soon, but she figured she could give them a few more minutes.

Her fingers brushed against something in her pocket. Pooled and forgotten in the corner. Her fingers were still too frozen to make out precisely what it was. She pinched the item between the tips of her index and middle fingers and fished it out. The item rested in the center of her palm, its chain entangled between her fingers.

And then she remembered—the necklace. It had a silver chain and medium-sized turquoise crucifix; at the center was a red stone she couldn't identify offhand. She'd found it the day Andrew had gone missing, half-buried at the base of the rock wall that separated the parking from the grassy area around the lake. She'd slipped it into her pocket that day and completely forgotten about it until this moment.

She stopped recording Justin and Andrew and dropped her phone into her pocket. She used both her hands now to work some of the easier knots from the chain. She rubbed some of the residual dirt from the round stones. Like the day she'd found it, she had the feeling she'd seen it before.

In her mind, it lay against tan skin at the base of the person's throat. It was sunny outside, and the light reflected off water. She was drinking wine, and there was the scent of a storm that was rolling in—

She remembered. In that instant, she saw the whole picture and setting. The last time she'd seen this necklace was the night she'd gone to book club. The night before Elijah's body had been discovered.

Discovered at the lake, where she'd found this necklace.

"Justin!"

CHAPTER FORTY

Alyson stood on the porch and hesitated. She was a wreck. Both nervous and nauseous, she considered turning around and leaving. And even though she'd imagined how she'd do this, maybe she simply didn't have the guts to go through with it. She closed her eyes and felt her body sway. It would be easier to run away.

But Alyson had promised herself, no more running away from conflict.

She opened her eyes and quickly reached out to press the doorbell before her half-buried cowardice won the day. Alyson could hear footsteps approaching on the other side of the door, and she took a deep breath to settle her nerves.

The door swung open before her, and on the other side of the glass storm door, her friend's expression broke open into a surprised but wide and warm smile.

"Alyson!" Gabby exclaimed. "Come in," she said as she opened the door and motioned for Alyson to come inside.

Alyson hesitated. In her mind, this entire scene had played out on Gabby's cold and wintery porch. She'd never imagined being inside Gabby's home. "Thank you," she said awkwardly as she stepped over the threshold, defaulting to ingrained social mores as her initial bravado failed her.

Gabby greeted her with a hug and then motioned for Alyson to follow her as she walked away. "I was just going to have another cup of coffee. Dennis took the kids out onto the golf course to sled. Thank God, because after yesterday, and this entire Christmas break, to be honest, I'm about to lose my mind with these kids." She stopped in her kitchen, opened a cupboard, and pulled out a pale blue mug. "Want one?" she asked over her shoulder.

Alyson shook her head. "No, thank you. Justin and Andrew are waiting for me. I only meant to stop by for a moment. I…found something. And I believe it belongs to you, so I wanted to return it."

At this, Gabby turned around with a curious expression. Alyson pulled the necklace from her pocket and held it up, letting the turquoise crucifix dangle from the chain.

Gabby's mouth fell open, and she rushed across the space between them. "My God, Alyson." Gabby reached and took hold of the crucifix and slipped it from Alyson's outstretched hand. "Where did you find it?" she asked as she inspected the pendant in her hands. "I lost it months ago. I've been tearing the house apart and wracking my brains." She looked up at Alyson with a huge smile and leaned in to hug her. "I even blamed the kids. They're always messing around in my jewelry box." Gabby pulled back from the hug. "My grandmother gave this to me for my sixteenth birthday. I've been sick about losing it."

Behind her, the Keurig coffee finished brewing and spit its final few steaming drops into her cup. Gabby kissed Alyson on the cheek and returned to the counter. "This is honestly the best day-after-Christmas present ever. Where did you say you found it?"

Alyson watched Gabby's back as she picked up her favorite creamer, French vanilla, and poured a generous dose into her cup. From almost the first day Alyson had moved into this neighborhood, Gabby had been her friend. When Alyson didn't know a soul, Gabby had been the one to reach out, extend her hand, invite Alyson along, and introduce her to others. She had watched Andrew, been a sounding board of motherly advice, and tried her best to help guide Alyson through The Enclave's backwater relationships.

Gabby was a good mother. Gabby was a wonderful friend. Gabby was a loving wife.

Because of all of this, there was a part of Alyson that didn't want to look beyond all that. She could have kept that necklace hidden away. She could have told herself she didn't remember why it was familiar. She could maybe even lie to herself and pretend she'd never read what Justin had dug up on her favorite new friend.

Except, the truth was, Alyson wasn't capable of that degree of deception. Not even with herself.

"That day Andrew went missing from school, and we scoured the neighborhood looking for him."

"My God, what a nightmare that was," Gabby commiserated as she wiped up whatever mess she'd made near her coffee maker.

Alyson took a breath. "I found it by the lake. At the base of the rock wall between the parking lot and the lake."

Gabby stopped wiping her countertop. Several seconds passed in which she didn't move. "That's weird," she finally said, struggling to hide the emotion in her voice. "I can't imagine how it got there.

Unless, you know, I bet one of my boys did have it. Probably playing with it, riding around the neighborhood—you know how they do—and it slipped right out of their pocket." When she finally turned around, her smile was too big, too bright, and did not match the terror in her eyes.

"Let me get you some coffee," she said, changing the subject. "The kids are all outside with Dennis." She gestured to the back windows that offered an unobstructed view of The Enclave's golf course behind them. Alyson could see them in the distance—Dennis and all four kids, bundled up in their snow gear and sledding on the small, manmade hills covered in snow. "It's a miracle we actually have a moment to ourselves." She opened her cupboard back up and took another mug down. "How was Christmas? Did Andrew just love the trampoline? My God, my kids are going to lose their minds when they find out he got one. They've been begging—"

"Gabby, stop," Alyson whispered.

Gabby froze, her hands trembling on her coffee pod rack.

"You lost it the night we went to book club at Jessica's. You were wearing it that night—I remember thinking how beautiful it was, very unique, and that it looked gorgeous against your tanned skin."

Gabby continued to make Alyson the cup of coffee she didn't want. "Oh, well, yes. But I don't think that's when I lost it. I've had it since then, for sure."

"You drove me home that night. I was so drunk, and I thought at first that I had left my car in front of Jessica's and just walked home. But it was raining that night. Pouring actually. And if I had walked home, my clothes, shoes, hair—all would have been soaking wet and probably muddy. But they weren't. I may have woken up on my bathroom floor that next morning, but I wasn't drenched or dirty the way I would have been if I'd not had a ride."

Gabby brought Alyson the coffee and set it down on the counter beside her.

"You hit Elijah Sloan with your car that night."

Gabby shook her head and turned away. "You were completely passed out, Alyson. You don't know what you're talking about."

"Maybe, but I know you were nervous when you came over the next morning. Then Dennis had to take your car into the shop to 'have some work done.' And now your necklace that you lost that same night has been found very close to the spot where Elijah's body was found. Gabby, I know you hit him with your car that night."

"There isn't any way you remember that."

"I don't have to remember it. The evidence speaks for itself. And I know about your DUIs. You've already had two. You hit a kid while under the influence… What would happen if the police found out how much you'd been drinking that night?"

Gabby turned to her, her desperation palpable, and pointed out the window to her family, happily racing up the snowy hills before launching themselves back down on their bellies. "What do you expect me to do? Turn myself in? Leave them without their mother? For fuck's sake, Alyson. You think I'm not sorry? You think I wouldn't take it back if I could?" Her voice broke, and her eyes welled up with tears. "But I can't! And getting myself locked up doesn't bring Elijah back. Do you think you'd make a different choice if you were in my shoes? Can you honestly tell me you'd leave Andrew to be raised without his mom?"

Alyson stood very still as she looked into Gabby's pleading eyes. The truth was, she couldn't say for sure what she would do if the roles were reversed. How would Alyson handle it? What lengths might she go to if she were the one with two prior DUI convictions who hit a child while under the influence? It was possible that Gabby was right. That if she had to make a series of choices and mistakes that had led her to the same corner Gabby had worked herself into, Alyson might also try to keep her life and her family while doing her best to forget and manage the burden of a catastrophic regret.

"Alyson? Please, I'm begging you. Don't do this. I am sorry for what happened. And actually, *sorry* doesn't even come close to capturing how much I hate myself for it. You have to believe that. What happened that night, that's something I'm going to carry with me for the rest of my life. Knowing that I'm the one responsible for Elijah's death. I *knew* that kid. Bonnie used to be one of my best friends. Believe me when I tell you I don't *feel* like I'm getting away with anything."

"So the guilt is punishment enough?" Alyson asked.

Gabby shook her head. "I know what you're thinking."

"And what about Bonnie and Bennet? What about Gracie and George? They're supposed to just live with never knowing what happened?"

Gabby opened her mouth to respond but was interrupted when the doorbell rang. She sighed her comment away and looked down the hallway toward the entrance. She held up her finger to Alyson. "Don't go anywhere, okay? Let me just get rid of whoever this is." She started to walk away. "Promise we can still talk about this."

Alyson nodded and watched Gabby disappear down the hallway.

She stared at the cup of coffee Gabby had offered her, watched the steam lift, curl, and disappear into the air as Gabby opened her front door.

"Hello?" Gabby asked. And even though Alyson couldn't see her friend's face, she could plainly hear the terror in her voice.

"Gabrielle Lawrence?" a man's voice boomed from the doorway.

Alyson closed her eyes.

"Denver Police Department—we have a warrant for your arrest. You have the right to remain silent. Anything you say may be used against you in a court of law. You have the right to consult an attorney..."

As the officer continued reading Gabby her Miranda rights, Alyson heard the ratcheting click of the handcuffs echo down the hallway.

"My family," Gabby protested, her voice sounding farther away, like she was already outside the door. "I need to speak to my husband," she wailed.

As she listened to her friend being dragged from her home, a tidal wave of sorrow washed over Alyson, and she grabbed the counter to keep herself upright. She looked out the window to see Dennis and the kids still racing up and down the snowy hills, laughing and smiling, completely unaware that the last time they saw their mother was the last time they'd see her as a free woman. Their lives were irrevocably changed, and they didn't know it yet.

CHAPTER FORTY-ONE

Alyson bent over and fastened the buckle beneath Andrew's chin. Predictably, he squirmed and gave her a dirty look, but he now knew better than to argue or take the helmet off. No helmet, no bike.

Despite his sour expression, she smiled at him anyway and tapped the top of his helmet gently. "Okay, you're all set. Go nuts."

He twisted the handlebars and turned his bike around. Once he got both his feet square with the pedals, he was off and racing away from her like lightning.

"God," Justin said beside her. "He really does cover a lot more ground on that bigger bike."

Alyson sighed and zipped up her coat. "Well, at least our yard opens onto a bike path now instead of a street." She took hold of Justin's gloved hand with her own mittened one and turned her cheek toward him when he bent to kiss it.

Their new home wasn't exactly a house—it was a townhouse. It was roughly half the square footage of their home in The Enclave, and it was also less than half the price. They'd done well on the sale of their house, much better than they both dared to hope, given they'd only bought the house six months before. But after the real estate fees and paying off most of the debt they'd acquired, they were left with a very small down payment for their next home.

The realization was bittersweet for Alyson. It was a relief to realize the equity they had could be used to offset all that credit card debt. But she was still angry with herself for allowing them to get into that situation in the first place.

"It's a lesson learned, for both of us," Justin had rationalized.

"You're right. I just wish that was one I didn't have to learn the hard way."

So their home was smaller, less private, and definitely not in a prestigious part of town, but Alyson was happy. Moreover, Justin and Andrew seemed happy too.

Since unloading their debt, and significantly reducing their mortgage payment, she and Justin had sat down and figured out a way for him to pursue his pilot's license. They still needed the income from his job, but for a few hours at night and on weekends, Justin worked toward his commercial rating. It would take a few years, but ever since he was openly pursuing the career he really wanted to have, and Alyson *knew* that's what he was doing, he was happier and more involved than ever before. They figured out that in three years, he'd be ready to apply for positions at the smaller regional airlines.

Ahead of them, Andrew stopped his bike on the path where it met a crossroads. Even though it wasn't a busy street, he knew he had to wait for them to cross with them. No waiting, no bike.

"I saw in the *Denver Post* this morning that Gabby's trial date is set for July," Alyson said.

Justin glanced down at her for a second before returning his watchful eyes to Andrew in the distance. "I can't imagine what that must be like. For her, yeah. But my God, Dennis, and the kids."

Alyson nodded and pushed down the swell of regret and sorrow she sometimes felt whenever she thought about Gabby, and especially when she thought about Gabby's kids growing up without her.

Because Christmas Day, standing in her backyard watching Justin and Andrew bounce on the trampoline, holding Gabby's necklace in her hand as all the pieces fell into place in her mind—Alyson had considered not calling the police. Very seriously considered it. She knew it would destroy her friend, decimate her family.

But isn't that exactly what had happened to Bonnie and her family when they found out Elijah had been killed? It had ruined Bonnie's life, wrecked her family. Alyson had heard that Sloan Investment was filing for bankruptcy. And the Sloans had been trying to sell their house since January but were having a hard time because it was overpriced and dated.

When Alyson learned that their house was on the market, her morbid curiosity had gotten the best of her. After dropping Andrew off at his new school, she'd returned to their townhouse and pulled up the listing on realtor.com. She had clicked through the thirty-five photos, imagining Bonnie and her family living and growing up in those rooms of 1990s palatial elegance. With its darkly papered walls, thick mahogany wood trim, and swooping brocade custom window treatments, Alyson understood why they were having a hard time selling. Now everyone wanted white, bright, happy, marbled spaces.

Bonnie's home looked like a haunted mansion by comparison.

That, coupled with the uncertainty about what the land directly behind the home would be used for, meant there just wasn't much interest from buyers looking to plop down several millions of dollars on a home that would need a gut renovation.

But Alyson hoped it would. As much as she had disliked Bonnie while living in her neighborhood, Alyson now felt deeply empathetic toward the woman. She had, after all, lost almost everything when she lost her son. If Jessica and Courtney were to be believed, Bonnie and Bennet were also going through a divorce.

It was a far more personal tragedy and horror than Alyson would ever wish upon even her worst enemy. And while Bonnie had made Alyson's life unpleasant at times, she was hardly an enemy. Bonnie was a mother navigating the single worst experience a mother ever has to endure. Any unkind thought Alyson had about the woman paled in comparison to that fact.

Justin squeezed her hand. "You okay? You look upset."

Alyson shook her head and put on a smile. "Just thinking."

Justin let go of her hand and put his arm around her instead. "Oh yeah? About what?"

She tilted her head and rested it against his shoulder as they walked. "I don't know. About how lucky we are, I guess."

"Really?" He sounded surprised. "Even though we couldn't keep your house, and your husband wants to be a pilot, and our son can't sit still for even five seconds? Lucky?"

She stopped him from walking and turned his body to face her. "Yes, actually." She reached up and placed her mittens on either side of his face. "Right now, I feel like the luckiest woman on the entire planet," she said, pulled him toward her, and kissed him.

AN EXCERPT FROM *HER PERFECT LIFE*

Eileen

She was having one of those *emotionally vulnerable* moments their therapist was often trying to get her to understand. All the signs were there: short temper, racing thoughts, catastrophic thinking—check, check, and check. All confirmed and completely undeniable in light of the huge fight she and Eric had last night.

The memory of it, with the morning hangover beginning to bloom, made her take a breath and hold it tight. Shit, what exactly had she been raving about? Because all of it was absolutely going to get rehashed at therapy next week. Eric certainly would not forget her every word; he never did. Eileen placed both her elbows on the desk and her head in her hands.

"A whole bottle of cab," she whispered to herself, shaking her head. "Come on, Eileen." The normally endearing expression broke her. The tears gathered and pooled behind her closed eyes. Eric hadn't sung her that song in years. No, not now. She sat up and checked the time on the computer screen. Shit and shit…what had she been doing? Twenty minutes before they were all supposed to be out the door, and not a single one of her kids was even out of bed. Lunches, the laundry she didn't move from the washer to the dryer last night, homework? Had she checked homework last night?

Time hated her—and it was so clearly personal.

Eighteen minutes. An impossibility. A series of miracles would not save them this morning. Everyone would be late, again. Well, everyone except Eric, of course. Eric was already out of the house, showered, dressed, pressed, and cologned. His lunch—the only one he ever packed—would be placed calmly and professionally onto the back seat of his immaculate and always client-ready car.

This, she remembered suddenly, is what had started the fight last night.

"I'm tired. I'm tired of doing everything," she had finally managed to say, standing at the sink and slamming a cast iron frying pan into the stainless steel tub hard enough to dent it.

"Just tell me!" Eric said, throwing both his hands over his head. "What the hell do you want me to do?"

"Why do I have to tell you? Look around, Eric. The *To Do* is all around you. For fuck's sake, pick *anything*! Because I can't manage the kids, the house, the bills, the yard, the every-fucking-thing any more. My car! My car has not had the oil changed in a year!"

"What?" Startled, he shook his head as if *this* was the most disturbing thing, the most pressing concern. "Eileen! A year?" His tone was accusing. "You're lucky it's still running. You can't let that go like that."

She stared at him. A swift and unexpected calm moved over her so fast it made the hair at the back of her neck stand up. She couldn't make him understand, but she absolutely knew what the next words out of her mouth needed to be.

"Will you please take my car and get the oil changed." It wasn't a question. It was a concession. She was telling him what to do. Never mind it solved nothing. Never mind her only thought was the impossibility of him ever understanding. Never mind the hopeless feeling creeping up her spine, squeezing her ribs, holding her breath and her words tight in her chest.

Eric looked relieved. "Yes. Yes, tomorrow I'll take it to my guy down by the office." For the briefest of moments, he had looked like he might have wanted to come to her at the sink, maybe kiss her forehead. *So happy we resolved all that. See, just tell me.*

She didn't want his kiss. She wanted him to know how hard it was to make all the pieces keep moving. She wanted him to help, not because she told him or gave him a list, but because he saw their life, their children…her. She wanted him to notice what needed attention because he cared—not because it was assigned.

That was the fight last night, and that was how it ended. Well, and with a bottle of cab as she finished the dishes and Eric retreated to his office for the work he'd brought home.

Fifteen minutes before everyone needed to be in the car.

She sat back in the kitchen chair she used when working on her laptop in the kitchen, felt the tears slide down her cheeks, and considered the implications of calling it a "mental health" day for everyone—not even waking the kids up. Let them sleep, the dogs sleep, the lunches go unmade, the laundry sit in the wash. Crawl back into bed herself even.

Twelve minutes.

An email alert slid onto the screen. News: Clare Collins

Eileen stared at the rectangular notice box for the full five seconds it remained on her screen until it slid back off. She shouldn't. She didn't have time. Plus, there was the whole already "emotionally vulnerable" state of affairs. Reading internet alerts about her sister was almost guaranteed to make her more "emotionally vulnerable." She had promised herself, weeks ago, that she was going to turn these notifications off.

She stood up and walked to the bottom of the stairs. "Ryan! Paige! Cameron! Get up! Get ready!" she shouted before heading back to her computer.

Just a quick look, she told herself.

When she had learned you could do this, years ago, she thought it would be an easy way to keep up on any of the latest news about her sister and her books. Eileen never dreamed she would end up getting anywhere between five to ten alerts a day. She had always known her sister was a successful author. She could plainly see the evidence of it on the shelves of every store she walked into that sold books. It was only after she started reading about every book tour, new book contract, foreign rights deal, charity luncheon, celebrity book club endorsement, film adaptation option—only after seeing regular and daily evidence in the news of her sister's extreme success—that Eileen realized Clare was much more than a successful author whose books flew off the shelves and into shopping carts.

No. Her sister, Clare Collins, was, according to *Forbes*, one of the *Ten highest paid authors in the world*. Eileen remembered that morning, four or five years ago, staring at that ridiculously high number next to her sister's name sitting at the number-six spot on the *Forbes* list.

Fourteen million.

Dollars.

In a single year.

Her sister, the girl who had once shared a bedroom with her… who had loved eating Kraft Macaroni & Cheese after school…who used to sit next to her on their sagging couch and fight with her over the remote, now earned lottery win–levels of dollars—every year.

Eileen clicked open the email and steeled herself for whatever fresh self-esteem low she was about to plunge into.

It was a picture of Clare, poised and statuesque, long neck, face turned slightly away from the camera so her chiseled cheekbones and prominent chin were captured perfectly. A long, pale blue dress looked poured over her toned body, revealing every tightly calculated proportion as it spilled into a short train over the red carpet beneath her silver-stilettoed feet. The second shot was from behind. Clare's long, auburn hair was styled in an updo so the dress's plunging back would not be hidden beneath her silky waves. The only flaw, if you could even call it that, was the hint of Clare's black inked tattoo, barely visible on her shoulder blade, creeping out from behind the dress. It hardly showed. Probably most people wouldn't even notice it—most people didn't even know Clare had that tattoo.

Eileen remembered the day she got it.

"Mom?"

Startled, Eileen jumped in her seat and turned to see her sleepy youngest son Cameron, nowhere even in the ballpark of ready for school. "You're not dressed."

"I don't have any clean shorts."

She sighed and closed her eyes. Cameron's load of clean clothes was still sitting in a damp lump in the middle of her washing machine. "I know, I'm sorry." She racked her brains for some alternative. "We'll just put what you're going to wear today in the dryer. It'll be faster."

"School starts in five minutes."

Defeated, and obviously with no good solutions for anything this morning, Eileen nodded at her son.

"Is that Aunt Clare?" he asked, his eyes focused on the screen behind her.

"Yes."

"Why's she so dressed up?"

"One of her books was made into a movie, and she went to the premiere last night."

"Another movie?" Cameron beamed, his excitement erasing the last traces of sleepiness from his face. "Can we go see it?"

The pain—it was a real thing. Jealousy wormed through her gut like an infection. Eileen gave him a weak smile. "Of course."

Cameron, her most sensitive and emotionally attuned kid, narrowed his eyes at her. "What's wrong?"

"Nothing." She turned in her seat and closed the internet browser on her screen so her glamorous sister was replaced by Eileen's tangled mess of desktop icons.

"Are you sick?" Both of his hands landed on her cheeks and drew her face back to his.

She looked into his bright blue eyes, took a deep breath, sat up straight in her chair, and conjured a real smile. "I'm only a little sick."

"Are you going to stay home today?" The hope in his voice gave away where this questioning would lead.

"No. And neither are you, or your brother, or your sister. We are all pulling it together and getting on with the day," she declared. She stood up and went to drag Ryan and Paige out of bed. "Go pick something to wear out of the washer and put it in the dryer."

Cameron, giving up any last hope that he might spend the day at home playing video games instead of at school, slumped his shoulders and moved like a snail toward the laundry room. "You know, class starts in two minutes," he called back to her.

"Just keep moving," Eileen yelled back. "Faster." Her own slippered feet raced up the stairs. "Paige! Ryan!"

An hour later, and after a frantic search for her car keys, which were eventually found in the sink of the downstairs bathroom, Eileen herded the last of her kids out the front door.

"I forgot my ID," Ryan said, rushing back inside the house.

Eileen closed her eyes and took a breath. Something was wrong with her… It simply wasn't this hard to get three kids to school and herself to work. She knew it. Every day, millions of families all over the world seemed to pull this off, on time.

Ryan finally came barreling back down the stairs, "Got it!" he said as he raced out the door. Eileen remembered to close the front door and lock it—something that hadn't happened yesterday.

She adjusted her tote and camera bags on her shoulder, leaning to counterbalance the weight, and pressed the unlock button on the key fob several times as she walked down the porch steps. When she rounded the edge of the house and could see the drive, she was surprised to see all three of her children, not inside her car waiting for her, but standing next to Eric's car.

Paige was pulling a large manila envelope from underneath one of the wiper blades on the windshield.

What is going on? Where is my car? Hasn't Eric already left for work? Then it hit her—their fight, her assignment for him. *"Will you please take my car and get the oil changed?"*

Ryan snatched the envelope from Paige and turned away from her, protecting the prize. "I'm opening it. It's probably for me!"

"I'm expecting something," Paige countered, trying to snatch the envelope back.

"I saw it first." Ryan clutched the envelope to his chest, his body turning and twisting against his sister's every attack attempt.

"Mom?" Cameron asked. "Can I open it? Please?"

They were about to get into a fight—a real one. She could practically smell kid fights rushing in, seconds before someone shoved just a bit too hard, initiating a return strike that actually hurt, leading to a defensive kick—running, arms flailing.

"Stop!" she commanded, rushing into the fray and grabbing the envelope from Ryan. "What is wrong with you two? Get in the car, now!"

"But—"

"Now!" Eileen finished. "For God's sake, we don't have time for this."

"Well, whose fault is that?" Paige added in a withering tone as she sauntered to the front passenger door.

"I'm sitting in front," Ryan called, rushing to get between his sister and the door. "I called it."

"You did not!"

"I did! Ask Cameron. I called it before we came outside."

"You can't call it when everyone's not there."

Movement across the street caught her attention. Her neighbor with her erect spine and size-two body was pretending to not hear this "poor parenting" episode unraveling. Eileen watched as she slipped into her shiny black Mercedes. Her children were already at school. The nanny got them there on time every morning.

"Stop it," Eileen hissed. "Get in the back, both of you. Cameron's sitting up front."

Paige turned on her. "Cameron's not even old enough—"

"I. Don't. Care. Get in the back. Now!"

Cameron beamed.

"It's not fair," Ryan whined.

Eileen ignored him and unlocked the doors. Finally, everyone got in the car—all unhappy except Cameron.

"What should we listen to?" he asked as he reached for the radio, defining the battleground for the fight that would happen on the drive.

Eileen put the key in the ignition and started the car, the envelope from the windshield still in her left hand. Eric's full name was handwritten across the front in black Sharpie.

"No!" Paige declared from the back. "We are not listening to country music, Cameron!"

Eileen turned her body in her seat and stuffed the envelope down the side of her tote so she could give it to Eric later.

"No radio." She pushed the off button on the console. "We are having a moment of silence," she finished as she shifted the car into reverse and backed down the drive.

READING GROUP GUIDE

1. Bonnie and Alyson hold different positions in The Enclave and in their families. How would you compare their ambitions? Who did you find more relatable?

2. Alyson's faux-innocent callout post for George Sloan on the community Facebook page does not earn her any friends. How does social media complicate interpersonal conflict? Do you think there are circumstances where a post like Alyson's could lead to a resolution without causing further tension?

3. The darkest corner of the school parking lot is the only place Bonnie feels invisible. Why does that make her feel so calm? Where do you go to hide from the world?

4. One of Alyson's biggest obstacles is her isolation. How did moving states contribute to her loneliness? Do you think she could have kept in touch with her old friends more effectively?

5. Compare Bonnie's anxiety to Elijah's. Why do you think they're so different?

6. Describe Alyson's parent-teacher conference with Andrew's teacher. Does her fear of being judged get in the way of supporting Andrew?

7. After Elijah's death, Bonnie's Senate campaign team has a comprehensive plan to keep her on track. Could you have gone along with their strategy if you were in Bonnie's position? Do you think we, as a society, value the grieving process? What effect does that have on us?

8. Alyson worries that her life has gotten unexpectedly "retro" when she thinks about her role as a housewife and mother. How does the new assumption that women can "have it all" affect women who work and women who prefer to stay home?

9. Who did you think should be the prime suspect in Elijah's murder throughout the book? How do you think The Enclave will react when the real killer's identity reaches the rumor mill? Will Bonnie get justice?

10. How would you describe Alyson and Justin's relationship at the beginning of the book? At the end? Which moment would you identify as the turning point for them?

A CONVERSATION WITH THE AUTHOR

Alyson and Bonnie are both very concerned with how their lives look to other people. How do you handle the fear of being judged?

I think being judged by others was something I was more concerned about earlier in my life. Middle age seems to have cured me of it.

Bonnie's crushing grief forces her to drop out of her political campaign. How did you get yourself into her headspace and tap into those devastating feelings? Did you consider having her try to continue the campaign?

As a mother, writing these scenes was a matter of putting myself in her shoes. It was not difficult to imagine my worst nightmare—the loss of one of my children—and then translate that fear and pain onto the page. No, I never considered her continuing with her campaign. It was hard enough to make her get out of bed.

The Enclave feels like a neighborhood you could find in the suburbs of any major city. How did you get a sense of the insular community and the types of people who live there?

I've lived in suburbs for a long time, and while The Enclave isn't modeled after any one of these in particular, there are probably aspects that are reminiscent of many neighborhoods.

Which character was the most challenging for you to write?

It was painful to write about Bonnie's grief. Additionally, as a woman who runs most everything in her own home, I found Alyson's need to fit in, blind materialism, and ignorance about their family finances disturbing at times.

How did the writing process for *The Secret Next Door* compare to the writing process for your first novel, *Her Perfect Life*?

There was definitely more pressure to write under contract, and trying to be creative during a pandemic was a hurdle I barely cleared.

What are you reading these days?

I just finished reading *The Push* by Ashley Audrain. It was a fantastic read, and I highly recommend it.

ACKNOWLEDGMENTS

I'd like to thank the Sourcebooks team and my editors, Shana Drehs, Erin McClary, Jessica Thelander, and Natalie Jones, for all their work to get *The Secret Next Door* ready for publication. Thank you also to my agent, Kevan Lyon, for the support and early edits. Thank you to my well-read friends Jill Arnhold, Lisa Sundling, and Amy Blevins for being the very first people to read this in rough draft form and for offering words of encouragement. Special thanks to Traci Lunsford, who creates a real life Christmas Garage every year. She was generous and allowed me to use her fun tradition in this book. (However, it should be noted that her festive garage is filled with much kinder guests than The Enclave version!)

ABOUT THE AUTHOR

Rebecca is the author of *The Secret Next Door* and *Her Perfect Life*. She lives in Colorado with her family. You can learn more about her writing at: rebeccataylorbooks.com.

HER PERFECT LIFE

How well do you
really know the
ones you love?

Reclusive Clare Collins crafts her novels like she crafts her life: perfectly. So the world is stunned when the famous author is found dead on a beach from a self-inflicted gunshot—the morning after her latest book hits the shelves.

Her sister, Eileen, is at a loss. Clare led a charmed life: success, mansions, money… Why would she throw it all away? But while reading through her sister's latest—and greatest—novel, Eileen discovers a clue that unravels the fiction of their perfect family and reveals the painful truth.

Suddenly, Clare's enviable life doesn't seem so sparkling, and Eileen must confront the shadows of the past that have hung over them both.

"Compulsively readable from the first page. Rebecca Taylor weaves an expertly layered story of family secrets and builds the suspense to an almost unbearable pace in this modern story of two sisters."

—Kelly Simmons, author of *One More Day* and *Where She Went*